NO HOPE

NO HOPE

No Justice Series: Book 3

NOLON KING
DAVID WRIGHT

STERLING & STONE

To YOU, the reader.
Thank you for your support.
Thank you for the wonderful emails.
Thank you for the thoughtful reviews.
Thank you for reading and loving our stories.

Prologue

HECTOR VARGAS HEFTED the gallon of milk up onto the counter at the Gas n' Stop. The cashier, an old woman who reminded him of his grandma, smiled.

"Will that be all?"

"Yes ma'am," Hector said.

"That'll be $3.59."

Hector reached into his jeans and grabbed the wad of bills, peeled off four, and handed them to the lady. He still had three dollars plus whatever change was coming.

He eyed the row of candy on the shelf, eyes locking on the King-Sized Reese's Cups. He loved Reese's, especially when you put them in the fridge and the edges got crispy.

As the lady made change, Hector wondered if he should get the candy and if his mom would be mad at him for using the leftover money on sugar. She hadn't said that he couldn't get anything else. And she usually let him keep the change when he went to the gas station, to get something for her. But she hadn't given permission, and he wasn't a sneaky kid.

"Here you go, young man." The cashier handed Hector his change. "Would you like a bag?"

"Yes, please." Hector kept eyeing the candy, his knee bouncing, increasingly sure that she would have said yes if he'd thought to ask.

He heard someone approaching from behind him. He turned to see a couple of teenagers, a blonde girl and a black girl, both about fifteen, maybe older, pretty, wearing white button-down shirts and blue skirts. That meant that they came from Chadwick, the nearby private high school. The girls were sipping slushies and chatting.

He didn't realize he was staring at them until he heard the cashier. Before he could turn, the girls looked over and saw him staring.

Busted!

He spun around, his cheeks burning.

The girls giggled behind him.

God, he hated when girls laughed at him. He was twelve. Girls his age and older always seemed to be doing exactly that. It was never because he had said something funny.

No, they were usually laughing because he'd tripped, or was caught looking at them, or just because he was fat, and had giant glasses with thick lenses that made his eyes look three times bigger than they were.

He took the milk, and as much as he wanted to get out of the store and away from the girls, he couldn't move.

"Is there anything else I can get for you?"

One of the girls sighed behind him.

Oh, look at the fat boy trying to decide if he should get candy or not. Spoiler alert, no, you shouldn't, Tubby!

He hated buying or eating junk food in front of pretty girls. But he really *really* wanted the candy.

Hector doubted that he'd get in trouble for buying the

Reese's, but his father might give him yet *another* lecture on sugar. As if Hector didn't know that candy wasn't good for you. *Duh.*

He grabbed the candy bar, put it on the counter, then paid.

"Would you like another bag?"

"No thank you." Hector grabbed the candy, shoved it into his front jeans pocket, and turned. The bag of milk slipped out of his hands.

Hector grabbed the handle before it could hit the floor and explode. His reflexes were decent for a fat kid. But the girls were still laughing at the stupid fat kid stumbling toward the door.

He left the store, glad to be out of sight, and headed toward the sidewalk leading past the woods and towards Fairlake Apartments.

He was about two blocks from the building's gated entrance when Hunter and Landon rode out of the complex on their bikes.

Crap!

Hector spun around, intending to head back to the gas station, where he could double back and take that path through the woods and escape the bullies' torment.

There was no telling what they'd do if he ran into them. They might be nice and just make him beg to pass. Or, they might be mean and make him hand over his money. Maybe they'd make him endure a round of punches in the arm, or smacks to his belly before letting him pass.

They'd never explicitly beaten him up, but they had done a lot of crap to Hector in the two years he'd lived there. He was sick of it. He'd spent most of his summer inside, just to reduce the odds of a random encounter. It was harder to hide now that school was back in session.

He didn't want this year to be like last, always going home and lying to his family about why his arm hurt. Why he was short a few dollars, or items of clothing. Hector had made the mistake of telling the truth last year. His dad yelled at him for not defending himself. Of course, it was easy for his father. He was big and strong. Nobody messed with him.

Now Hector kept the abuse to himself.

He walked quickly, hoping to reach the gas station parking lot without being spotted.

Too late.

"Hey, Fatty!" Hunter bellowed from behind.

Hector walked faster, about ten feet from where the woods ended. He could make a quick left once there, then escape toward the path.

"Hector!" Landon yelled. "Wait up!"

Their bikes were getting louder. Hector didn't dare turn around and acknowledge that he'd heard them.

Keep walking faster.

He reached the edge of the woods, then turned, and sprinted as fast as he could with the bulky, awkwardly held gallon of milk.

Hector passed the girls with their slushies, ignoring their gawking, eager to reach the forest.

He kept running when he got there.

The woods between the store and his apartment complex were roughly a block long, a wide swath of trees which Hector liked to pretend was part of a much larger, perhaps magical, forest. He rarely entered alone. Some of the mean kids, like Hunter and Landon, hung out there, smoking and doing other stuff that bad kids liked to do.

But with Hunter and Landon on their bikes, the woods offered safe passage today. The path was well worn, and a

fairly straight shot through to the neighborhood park abut-
ting his complex.

His heart raced. He was out of breath, struggling to
push himself forward. Hector wished he could lose the
milk. But he couldn't come home empty handed without
telling his parents why.

He had to keep running and hope the bullies would
give up.

Hector heard laughing behind him. He turned
around.

Hunter and Landon were riding their bikes in the
woods.

Kids *never* rode their bikes in the woods. There were too
many branches and rocks. It was easy to get hurt or pop a
tire.

But clearly, they didn't care.

They were hurtling forward, eyes locked onto him like
wolves in pursuit.

They sped up, their smiles vicious.

The woods yawned into the park 100 yards ahead.
They were less than forty behind. There was no way he'd
beat them out of the woods.

They'd probably beat him *in* the woods.

Hector's only option was to turn off the path, run into
the knotted tangle of trees and brush, and navigate his way
back to the sidewalk, or into the park.

He hoped Hunter and Landon would be annoyed
enough to surrender. They couldn't possibly be willing to
ditch their bikes and chase him on foot.

Hector turned off the path, tripping and stumbling
through the vegetation, working to put as much distance as
possible between him and his pursuers.

Hunter and Landon were tall and lean. Much faster

than him. But Hector figured if they couldn't see him, they couldn't catch him.

He ran blindly, turning left, right, then left again, navigating openings as they came.

"We're gonna get you, Fat Boy!" Hunter yelled.

Hector couldn't tell where his voice was coming from. The trees played with sound and rendered his senses unreliable.

He ran faster, branches scraping his arms and his face.

He caught a glimpse of movement to his right — Landon's red shirt.

Landon yelled, "I got him!"

Hector panicked, his heart pounding hard enough to explode. He turned left, away from Landon.

The stupidity of running into the woods became all too evident. He'd traded the relative safety of the street for a forest where no one could see him. Or answer his cries.

Hector raced blindly into a small clearing, and glimpsed daylight ahead, either the park or the road. He had to make it out of the woods. He was safer in a public place.

The laughter and footsteps grew closer.

Landon was gaining on him.

Hector dropped the milk and ran faster.

Daylight was within reach.

He tripped over something and fell face first, hard. Hector sat up, gasping, struggling to recover his breath. He held up a finger up to his bullies, still closing in behind him.

"W…wait," he stuttered, hoping they'd at least let him catch his breath before kicking his ass.

But to his surprise, their punches hadn't landed.

He slowly turned, almost afraid that doing so would invite a fist to his face.

But Hunter and Landon were standing there wide-eyed and sheet-white, staring at Hector.

No, not at him. The bullies were staring down.

He followed their gaze.

And then Hector's heart followed the breath from his body.

Chapter 1 - Mallory Black

DESPITE THE BLAZING AUGUST HEAT, a chill ran through Detective Mallory Black as she and her partner, Mike Cortez, approached the cordoned-off crime scene in the woods.

They were met by Deputy Harrison, an officer who'd been with the Creek County Sheriff's Office for three years.

"What do we have?" Mal asked.

"Dead girl, eight- or nine-years-old, found by three boys about forty minutes ago. The kids say her name is Chloe Conlan, lives, er, *lived*, in the apartment complex over there."

Mal followed Harrison's finger, back to the opening where she and Mike had entered the woods leading into the park. Three kids stood mostly together, all of them looking shaken, but none so much as the heavyset Hispanic in tears, standing slightly apart from the other two.

"Those the kids that found her?" Mal asked.

"Yes, Deputy Thomas took statements."

"Who called it in?"

"The kid in red, Landon Bowman. Said they were playing in the woods and stumbled over the girl. The kid standing next to him is Hunter Lawson. The fat kid, Hector Vargas, said Chloe was a good friend of his. He's really broken up."

Given the distance between the skinny kids and Hector, and the scratches all over Hector's arms and face, Mal doubted they were friends or merely *playing* in the woods. She wondered if Hector, or the others, had anything to do with the crime. Maybe they were playing, and things got out of hand?

Mal stepped past the yellow tape and approached the body, careful not to screw up the crime scene any more than the trio of kids who claimed to have found the girl had already done.

Mal opened the app on her phone to record audio as she walked the scene, noting every detail as it came. You could never be certain which details would matter most in a murder investigation. Mal preferred audio of her findings to those old scribbled notes. She could record so many more details when not limited by her slow handwriting.

The victim was pale, with long dark curly hair, matted with leaves, dirt stuck to her bloody, and a severed throat. Her white school shirt was ripped open, exposing a sports bra, though the girl hadn't started puberty. Mal noted a button was missing from the girl's shirt.

She was half-covered in a black blanket that looked like it had been in the woods for months, caked with dirt and leaves. Her left arm was under the blanket, and her right arm was extended above her head, scratches along her anterior forearm. A fraying friendship bracelet hung loosely from her right wrist, the purple so faded that it looked almost pink.

Mal couldn't tell what the girl was wearing beneath the

blanket, and didn't dare move her until the techs showed up and processed the scene, but she figured if the girl's shirt was ripped open, there was a good chance that she'd been sexually assaulted.

As Mal walked the scene, taking pictures and waiting for the crime scene tech to arrive, she tried to ignore the three sets of eyes she felt raking her from the boys standing behind her. She glanced up. The two taller kids looked guiltily away.

The fat kid just stared, crying and shaking.

Mal wasn't sure what they had said in their statements, but she had a feeling that they knew something. She'd get them alone and separated, see what she could find out.

Mal went over to Mike and pulled him aside. "I want the cryer. You take the other two."

They approached the boys, Mal using her notebook instead of the recording app. Shoving a phone in someone's face usually didn't invite the geniality that could butter an interview's bread.

"So, who knew Chloe best?"

Hector raised his hand like he was in school.

"Okay, I'll talk with you first." Mal put an arm on Hector's shoulder and led him away from the other two boys. She stopped just short of leaving the woods. Mal didn't want to bring Hector out into the park where she'd passed several other kids, and a few huddled adults, trying to figure out what was going on.

She went over some basic stuff, then asked him how he knew Chloe.

"We were friends. She was nice. Do you know who did this? Do you know why?"

"Not yet."

Whenever Mal interviewed someone who knew the murder victim, she looked for signs that pointed to them as the killer. It was easier with adults than kids. You could never fully anticipate a child's reaction. When it came to children, there wasn't a normal response to something as brutally shocking as a murder.

"How did you know her? Did you go to the same school?"

"No. She's in elementary school. I'm in middle school. I just knew her from around here. I don't have many friends. Neither did she. So, we'd play together whenever she was home."

"Was she not home a lot?"

"Sometimes she'd go to her grandmother's house for a week or more."

Mal scribbled on her pad then looked back up at Hector. "What did you play?"

"Hide and seek, or we'd ride bikes, or play in the woods."

"What did you play in the woods?"

"If we weren't playing Hide and Seek then we would make up games. Or sometimes we'd play in the tree house."

"The tree house? Where's that?"

"You follow the path then go left." Hector pointed deeper into the woods, past Mike interviewing Landon and Hunter. "Then you follow the smaller path until you have to go right. But a lot of times we can't play at the tree house because bullies are hanging out there, usually smoking or something."

"Bullies? Do you know any of their names?"

Mal kept her pen moving as Hector delivered names. Neither Hunter nor Landon made his list.

"Did any of them ever mess with Chloe?"

"A lot of kids were mean to Chloe."

"How so?"

"They called her stupid, freak, and other mean names. But she wasn't stupid. Chloe was just different."

"How so?"

"I'm not sure what it's called … artistic?"

"Autistic?"

"Yeah, that's it. She was autistic. She would make weird noises, and then sometimes she'd just stare off. People thought she was dumb. But she was actually smart. Just different. We got along good."

"But kids made fun of her?"

"Oh yeah."

"Did any of them ever hit her or do anything physical that you know of?"

"She said that some girls at school had pushed her. I don't know if anyone around here ever hurt her, but a lot of them said mean things. And they thought it was funny to make her cry."

"Do you have names of those people?"

"It would be easier to tell you who didn't," Hector said, his eyes on the ground.

"Okay, who didn't?"

"Me, John, and Lucas were Chloe's only friends."

"Who are John and Lucas?"

"John and Lucas Sutherland. John's my age, twelve. Lucas is eight. He went to school with Chloe and spent almost as much time with her as I did. He's fat, too. Sometimes all three of us would get together. John didn't hang out with us all that much, though."

"Okay," Mal said. "Did you see anybody else in the woods today?"

"No." Hector looked back at the ground.

"Okay. Can you tell me how you found Chloe?"

Without looking up, he said, "Do I have to?"

Mal hadn't seen Hector's statement yet. Later she'd look for inconsistencies.

"Well, we can't catch whoever did this if you don't tell me."

"But I didn't see anything."

"You might not *think* you saw anything, but you'd be surprised how many times people didn't think they saw anything, but they give us an important clue which helps us solve a crime."

"Really?"

"Really."

"Do you have to tell my dad?"

"I don't know. What don't you want to tell your dad?"

"Why I was in the woods."

"Why were you in the woods, Hector?"

"Running."

Mal looked past him, glancing at Hunter and Landon. Both boys were pretending not to be watching her interview Hector, and doing an awful job of pretending.

"Running from who?" Like she needed to ask.

"Hunter and Landon."

"Why?"

"Because I didn't want them to bully me again. And I can't tell my dad because he told me that next time they did something to me, I ought to just punch one of them in the nose so that they'll finally stop messing with me. But I was too scared. I don't know how to punch, and they're bigger than me. And there's two of them and one of me!"

Hector started bawling.

Mal gave him a moment then put a hand on his shoulder. "It's okay. You're doing a brave thing by telling me what you saw."

"I am?"

"Oh yeah. And I'm sure Chloe would be proud of you for telling me what happened."

Hector wiped at his tears, then finished telling his story to Mal.

After he finished, she said, "Good job, Hector."

He looked up to meet Mal's eyes, and she asked a final question. "Did Hunter and Landon seem surprised when they saw Chloe on the ground?"

"Oh yeah. They looked like ghosts! I thought Landon was going to hurl."

"Thank you," Mal said. "You can go home now. Do you need a ride?"

"No, I live right over there." Hector pointed towards the park.

Mal gazed through a break in the trees at the third and fourth floors of the apartment complex. So many windows looking down on the crime scene. The trees were thick, but someone might have seen the killer enter the woods.

Or maybe the killer was watching her now.

Chapter 2 - Mallory Black

MAL APPROACHED the first-floor apartment with Mike, her stomach on its seventh somersault.

There was nothing she hated more about her job than informing a parent that their child had died. Every knock started the rollercoaster — anxiety as the door opened, the confusion that marred the parents' faces, wondering why detectives were knocking, and then their eyes, as reality set like a sun on their old lives.

That look haunted Mal and had ruined countless hours of sleep.

It was surely the same expression that had claimed her face when she got her own knock on the door two years ago.

We found her. We found Ashley.

But it wasn't the right kind of found.

It was the kind you could never forget, even with eons behind you.

A punch in the gut, an endless nightmare, a roaring wildfire that tore through the forest of your life and never stopped burning.

16

There was one look even worse than the realization that a child was never coming home. The look in a parent's eyes when they already knew.

When they were the one that killed their own innocent flesh and blood.

And every time Mal approached the door of a victim's home, she hoped to God she wouldn't be staring into that Arctic gaze.

A tired woman's voice answered from the other side. "Who is it?"

"Creek County Sheriff's Office," Mike said. "We need to speak to you, ma'am."

"Got a badge?" asked the woman's muffled voice.

Mike, looking annoyed, pulled his badge from his pants pocket, and held it up to the peephole.

The door slowly opened.

Mal's first impression of Kelly, standing in sweatpants and a tank top, an unlit cigarette dangling from her pursed lips, was that the woman looked like a model.

Sure, her long hair was a tangled mess, dark circles at war with her eyes, and the cigarette an aesthetic bruise, but her sort of beauty was born for the big screen.

"Yeah?" She lit her cigarette. "How can I help you?"

"Is your daughter home?"

"Chloe?" Kelly said, looking at Mike oddly as if to say *what the fuck do you want with my kid?*

"Yes, ma'am."

"Um, hold on." She turned, looked down the hall, and shouted, "Chloe! Get out here!"

Mal looked inside. The apartment was dark. The shades were all drawn, but it looked nice enough. Fairlake Apartments was one of the more upscale complexes in Pine Harbour, home to middle and upper-middle-class families. A place where road deputies rarely had to travel.

Chloe didn't come. Kelly sighed, said "hold on" without looking back at Mike or Mal, and marched toward the rear of her apartment.

"Chloe!"

The tone of her voice, a mother sick of her kid, felt like knives carving into Mal's spine. Sure, every parent is occasionally annoyed with their child, but agitation seemed like the default all too often. Was it any wonder that so many kids who felt unloved, or like an inconvenience, took that pain out on others?

Annoyances aside, Mal figured if Kelly was putting on a show of not knowing her daughter was dead, it was worth the price of admission.

She went into a bedroom in the back, then crossed the hall into another room. And then a third, constantly calling for Chloe.

She returned to the front door, looking baffled, the realization not yet dawning. Soon it would come in a wave.

"Um, she's not here. Maybe she's out there at the playground. Did you check there? What's this even about? What did she do now?"

"What do you mean, *now?*" Mal asked.

"Did she break something? Did one of these fuckers complain about her bothering them again?"

Mal took a deep breath as she palmed the phone in her jacket pocket. "When's the last time you saw Chloe?"

"Um, this morning as she was getting ready for school. I work nights. Was sleeping until you all knocked. What's going on?"

A detective was charged with the dual tasks of informing the next of kin that a loved one was dead while registering their initial response for signs of guilt. Did they seem surprised? Was their response appropriate, or staged?

Given that no two people processed grief the same way, with responses ranging from stone cold silence to hysterics and fainting, it was never easy. But it was essential to see the next of kin's reaction and weigh it against what you eventually learn about the person.

Mal pulled out her phone, found the least gruesome photos, and held it up to Kelly. "Is this your daughter?"

Kelly's eyes went wide. She reached for the phone, touched the screen, shook her head. "What is this?"

"We believe we found your daughter's body in the woods."

"No, no …" Kelly fell to her knees, shaking her head. "I want to see her."

"You'll get your chance, but right now our crime scene technicians are working the case."

"I want to see her!" Kelly stood and started toward the door.

Mike raised his hands to block her.

She shoved him. "Let me see my daughter!"

Mike tried to calm her, but Kelly pushed straight past him and into the yard outside her first-floor apartment.

Mal caught up with Kelly — it would be better for a woman to calm her. "You'll get a chance to see her. But not now. Not if you want us to catch the person that did this. We need you down at the station. You can help by telling us everything you can about your daughter, and anyone who might have had anything to do with this."

Kelly turned to Mal, tears streaming down her face, "I …"

Then she puked in the grass.

Mal and Mike waited for her to finish.

Once done she looked up. "I need to shower and change."

"I'm sorry," Mal said. "We'll need you to stay as you are. We'll want to check you over and take your clothing."

"What? What are you talk — Wait, you think I killed my little girl?"

She backed away, her hands raised as if guarding the air between them. For a moment, Mal thought she might run.

"It's too early to think anything, but we need to rule out suspects before we can narrow our search."

"I did not kill my daughter. I love her!"

Mal noted the present tense of the word, *love*, rather than *loved*, something the girl's killer may not say. A minor detail, but one of many you notice when interviewing next of kin.

A skinny, dark-haired man in his late thirties or early forties approached. He looked vaguely European. Trendy, his dress shirt tucked into skinny jeans, bunched above gleaming yellow sneakers.

"What's going on?" he asked Kelly, practically ignoring Mal and Mike.

"They're saying that Chloe's dead. They found her in the woods! And they think *I* killed her!"

"What?" he said to Mal, the closest to him. "There's no way she killed her daughter."

The man's right hand was in his pocket. Peculiar. Mal didn't notice a bulge beyond the size of his hand, so *maybe* it was a casual manner of standing. But it could be something else.

She saw a blood stain on his shiny yellow sneaker and said, "What's your name, sir?"

"Scott, Scott Isaacson. Why?"

His nervous blue eyes flitted from her to Mike and back to her. Mal turned to Mike and winked.

Mike eyed the guy then stepped toward him. "Where do you live, sir?"

"In Building B. Why?"

Mike asked, "When's the last time you saw Chloe?"

"Um, I dunno. Yesterday? The day before? On the way to school."

"Do you remember seeing her talking to anyone else? Or did you notice anything odd about her?"

Mal sensed Kelly staring at them, waiting for Scott's response, likely desperate for any information he might have.

"Um, no. She was just walking to the bus stop, same as usual, alone."

"Thank you." Mal reached into her jacket. "Here's my card. If you think of anything else, give me a call, anytime."

Mal specifically held the card far to the left so Scott would have to pull out his right hand to get it. Turning to reach with his left would be way too suspicious.

He drew his right and reached for the card. It was bandaged with thick gauze, enough to cover a knife wound.

"What happened to your hand, Scott?" Mal asked, handing him the card.

"Um," he looked down as if he didn't know it had been dressed. "I cut myself."

"When?"

"This morning, making breakfast."

"And what do you wear when you make breakfast?"

"What?" His nostrils flared. "Why?"

"I'm curious."

"I dunno. Boxers and a tee shirt."

"What else?"

"What does this have to do with anything?"

Mike came closer. "Just answer the question, man."

"I dunno, nothing."

"So, no socks or anything?" Mal asked.

"No. I get up, put on a tee shirt and make breakfast. I don't see why this matters."

Mal locked eyes with him. "I'm just wondering how you got blood on your sneakers."

Scott looked down.

Then he looked up.

And then he ran.

Chapter 3 - Jasper Parish

JASPER WOKE to movement beside him.

He was surprised to find himself naked, covered in a down comforter, lying in bed next to a woman, whose mocha-colored nude back and curly shoulder-length dark hair was turned to him.

His heart raced. He tried to remember last night but came up blank.

Jasper looked around the bedroom. It was large, with white walls and all white furniture. A tall plant near the closet offered the room its only color. It was a clean, minimalistic look that reminded him of his bedroom back home. The morning sun streamed through sheer white curtains. And behind them, the outline of treetops. He was on a second story or higher.

He couldn't see the woman's face, so he turned, searching for other clues to jar his memory.

On the nightstand to his right, Jasper saw his phone and a silver-framed photo of a woman in her thirties and a light-skinned mixed girl with pigtails and a pink jacket standing in the sand with an ocean behind them. Both were smiling, happy. The girl looked to be around seven or eight.

Who are these people?

Jasper had woken up a few times in the past couple of years with no memory of how he got there, but he was usually in his car or in someone's backyard. He'd always figured it was one of the side effects of his condition, or maybe the medication, but he'd never found himself in trouble. He'd also never blacked out after a kill, which was one of his greatest fears. Being a vigilante was difficult enough without fainting then waking up hours later without any memory.

Fortunately, the blackouts were rare, and usually only happened when Jasper was losing sleep.

This was the first time he'd woken in bed with someone. He wondered who the woman was, where she lived, what he'd said to get her into bed, and how he'd extract himself.

She turned over, smiling at him.

And that smile triggered something inside him. Not a memory so much as an odd familiarity.

"Hey," she said, leaning forward to kiss him.

It wasn't the kiss of a one-night-stand. It too was *familiar*.

"What's wrong?"

"Um, just a headache," Jasper said, not entirely lying.

She slid out of bed, the white down comforter slipping off of her naked body. The woman was breathtaking. Jasper was instantly, uncomfortably, aroused.

She went to the bathroom then returned with a bottle of Tylenol and a paper cup half-filled with water.

"Here ya' go." She handed him the cup then unscrewed the bottle's cap and spilled a pair of pills into his palm.

"Two enough?"

"Yes," he said, looking up and meeting her kind, soft eyes. "Thank you."

She closed the bottle and set it on her nightstand, then slid back under the comforter. She ran a hand over Jasper's arm.

She probably wanted to continue whatever they were doing last night. He was physically ready. But mentally, no.

Jasper had never been the sort of man who could have sex with a stranger. He married his first love, Carissa. He'd never thought of straying. And even in the years after cancer had claimed her, it still felt like cheating.

He wasn't sure if that was because he still saw his wife's ghost, or whatever she was, or if it was just that he couldn't move on.

The woman was staring at Jasper, concerned. "Don't tell me you're thinking about leaving already."

Jasper said nothing.

She sat up, crossing her arms over her breasts. "Come on, at least stay for the weekend. Ophelia wants to see you again."

Ophelia?

His mind flashed on the girl in the picture.

Have I been here before?

It seemed impossible, but the personal way this woman — Alicia, her name popped into his head like a computer helper prompt — was talking to him, this couldn't have been a one-night stand.

He felt dizzy, trying to sort through what was happening.

"You don't look so good. When's the last time you ate?"

He shook his head. "I … I dunno."

"I'm making you breakfast. And you're staying for the weekend. I don't want to hear any of your usual excuses.

Now take a shower then come out and have breakfast with us."

She stood without another word, or an answer from Jasper, and then got dressed and left the bedroom.

Jasper stared at the door as it closed. His small travel suitcase sat behind it. He'd planned this trip, despite not having any memory of doing so.

He grabbed his phone, but it was different from the one he usually carried. One of the decoy phones he used while hunting monsters.

He checked his last dialed numbers — two calls to a 954 area code.

If those were to Alicia, that meant he was in South Florida. He tried to remember if there was anyone on his Kill List in South Florida. There had to be a few, but Jasper couldn't remember if any were ones he was ready to move on.

He tried to space his kills, not just from each other, but also from those crimes that earned the monsters a spot on his List. He usually worked to make the deaths look random or like a suicide, or perhaps at the hands a rival criminal. The fewer people looking for a vigilante, the easier it was to stay invisible.

He quickly showered, then dressed in a pair of jeans and a long-sleeve black button down. He still had clothes in his suitcase for another day or two, which made him wonder how long this trip was supposed to be.

Jasper descended the stairs to the pleasant scent of frying eggs and bacon. His stomach rumbled.

When he reached the bottom, the young girl with pigtails at the dining room table looked up from her coloring with a giant smile.

"Dennis!" she yelled, practically knocking her chair to

the floor as she launched herself from the table toward him.

She leaped into his arms, hugging him fiercely.

Jasper hugged her back, but it was no match for her intensity.

He felt like he'd woken up in someone else's body, with someone else's family. A pretender wearing another man's skin, reaping the love of a family earned by some other man.

The child — *Ophelia* — asked, "How long are you here, Dennis?"

She took his hand and led him to the table.

He pulled out the chair next to her and sat.

Ophelia hopped into her chair, full of a buzzing energy he hadn't seen since Jordyn was a kid.

"I made you some pictures." She slid a pile of drawings toward him.

Alicia appeared and sat a wire basket of muffins on the table. She winked at Jasper. "Told you she was excited to see you."

He smiled.

"This one is a unicorn, like the one in that story you read to me last time you were here." Ophelia jabbed her fingers on one of the pages.

He held it up and examined the crayon drawing of a unicorn running through a forest, smiling a big goofy smile. A young girl was clinging to the unicorn's saddle. She looked suspiciously like Ophelia.

"Is that you?"

"Yeah, don't you remember? You changed the story so that it was me instead of the boy?"

"Of course," he said, racking his brain for any memory of this girl at all. "I just wanted to hear you say it."

"And here's one of you in the Bahamas." She pointed

to a drawing of a man sitting in a hammock, sipping a giant pink drink with umbrellas.

"Thank you. That looks just like me."

"And here's one of mommy and me, so you can remember us when you're traveling around the world."

The drawing was of Ophelia and her mom standing in what appeared to be a garden full of flowers and trees. A rainbow paired two sides of the sky. Both were smiling, with flowers in their hair.

"Aw, thank you, sweetie." Jasper leaned over and kissed the girl on her head. "I'll take these with me everywhere I go."

"Promise?"

"Yes, ma'am."

She frowned, her nose scrunching.

"What?" he asked.

"Mom only calls me ma'am when I'm in trouble."

"That's not true," Alicia said from the kitchen, loading bacon from the frying pan onto a large plate, "*ma'am.*"

Ophelia giggled. Her raspy voice and laugh reminded Jasper so much of Jordyn when she was the girl's age.

A sadness descended as he remembered his argument with Jordyn's ghost.

She'd begged him not to kill Calum Kozack, the young man who raped her and drove her to suicide. She'd said it was too dangerous to kill him, that Jasper would draw attention to himself because Calum would be linked to her, which would lead detectives to finding him. He ignored her, so she threatened not to come around anymore.

He thought she was bluffing, saying what she had to, doing what she thought she should to protect him. But it had been a while since Calum "vanished" and Jordyn along with him.

And now Jasper found himself wondering if the

vengeance was worth it. He'd killed the man who had destroyed his daughter's life and essentially caused Calum to kill his sadistic girlfriend who had orchestrated the rape.

And while Jasper still had one more name on the list of Jordyn's rapists, Calum's cousin, Perry, Jasper had taken care of the two most responsible. Despite Jordyn's fears, nobody had found Calum's body, let alone linked Jasper to the crime. The common consensus was that Calum and his girlfriend took off together, maybe eloped. Nobody was looking for Jasper, whom the world believed to have perished in a fire years ago.

Justice was done and the world still spun. And Jasper felt empty. And now Jordyn refused to talk.

It was an odd sensation to miss someone who might not exist. Who might be merely a figment of his imagination, if the shrinks were to be believed. He missed her all the same.

"Earth to Dennis," Ophelia said, snapping Jasper from his thoughts. "What do you want to drink?"

She was standing next to him, one arm on her hip, tapping her foot like a sassy little miss.

"Oh. Sorry. Do you have milk?"

"Yes, sir."

"Thank you, ma'am," he said with a wink.

Ophelia smirked then bounded toward the kitchen.

Alicia set a large blue bowl of scrambled eggs next to a plate overflowing with bacon. There was enough food to feed them three times over.

"Are we having an army over?" Jasper joked.

Ophelia laughed as she returned to the dining room holding a tall glass of milk filled to nearly the rim.

She handed it to him carefully. As she focused on not spilling the drink, he noticed the tip of her tongue sticking out the right corner of her mouth.

"Here you go, sir," she smiled.

He resisted another *ma'am* and simply said, "Thank you."

BREAKFAST WAS PERFECT, and not just the food.

As they talked, Jasper assembled some of *Dennis's* back-story. Apparently, he was a travel writer, which explained why he only came into town every so often. He'd also told them that he lived in Washington State, enough of a distance to prevent more frequent visits.

Alicia was a realtor, though he wasn't quite sure how they'd met, or how long he'd been seeing her.

As breakfast was winding down, Jasper risked asking a question that he hoped wouldn't reveal his lack of memories.

"How long have I been coming here? Time is so weird when you're living out of hotels for most of the year."

"You started coming here last year," Ophelia said. "You don't remember?"

"It's all a blur after a while."

Ophelia frowned, turning her attention back to the remnants of eggs on her plate.

Jasper was trying to think of something to say, anything that might move the conversation from awkward back to pleasant. His phone buzzed.

He fished it out of his pocket, looked at the screen, and was confused when he saw his mentor, Lenny Barnes' name next to a text:

Confused, Dennis? Meet me at the 5th Street Park at 11.

What was Lenny doing in town?

Jasper didn't think it was possible to be more confused.

He stuffed the phone back in his pocket and smiled.

Chapter 4 - Mallory Black

MAL BOLTED, a beat behind Isaacson.

Mike and deputy Nestor Lorenzo were trailing Mal by at least ten yards. Nestor was probably already panting.

Scott slalomed through the maze-like spaces between buildings, far more familiar with his surroundings than Mal.

He reached the parking lot surrounding the complex, twenty yards away and not slowing.

Mal's only hope was cornering him toward the nine-foot brick wall separating the gated community from the woods beyond.

The gates leading out of the complex were behind them. His only option was to surrender, or turn right along the parking lot and navigate his way back into the maze.

But that nearly killed his odds of escape. Other deputies had joined the chase, and he was likely to find them.

"Stop!" Mal shouted, out of breath, as if he might hear her desperate plea, then stop, turn, and apologize with his wrists raised and waiting.

He reached the corners where the north and western walls met. To Mal's utter dismay, he didn't stop.

He planted his left foot on the west wall, pivoted, and exploded off the left wall and onto the right, performing a perfectly executed wall run, before reaching up, grabbing the ledge with both hands, and hauling himself over the edge.

"Fuck!" Mal shouted. Just her luck that one of her few foot chases is behind Parkour Pete.

The man vanished over the top of the wall and dropped into the woods, where he could easily disappear.

This was escalating quickly. She'd have to call backup. Choppers. Even then, they would probably lose their only suspect.

Mal raced toward the wall, considering only two options: wait for Mike and Lorenzo to give her a hand up, or follow the leader.

She was out of practice, but Mal bet on muscle memory as she approached the corner. She'd either execute the wall run, smack face first into the wall, or fall flat on her ass and never hear the end of it.

Mal reached the wall and leaped, planting her left foot into the left wall, then pivoted off, digging her right one into the north face. She reached up and grabbed the lip of the wall, gasping as her fingers found purchase.

She hefted herself over the wall then scanned the woods for movement.

She saw Scott, twenty yards deep in the woods.

She dropped to the ground and rolled, then leaped to her feet.

A splintering pain tore through her spine.

She froze.

"Dammit!" She clutched at her back.

She must have pulled something. But there was no time for pain.

Scott was getting away.

Mal shoved the pain as low as it would go and started running, wincing as every step echoed through her back in seismic waves of pain.

Must.

Keep.

Going.

She gritted her teeth, pushing herself forward, faster and harder until he was only ten yards ahead, heading toward where the woods thinned then ended at a four-lane street that would likely be bustling right about now.

That might be enough to slow him. Unless Scott was crazy enough to run right into traffic.

I hope not.

Mal wasn't in the mood to play *Frogger*.

Scott reached the edge of the woods, stepped onto the sidewalk, and then looked back.

His eyes went wide as he saw her closing in.

He turned to run but stopped dead in his tracks as a red pickup whizzed by. That was all the time she needed to close most of the distance.

Instead of trying to cross the road, Scott started to run north on the sidewalk.

Mal followed, ignoring the sharp pain pinching her back hard enough to start the tears.

"Stop!" she shouted.

Mal considered reaching for her radio, but that would only slow her down. She hoped that Mike and Lorenzo had figured out where she was and were sending cars to intercept.

They were approaching an intersection and heavy traffic.

Scott had to stop.

And she caught up.

Scott knew he was trapped, and didn't put up a fight.

Still, she flung him to the sidewalk, certain she'd have to explain his bruised face. But right now, she didn't care. He needed to share her pain.

She dug her knee into the small of his back and cuffed him.

"I didn't do anything!" he cried out.

"Then why the fuck are you running?" She buried her knee deeper into his back until he cried out.

She was tempted to grab him by his hair and yank his head back, scream at him some more, but then a siren blurted behind her.

Mal turned to see a squad car pull up, light bar flashing.

The cruiser stopped, and the driver, a rookie named Mary Reese, was talking to dispatch as the passenger door opened to Sergeant Randal Greer.

She looked down to see Scott's eyes widen as he took in all six foot seven inches of Greer, whose dedication to the weight room only paled in comparison to his time at the gun range. He was one of the top deputies on the road, and would surely make detective soon.

"I bet you wouldn't have run from him, eh?" Mal said as she stood, trying to hide her pain.

Greer smiled. "I heard you scaled a wall?"

"Yeah," Mal said. "No big deal."

"Wow, I'm impressed." Greer yanked Scott up with one hand and shoved him toward the car. "That means I'll be seeing you in the gym more?"

"Yeah, I'll get right on that." Mal laughed.

She wasn't sure if Greer was being flirtatious, but he loved to give her a hard time whenever he saw her eating junk food or drinking a sugary coffee. He'd invited her to work out with him a few times, too.

"You shouldn't run," Greer said as he opened the rear door and shoved Scott in, bumping his head against the doorframe on his way.

"Whoops." Greer slammed the door and turned to Mal, still smiling, "You alright?"

She didn't want to admit she was in pain. She'd probably be met with a too enthusiastic *No pain no gain!*

"Yeah, I'll be fine. Thanks."

"No problem. Seeya back at the station."

She nodded, returning his smile, just as Mike and Lorenzo emerged from the woods like clueless kids who'd missed all the action.

Mike looked at the squad car, then at Mal. "So, you caught him?"

"You doubted?"

"Well, I didn't realize my partner was Spiderman."

Lorenzo laughed. "*I* didn't doubt you. By the way, that was fucking awesome. Where'd you learn those parkour moves?"

"I tried out for that *American Ninja* show back in the day."

"Bullshit," Lorenzo said as they started walking back to the apartment complex, though he seemed unsure.

He was a sweet guy, but incredibly naive, especially for a cop. Mal liked to mess with his head, spinning tall tales to see how far she could go before he caught on.

Lorenzo turned to Mike. "Seriously?"

Mike shrugged, then turned and winked at Mal.

Mal winked back.

∾

THE APARTMENT COMPLEX WAS ELECTRIC. Word had spread about the body. This was typical of any murder and amplified a hundredfold when the victim was a child.

But she sensed another energy — something in the air insisting that this case was different. Mal wasn't sure if it was the number of spellbound neighbors gathered outside the caution tape, the dozens of news vans already lined up just outside the staging area, or the increased presence of the Creek County Sheriff's Office.

In addition to the mobile command unit, there had to be three dozen CCSO vehicles. Detectives were interviewing everyone they could while deputies walked the complex, searching for anything worthy of investigation. Techs processed the crime scene, and would soon be processing the Conlan apartment. Then, after Mal got a search warrant, Scott Isaacson's place.

But on top of that, both other homicide units were on duty.

Captain Wilson stepped out of the mobile command unit and made a beeline toward them. "This neighbor guy, Isaacson, do we like him?"

"It's too soon to say," Mal said. "Why?"

"Because we've got a Category Five shit storm gathering, and I need answers yesterday."

"What the hell is going on?" Mal asked, confused.

"You mean you don't know?" Wilson asked, his fluffy dark gray eyebrows arched.

"Know what?"

"The dead girl's mom is Councilman Conlan's daughter."

"Oh, fuck," Mal said.

"Oh, fuck indeed. So, we like this guy for the murder?"

"We haven't even searched his place, much less interviewed him."

"What the fuck is the hold-up?"

Mal didn't even bother explaining that she just chased the neighbor down and hadn't had a chance to call the judge for a warrant. Wilson was on fire, and only wanted to hear "Yes, sir!"

Councilman Harry Conlan wasn't just one of the most powerful council members in Pine Harbour, he was also one of Sheriff Bell's biggest critics, and good friends with the former sheriff, Claude Barry, running for his old job in the November election.

This was the sort of perfect storm that could change the face of the sheriff's department. Good deputies and detectives, like Mal, who had supported Gloria Bell in her bid to win would be ousted in a heartbeat if Barry weaseled his way back in.

"On it, sir," Mal said.

"Good. I'm gonna go call the sheriff and calm her down."

Alone with Mike in front of the command unit, Mal asked, "Can you walk the Conlan apartment? I'm going to call Judge Harrison and see if I can get a warrant. Plus, I need to sit for a minute."

"You okay?"

"Yeah, I think I pulled something when I landed."

"Yeah, I got it, you go recover, *American Ninja*." Mike laughed.

Mal thanked him, then went to her car. She called Harrison on the way. He didn't answer, so she left a message on his voicemail explaining that she needed a warrant fast. Among the Creek County judges, she liked Harrison most. He was younger than the others and not part of the Good Ol' Boy network that was always grumpy as shit when you called after hours.

Mal got inside her car — thankfully parked away from

NOLON KING & DAVID WRIGHT

most of the action then leaned the seat back. She cranked the cold to full blast and closed her eyes, waiting for the pain to pass.

But, as she sat, the agony worsened, every movement lighting fireworks on her spine.

Mal rarely had back pain, maybe once or twice a year, but it was intense on the rare cases it came. Thankfully, it was usually brief, lasting less than an hour. Only a couple of times was she laid up an entire day. And she usually woke up feeling *great* the next day, as if the pain had never been there.

She'd seen chiropractors, each with different diagnoses and suggested remedies, including surgery she refused to have. And she'd seen ineffective acupuncturists. She'd mostly given up on a cure. Back pain was just something you occasionally suffered.

The longer Mal sat in the car, the worse the pain seemed to get.

Of course, the itch came.

Because the pills *always* offered relief.

She'd managed two weeks without one, and hated to give in, but surely this was a legitimate need. She couldn't function with this level of pain. And if she couldn't function, then Mal couldn't find Chloe's killer.

A voice admonished her.

Oh, come on. You don't need these. Grab some Tylenol from the trunk.

She reached for the trunk release, but someone was sliding a blade into her spine. She cried out, freezing in place, waiting for the fresh wave to roll on by.

As the pain receded, she gingerly reached into her pants pocket, retrieved the small plastic pill case, and opened it.

She dumped two pills into her palm, then popped them

into her mouth, washing them down with a tepid bottle of Diet Pepsi sitting in the console.

Mal hated surrendering to the pills, but there was no time for guilt. And for the first time, she felt grateful for her constant self-inflicted torment by keeping the pills so close to her side.

Her phone rang, the judge with a yes.

Time to work.

Chapter 5 - Mallory Black

MAL KNOCKED on Scott's door, hiding her pain. The neighbors said that he had a fiancée, but that Scott still lived alone.

Mal nodded to the older redheaded beside her, the apartment complex's manager. She unlocked the door, "Here you go, Officer."

"Thank you," Mal said.

"Should I wait here or …"

"I'll get you when I'm done." Mal watched the woman leave, then slowly slipped on her gloves and booties. A young brunette woman jogged up to her, carrying an evidence tech kit.

"Sorry, I got stuck in traffic and then couldn't find a spot." The woman barely looked old enough to have graduated high school. A lanyard dangled from her neck: *Charley Eaves, Evidence Technician.*

"No problem," Mal said. "Haven't seen you before. You new?"

"Yeah, I was working in St. Johns, but got a transfer here last month."

"Welcome," Mal said, stepping into the cold apartment without waiting for the woman to put on her gloves and booties.

She turned on the lights and was immediately and thoroughly surprised. The house was immaculate. Everything gleamed. The walls, the furniture, and the appliances. The place was porn for minimalists, and so perfectly clean that Mal figured Scott either had a great cleaning service or was obsessive about his housework.

The apartment walls were all clean shades of taupe and sand. Most of the color came from photos on the walls in the living room and kitchen, most of them nudes.

Mal went to the kitchen to see if Scott's story about cutting himself during breakfast held up. Of course, being a clean freak, his sink was spotless.

She opened the dishwasher. Also empty.

"You ever date a guy this clean?" Mal made small talk while Charley unpacked her kit.

She laughed. "I've got two brothers, both bachelors, and this is pretty much the opposite of their places."

Mal laughed, then stopped because it hurt too much.

She walked the house, searching for evidence tying Scott to either the woods or Chloe. One good thing about searching a place with so few things — the work went quickly. Good, because Mal wasn't sure how much bending she could do before crying for mercy and begging Mike to take over.

The apartment had two bedrooms, the second being used as a home office/photo studio.

Mal searched obvious hiding spots in each room. Finding nothing, she went to a kitchen closet which housed a washer and dryer.

She opened the washer. Nothing.

But the dryer still had clothes. And not a full load. Two

items — jeans and a tee shirt. Not warm, but judging how quickly Scott probably put stuff away, likely laundered today.

Mal took photos of the clothes then instructed Charley to collect both them and the lint trap.

"Got it," Charley said, retrieving the evidence bags.

Mal went back into the home office and approached a large row of drawers. She opened the first one and immediately felt sick to her stomach.

She was greeted by a large photo print of a nude boy and girl, probably around six and seven, building a sand castle on the beach.

There were more photos of those kids beneath it. And others. There were also some of adults, but most of the attention seemed to be on the children.

The nearest pier was clear in the background. There's a good chance these photos were taken by Isaacson himself.

She went through more than forty photos, some printed as eight by tens, feeling nauseous. While none of the photos were pornographic or zoomed in on the children's genitals, they showed admiration for their bodies.

She looked at the computer on the pristine desk, and the cameras lining the shelves to the right, wondering how many other photos of a similar, or worse, nature forensics would find.

And would they find any photos of Chloe?

Chapter 6 - Jasper Parish

JASPER HAD TOLD Alicia and Ophelia that he had an errand to run, then followed his phone's directions to the park where Lenny asked to meet him.

The old man was sitting on a bench near the jogging trail entrance, wearing dark blue cargos and a gray hoodie, holding a bag of popcorn and feeding the mass of pigeons at his feet.

"Hello," Jasper said, taking a seat next to Lenny. "What are you doing here?"

They were in Barlow Springs, a small town about two and a half hours south of Pine Harbour.

"I figured you'd need me."

"So, you *knew* I was coming here? Did I tell you?"

"No."

"So, how did you know?"

"You haven't figured this out yet?"

"Man, don't talk to me in riddles."

Lenny smiled and took a bite of popcorn. "What do you remember?"

"Nothing. I woke up next to a strange woman who's acting like she knows me."

"Because she does."

"Well, that's nice, I have no memory of her at all. Who the hell is she? How many times have I been here?"

"Her name is Alicia. Nice woman, from what you've told me. You met her after a difficult time, about a year and a half ago. She thinks you're a travel writer. Married, but miserable."

"Wait. I—"

"You were stressed out. You got in the car and drove. You met Alicia in the hotel restaurant, where you were staying. You hit it off, and one thing led to another."

"How many times have I been here?"

"Four."

"Four times and I don't remember any of them? What the hell?"

"My guess is that it's part of whatever's wrong with you. Maybe you needed a break after what happened with …" Lenny lowered his voice as two women jogged by, glancing at them. "Calum."

Jasper nodded. "I don't get it. How can I have this whole other relationship going on and not remember any of it?"

"Do I look like a shrink?" Lenny met Jasper's eyes. "I don't know why. Maybe some part of your brain is protecting this, wanting to keep it separate from … well, your other activities."

"So, what? I'm usually someone else while I'm on these little vacations?"

"For all intents and purposes, yes."

"What happened this time? Why did I wake up before I returned home?"

Lenny shrugged.

"And how did you know to come here?"

Lenny laughed. "You still don't get it?"

"Get what?" Jasper asked, growing increasingly annoyed with the old man.

"Look, Son, here's my advice — don't overthink this. Just enjoy the good times while they last."

Lenny stood and handed the popcorn to Jasper. "I've gotta go. Text if you need anything."

"Where are you going?"

"May as well get a jog in while I'm here." Lenny pulled the hoodie over his head and ran into the woods along the path.

Jasper stared down at the bag of popcorn, then at the cooing pigeons strutting beneath him, waiting.

He emptied the bag onto the ground and tossed it into a trash can.

Then he went back to Alicia's.

"WHAT *IS* IT?" Ophelia scrunched her nose across the table from Jasper.

They were sitting under the warm sun and a clear blue sky, at one of the beach tables at The Fat Porpoise, a trendy, family-friendly seafood joint.

"Just try it," he said, offering the basket with pieces of fried calamari nestled on a large lettuce leaf.

Alicia, sitting next to Ophelia, laughed. "She doesn't like to try new things."

Sounds like someone else I know, he thought, thinking of Jordyn's notoriously limited menu when she was Ophelia's age. And older.

"The fact that you're not telling me what calamari is makes me highly suspicious." Ophelia returned her attention to the crayons and canvas on her kid's menu. She was hard at work drawing an anime looking girl with oversized eyes.

"Okay, calamari are fried squid," Jasper admitted.

"Ewww, like the squid in the ocean?"

"Yeah," he said, barely able to contain his laughter through Ophelia's series of horrified faces.

"No way I am eating *that*. And you two are disgusting!"

Alicia took a piece of calamari out of the basket, dipped it in the aioli, then took a bite right in Ophelia's face. "Mmmm, *sooooooo* yummy!"

Ophelia retched dramatically like a cat about to serve up a hairball.

Alicia laughed. "Such a drama queen!"

"Am not," Ophelia said, coloring the girl's hair pink with blue streaks.

"So, what *do* you like?" Jasper asked. Ophelia had ordered chicken fingers and fries for her entree, but every kid probably liked that.

"Um, chicken fingers."

"Besides chicken fingers … and, before you say it, french fries. Maybe something not fried?"

She looked up thoughtfully, then met his eyes. "Mac n' cheese."

"Okay, something healthy?"

"Mac n' cheese *is* healthy. It's got milk and milk is good for you."

"Mac n' cheese is not good for you."

"Yes, it is. My teacher said anything is healthy, that it's all about the serving size."

Jasper shook his head.

Alicia said, "Are you really going to try to argue food with a nine-year-old?"

"Okay. How about fruits and veggies. Do you like any of those?"

"Um, fruit, yes. Veggies no. Yuck." Ophelia made a gagging gesture.

He laughed. "Okay, what fruits?"

"All the fruits."

"Wow, *all* the fruits?"

"Yep! Apples, bananas, pears, grapes, kiwi, melon, oranges, strawberries, blueberries, pineapple, raspberries, kumquats, blackberries, and mango, and …" she paused to think of more, then held up the drawing, completed. "You like?"

"Yes, that's very good," Jasper said. "Who is it?"

"I dunno. I made her up."

"She's not from a cartoon or comic?"

"No." Ophelia handed the drawing to her mom for inspection.

"Great drawing. You're improving on hands."

"Thank you," she said, retrieving her drawing. She started to fill the background with blue.

"She loves drawing," Alicia said. "She wants to be an animator."

"And a veterinarian," Ophelia added, not taking her eyes from the paper.

"And an astronaut," Alicia said, smiling.

"Wow, that's quite the range," Jasper said.

"Range? What do you mean?"

As he explained, the server came with the food.

They ate and laughed, enjoying the soothing salt water wind, the crashing surf, and the occasional squawk of a seagull searching for scraps along the boardwalk and beach beyond it. Jasper wanted to freeze the moment and hold it.

Look, Son, here's my advice — don't overthink this. Just enjoy the good times while they last.

47

But even at the moment's joy, the shine in both girls' eyes, and the peaceful surroundings, Jasper felt a darkness chattering at the edges, like storm clouds about to roll in.

And those clouds came literally as they returned home amid a sudden, heavy downpour. As they approached Alicia's house, Jasper noticed a new addition to the driveway, a small car stuffed with bags, boxes, and clothing.

A woman lay slumped inside, her head on the steering wheel.

"Shit," Alicia said.

"Who is it?"

"Trouble."

Chapter 7 - Mallory Black

IT WAS NEARLY seven o'clock when the pain in Mal's back finally began to relent.

She sat in the observation room adjacent to the interview room where Kelly waited. Mal stared at the photos Mike had printed, evidence from Kelly's apartment. No signs of a struggle or a murder taking place. But they did find a stash of drugs. Pills, weed, coke, and heroin. Plus, five grand in a cereal box atop the fridge.

"You think she's dealing?" Mal asked.

"Well, there wasn't any paraphernalia. And from my interviews, and paperwork from the others I saw, nobody said she was. Had a few other accusations, but not dealing."

"What sorts of accusations?"

"That she was a prostitute."

"Really? And you find anything to support that?"

"Forensics has her computer. I didn't find ledgers or anything, but there were quite a few condoms and sex toys."

"Well, if rubbers and toys make you a whore, book me now."

Mike shook his head. "Well, thanks for *that*."

"Such a prude. Your poor wife."

Mike pushed some of the photos aside, then slid one of the little girl's room over to her.

The bedroom was clean. Pink walls, cute furniture, pictures of puppies and unicorns gracing the wall. The bed was neatly made, a dozen stuffed animals lined along the wall, reminding Mal of how Ashley used to organize her "stuffies" before leaving her room in the morning.

"Notice anything?" Mike asked.

Mal looked at the photo searching for anything out of the ordinary. Nothing stuck out. "No. What?"

"The closet door."

Mal picked the photo up and brought it closer, noticing that one of the two sliding doors was ajar, just a few inches. Another line of stuffed animals was lined in front of the door. In the gap between it and the frame, she noticed something sticking out. A pillowcase?

Mike handed her a second photo, this one with the door open. Inside the closet were a pillow and sleeping bag, with a string of colored lights dangling above it. There were no clothes, nor toys or boxes.

"She slept in the closet?"

"I think so. We recovered hair strands on the pillowcase. "Does her sleeping in there strike you as odd?"

"Maybe, though Ashley used to like sleeping in a chair and blanket fort in the living room sometimes. But that was when she was like four or five. Definitely want to ask mom about this."

"You want to take lead on the interview, or should I?"

Mal stared through the one-way mirror. The young

mother sat at the table, staring down at her hands, long dark hair falling in her face.

There was something Mal didn't like about Kelly from the minute she met her. She wasn't sure if she was picking up on the woman's guilt or if Mal was simply pissed that the woman had just woken up, more than an hour after her daughter was supposed to be getting home from school.

Being a single mom was difficult. Mal could appreciate it. She had nothing but respect for anyone who managed to raise kids on their own. And sleep was probably tough to come by, but Mal couldn't imagine herself sleeping so late in the day while her young daughter was playing outside without adult supervision.

School had let out more than an hour and a half prior to them knocking on Kelly's door, and she was *still* sleeping. Had no idea her daughter was missing. She seemed annoyed by Chloe's existence until she found out about her body being found in the woods.

To Kelly's credit, she seemed to be in genuine pain after that. Still, Mal was annoyed with the woman, and reasonably sure that her irritation would affect the interview.

"I think you should lead."

"All right," he nodded. "Let's do this."

THE INTERVIEW ROOM WAS CLAUSTROPHOBIC, with three of the four white walls soundproof, and the fourth mostly a one-way mirror. The only furniture was a heavy metal table bolted to the ground and two chairs. Bright, unforgiving neon lights poured oppression from the ceiling. Cameras hung from two of the corners.

Despite this, Mal always felt at home in the interview room. The place where most suspects sealed their fate, confessing to the crime or fumbling enough to earn a conviction. As much as she liked the challenge of working a crime scene, trying to figure out what happened from disparate clues, Mal enjoyed the raw energy of the interview room even more.

Here the law gave her an advantage. Here her skills were truly tested. Figuring out a person was sometimes as much of a challenge as putting the pieces together at a murder scene.

Should she go in hard and intimidate someone into a confession? Or should she sympathize, and work to earn their trust?

Each suspect was a lock. She and Mike were locksmiths, trying to find the right combination of poking and pressure to tumble their secrets loose. Even when Mike took the lead, Mal worked the subject in other, subtler, ways.

She stood in the corner, hands in her pockets, non-threatening, listening, making all the right facial expressions to convey sympathy for Kelly's plight. But inside, Mal was watching, waiting for tell-tale signs that might indicate guilt.

When they first entered the room, Kelly wanted to know about her neighbor, Scott. Did he do it? Why did he run? And a dozen other questions.

Mike explained that they were investigating the situation, but couldn't go into more detail yet. For now, they just needed to rule Kelly out as a suspect, which meant a lot of questions. He apologized for the inconvenience.

Mal listened as Mike and Kelly worked from the beginning of the day, through the moment they knocked, sifting through Kelly's story for holes — anything she could use to leverage the truth.

But so far, her facts seemed to line up.

Kelly last saw Chloe in the morning, helping to get her ready for school, just like every morning. She walked her to the bus stop because kids sometimes teased Chloe for being autistic. After she got her daughter on the bus, Kelly went back to her apartment and then to bed.

That was at seven thirty in the morning.

And she didn't wake up until Mike and Mal knocked on her door at five fifteen.

"You said you work at night. Where do you work?" Mike asked. "Who watches Chloe?"

"I work from home. I'm a cam model."

"A cam model?" Mike repeated. "What's that?"

"I do cam shows."

"What does that mean?" Mike said, playing dumb.

"I get naked for guys who tip me," she said with the sort of indignation of someone who's had to explain her job far too often.

Kelly looked at Mal as if expecting her to be looking down her nose.

But matter-of-factly she said, "How many hours do you work a night?"

"I dunno. Half the night I'm chatting in the free rooms, looking for someone to go private. That's where the money is. On a good night, I can work a few hours and make enough. Other nights, you get cheap bastards looking to bust a nut for free. I can go all night and make nothing. It's a shit job, but the hours are flexible, and that's important with Chloe. I used to have a real job, but they got sick of me calling in."

"What was that job?" Mal asked. "And why'd you call in?"

"I worked as a server at the Boat Yard Cafe until about a year ago. Chloe used to get night terrors, a lot. And it would take forever to get her back to sleep. There was no way she could go to school after that, so our schedule was a mess. No regular job will put up with that. So, I started camming."

Mal nodded. "How does the camming thing work? Do the guys know your name or where you live?"

"No, I have a screen name, and a different email I use for work and everything else, so no chance of stalkers finding me if that's what you're suggesting."

"Did you have stalkers?"

"Yeah. Most guys are harmless, though. Some are even fun to talk to. But you also have your nut jobs, men who hate women, or who want you to act out sick fantasies."

"Like what?" Mike asked.

"Lots of age play shit."

"What's that?" Mike asked.

"Asking me to act like a little girl. Sometimes even asking me to act like a baby."

"And, do you?" Mike asked.

"I did some daddy and daughter role play, sure, but I refused to act like a little girl, let alone a baby. Fuck that shit."

Mal asked, "Did any of your clients know about Chloe, or ever see her?"

"God no," Kelly said, clearly offended. "I didn't tell people I had a kid. It kinda went against the whole college girl vibe."

Mal nodded. "So, nobody ever contacted you or sent you anything?"

"Well, yeah, people sent me stuff. I have a wish list that people can shop from and send me things. But I don't think they can get my address from that. Right?"

"Actually, I think they can see where the order shipped to," Mal said. "We'll want to get a list of anything sent to you so we can look into these people."

"You think one of *them* did it?" Kelly looked nauseous, as if she'd personally invited some pervert to her house to kill her kid.

"It's too early to say anything," Mike said. "Right now, we've got to explore all possibilities. Start ruling out suspects. Speaking of which, what's the story with the girl's father?"

She paused a beat, then asked, "What do you mean?"

"Is he in the picture at all? Does he see her? We'd like his name."

"I don't know her father. Just some random hook-up years ago."

"Do you have a name?" Mike pressed.

Kelly glared at Mike. Mal could sense Kelly's anger brewing. She wondered if maybe she should take the lead after a break. A single mom and cam girl who likely had to deal with shit from guys all the time probably didn't want another man judging her.

"I'm trying to tell you that I don't know who he was. I was sixteen, a wild girl back then. It could've been anyone."

"Ah," Mike said. "What about now? Is there a boyfriend?"

She crossed her arms. "Yes, there is a boyfriend."

"Can you give us a name?" Mike asked, also growing testy.

"Yeah, Eddie Dixon. You know him?"

Mike shook his head. "Should I?"

"He's been in and out of trouble ever since he was a kid. But he's not a bad guy."

Mal barely concealed a snicker. Eddie Dixon was about

as far as you got from "not a bad guy." He was a dirt bag drug dealer she busted for a DUI while working patrol. Eddie called her a "fucking cunt pig" when she pulled him over. He looked like he wanted to murder her. Maybe would have tried if she weren't wearing a badge.

Dixon had a rap sheet, though most of it was possession, a few assault and batteries. Never intent to sell, so thanks to overcrowded jails and lenient judges, he'd thus far avoided serious time. Mal figured he'd get popped for something serious eventually, or he'd piss off the wrong person and end up dead. But for now, he was just one of way too many dangerous scumbags walking the streets.

Mike steered the conversation to Kelly's neighbor. "What can you tell me about Scott?"

"I don't know much about him. He's a photographer, and he was always nice to us."

"Did you ever have him over to your house?"

"No. I don't entertain much. It's usually just Chloe and me. On weekends, I'll take her to my mom's house."

"Your mom is Gayle Conlan?"

"Yes."

"And your dad is Harry Conlan?"

"Yes."

"They're divorced?" Mike asked.

"Yeah, a long time ago. Why?"

"Just getting the facts," Mike said.

"When's the last time they saw Chloe?"

"We were at my mom's last weekend. She's out of town now, though. My dad, I don't know. I think he's in Georgia at some political conference."

"So, how often did you see Scott?"

"I dunno. We ran into him from time to time. Some of the parents would ask him to take portraits of their kids when their school photo sucked. And he always gave people a discount."

I bet he did.

"What about friends? Did Chloe have friends? Enemies? Anyone that would want to hurt her?"

"I wouldn't say she had any friends so much as kids who weren't mean to her. Wait, there was a little pudgy kid, Lucas. I guess he'd be her closest friend. Most of the kids were mean. Because she was different."

"You said she was autistic, right? Was she high functioning? What issues did she have?"

"She was mostly high-functioning. But now and then she'd freak out or have a meltdown over some texture or noise or whatever. And all of a sudden, she'd be a little kid having a tantrum. Other times, it wasn't so bad. She made weird noises and sung a lot, which seemed to make her a target, you know, because she was a little bit different. Kids suck."

"Can you tell us names of her friends, or of the kids who weren't mean to her? We'll want to talk to them. Also, the ones who were mean, and what they did to her?"

"Yeah, I can …" She stopped, her eyes widening. "Shit. I forgot."

"What?" Mike asked.

"There was an incident with Scott earlier in the year."

"What?"

"I don't remember all the details, but there's a little girl that lives in the apartment complex, Megan Hudson. She claimed that Scott locked her in the bathroom or something. They called the police and everything, but everyone, including her mom, said it was all a big misunderstanding. Ever since then, I hadn't seen too much of Scott. Do you think he might have been practicing before he went after my daughter?"

Kelly started to cry and asked for a tissue to blow her nose. Mike handed her a box from the table beside him. "Can I get a drink?" she asked, wiping her cheeks.

"Sure," Mal said. "What do you want? Coffee? Soda?"

"A Coke."

"You want anything?" Mal asked Mike.

"I need a break, so I'll join you."

They left Kelly alone in the room.

On their way to the break room, Mike asked Mal what she thought.

"Well, Eddie Dixon might explain the cash and drugs. But I want to know more about Isaacson locking a little girl in his bathroom. We need to find that report, and why charges weren't pressed."

On their way back, they ran into Aanya Batra in the hallway. She'd been working late, going through the digital evidence collected from the homes of Kelly and Scott.

"Find anything?" Mal asked.

"Nothing yet. Scott's computer was clean, but his hard drives are all encrypted, so that will take time to crack, assuming I can get anything."

"What about the mom?"

"Her computer, iPad, and phone were all clean. But there is something that struck me as odd. She *barely* had any photos of Chloe."

"What do you mean?" Mike asked.

"Well, usually a parent, especially a parent with just one kid, has a ton of photos, going all the way back to when they were a baby. Her gallery has a lot of selfies and pictures of her partying. A lot of pictures of her friends. She has more of her boyfriend than she has of her daughter."

Mal asked, "Any chance she has more photos somewhere else?"

"Well, I haven't had time to go through everything. She could have some in an online backup or something. I don't know. Just struck me as odd to only have a few pictures, and incidental ones at that, on her phone, the thing she carries with her all the time."

"You're right," Mal said. "Definitely something to look into. Anything else?"

"Not yet. I'm going to get a hot cocoa then head home. You need anything, give me a call."

"Sure thing," Mal said. "Thanks."

A few more steps down the hallway, they saw the last person either of them wanted to see — Jack Shapiro, the county's shadiest lawyer, and Harry Conlan's personal attorney. Shapiro was short, bald, and wore expensive dark suits that made him look like a mobster.

"Where is she?" Shapiro asked.

Mike said, "We're talking to her right now" before Mal could respond.

"You're done," Shapiro said. "You want to ask any more questions, call my office and arrange it."

Mal met the lawyer's beady eyes. "She's helping us find out what happened to her daughter. All we need is—"

"You're done. Now bring her out. And anything she's said to you already, I'll get thrown out of court."

"Excuse me?" Mal snapped. "It's an interview, not an interrogation."

"Yeah, I know how you operate. Now, please go get my client."

Mal spun around, not allowing Shapiro to see her disappointment.

Chapter 8 - Jasper Parish

THE CAR DOOR OPENED AND "TROUBLE" stepped into the rain. A skinny blonde wearing jeans and a sleeveless black tee with some band logo Jasper was unfamiliar with. Her arms were painted in tattoos.

Ophelia jumped out of the back of the car and ran to greet the woman with a big hug.

"Who is *that?*" Jasper asked.

"My younger sister. Well, step-sister, Karen. We stopped talking two years ago after a big fight."

"Ah," Jasper said. "Well, Ophelia seems to like her."

"Ophelia likes everyone." Alicia grinned. "She loves you, after all."

"Yeah, good point."

"I like her, too. Hell, I *love* her. Just too much drama. Always with the drama. I'm getting too old for drama."

"I hear that," Jasper said, watching Ophelia lead Karen toward the porch and out of the rain.

Alicia sighed. "Well, may as well see what she wants."

She killed the engine and got out of the car.

Jasper followed her to the house. They gathered under

the porch, rain pelting the roof, a cool breeze gathering strength around them.

"Alicia!" Karen said, hugging her as if they'd not spent two years apart. She looked at Jasper and smiled. "And who might you be?"

"This is Dennis. Mom's boyfriend."

"Ah, well *hello* Dennis," she said, shaking his hand.

"Hello, Karen. Nice to meet you," Jasper said, trying to hide his distaste for her flirtatious manner.

He'd seen a hundred, if not a thousand women just like her when he was a cop. Though she was Alicia's younger sister, hard drinking, and likely drugs, had done a number on her. She clung to her youth with too much makeup, disposable clothes, and cool tattoos, stuffing it all into an empty husk, terrified to grow up, or get old.

Women like this were always surrounded by drama, wreaking havoc in the lives of anyone close to them, until they had nobody left.

Jasper felt a bit guilty for his quick, even if only internal, dismissiveness of Alicia's sister, but he was rarely wrong when sizing someone up. She said it herself; the girl brought drama.

Alicia opened the front door. "Come inside."

Jasper followed with a sigh, wondering if he should cut this little vacation from his regular life short.

THEY SAT around the kitchen table, the adults drinking coffee and Ophelia hot cocoa, catching up on little things before Karen eventually got to the point and told them why she showed up on Alicia's doorstep.

"I need a place to crash for a few days, just until shit blows over with Clay. Whoops, sorry, O."

"That's okay. "Mom doesn't hide swear words from me."

"Really?" Karen said, her eyebrows arched. "Dad would be *soooo* disappointed."

Alicia smiled. "And that's exactly why I don't shield my child from adult words. I figure if she's exposed to them around me, I can give her context and make them less sexy. Hell, Dad was a control freak, and that didn't stop us from swearing."

"Or becoming dancers," Karen said, taking a drink.

"Oh, you dance?" Ophelia asked. "Like on Broadway?"

"Um, not quite." Karen looked at Alicia.

Alicia, for all her progressive parenting, nipped this one in the bud. "Hey, Ophelia, why don't you show Dennis your new game."

"Okay!" Ophelia grabbed Jasper's hand and led him away from the table.

Alicia winked at Jasper as he was pulled away. She mouthed, *Thank you.*

He nodded as he followed Ophelia to a room in the back of the house, dressed with a large L-shaped sectional couch, bean bags, and a 64" TV with two different gaming consoles connected to it.

Ophelia shut the door and whispered, "They want to talk about grownup stuff, I think."

"Yeah, probably. So, what games do you have?"

"Sit down, and I'll show you."

Jasper sat on one of two bean bags closest to the TV. Ophelia turned on the XBox One and navigated to a list of games, naming them off and explaining each one.

"I dunno, do you have anything simple? I'm old, remember?"

She laughed. "Oh, yeah, sometimes I forget."

He wasn't sure if she was kidding or if Ophelia considered him old. Of course, when he was her age, he remembered thinking twenty-year-olds had it all figured out. They were adults who had their shit together. Anything over forty was ancient.

"I got Pac-Man. Mom plays it sometimes, but it's kinda hard."

"Never heard of it. I'll give it a try."

"Okay … good luck." She started a two-player game. "You go first."

He took the controller. "What do I do?"

She explained how he was the "big yellow smiley guy" and he had to avoid the colorful ghosts.

He proceeded to crash his Pac-Man straight into a ghost.

She laughed. "Wow, I don't even die that quickly! Here, let me show you how it's done."

On her turn, she managed to get almost to the third level before her Pac-Man got killed.

"Okay," Jasper said, "Lemme see if I can do it."

He headed toward another ghost. "You said I'm supposed to chase them, right?"

"Noooo!" She grabbed his controller and steered him away from the ghosts. "Only when you eat one of those things that makes them blink."

He throttled his laughter as she handed back the controller and said, "You need to pay attention."

"Okay. I'll try."

He blazed through twenty-five levels, while Ophelia watched in amazement, leaning forward, her mouth agape.

When Jasper finally died, he turned, fighting the urge to grin, and asked, "Was that okay?"

"Okay? That was amazing!"

Ophelia jumped up, then ran out of the room and into the dining room.

Jasper followed.

"Mom, mom, Dennis got to level twenty-five in Pac-Man, and he never even played before tonight!"

"Wow," Alicia said, a twinkle in her eye as she met his. "Never played before, eh?"

He smiled. "Nope. Never even heard of it."

Ophelia caught their smiles. She threw her hands on her hips and glared at Jasper. "Wait a second! You *have* played before, haven't you?"

He smiled. "Maybe a time or hundred."

"You jerk!" She punched him in the arm. "I thought you were a noob!"

He laughed as she ran back to the TV. "Okay, I want a re-match!"

Before following Ophelia, Jasper looked at the sisters to get a sense of the room. Things were definitely tense. Not between them, they seemed to be getting along fine, but Karen's problem seemed to be vexing them both.

He leaned in and kissed Alicia on the cheek. She squeezed his hand.

～

AFTER DINNER, they settled Karen in the guest room. Jasper read Ophelia a bedtime story, one of the classic *Choose Your Own Adventures* on her shelf. Then he and Alicia went to her room, across the hall from the guest room, so they kept their voices low as they eased into bed. Alicia gave him the latest.

Karen had been dating a scumbag named Clay Barlow, who wasn't just a meth dealer but also was part of some redneck biker gang. He started hitting her, more than usual. She got scared, took all her shit, and left. Now she was looking for somewhere to start over.

"Is she moving here?" Jasper asked.

"No. She has a friend in upstate New York who's looking into jobs. But it's not like she has a lot of experience, other than stripping."

"Is she on meth?"

"She says no. And I don't think she is. But I'm sure she's doing other stuff. She was into pills when I saw her last."

"And how is this Clay dude taking her leaving?"

"I dunno. She left while he was out. From as scared as she was talking about him, though, she's afraid he'll find her."

"Does he know where you live? Or that she has a sister?"

"She said he knows about me, but not where I live, or even my name."

"Is she sure?" Jasper said, something ugly burrowing into his gut.

"She said she never trusted him, so she kept her private life private."

"Never trusted him, but went out with him? Sounds consistent."

Alicia sighed. "That's Karen for you. Growing up, she was always seeking attention. I think part of it was because her father died when she was a baby. Then my dad married her mom when Karen was eleven and I was seventeen. And she was always trying to get between my dad and me."

"So, did you all fight a lot?"

"Yeah, early on. But after a while, I was going to college and only home on weekends. Then, things changed. We were like best friends. And now that she had my dad's attention pretty much all week, she started not to want it. He was sweet to her when she was a kid, but the minute she turned into a rebellious teen, he put his foot down. Stomped it, really. Very overbearing, and, after a while, she hated him. We had that in common."

"Why'd you hate him?" Jasper asked, hoping it wasn't something she'd told him before, in which case she'd probably get pissed that he didn't remember.

She shook her head. "Not something I want to get into now. Let's just say he was cruel to my mom and drove her into an asylum."

"Oh. Sorry."

Alicia stared out the window and the moonlight bleeding through the branches. Silence draped the bedroom.

Jasper wasn't sure what to say, so he held Alicia as she drifted to sleep in his arms. He stared, admiring her features in the soft moonlight, feeling the warmth of her skin against his.

It had been a long time since he'd felt this sort of intimacy. And while he still felt guilty for being with anyone other than Carissa, he also felt something he hadn't felt in a long time: happiness.

And that emotion invited a more familiar one.

Fear that he could lose it all.

Chapter 9 - Mallory Black

SCOTT ISAACSON WAS an obvious wreck in Interview Room Three. He'd gone through the humiliation of a strip search and having his nude body photographed. Provided a DNA swab. His clothes had been taken, and he was wearing orange prison coveralls. He looked like a wounded animal, and surely must feel like the walls were closing in on him.

If he was guilty, Mal counted on all of these elements to help break him. This time, she was taking lead on the interview.

"So, Mr. Isaacson, how's *your* day going?"

"Just wonderful. I'd like to know when I can leave."

Mal ignored his question. Mike shook his head.

The right side of Scott's face was scratched and bruised from when she threw him to the ground. But the scrapes were nothing compared to the ass whooping other deputies might have given him for running and resisting.

"I didn't do anything," he whined.

"Then why'd you run?" Mal took a seat across from Scott while Mike continued to stand in the corner next to the closed door behind her.

"I … I don't know."

"Sheesh, all this time sitting in here and that's the best you could come up with, *I don't know?* Come on, give me something to work with."

"I ran because you're going to take one look at my art and think I'm a pedophile or a rapist."

"Ah, *art.* Is that what you call the naked kid pics?"

"It's not just kids; I have plenty of adult subjects. And I get parental consent for all models under eighteen."

Mal turned to Mike "Who lets some weirdo with a camera take photos of their naked kid?"

Mike shrugged.

"*Nudists.* I take photos of nudists. Since when did that become a crime?"

"Come on, let's cut the shit, you're into little kids. It's okay. I understand. Some of those girls, it is girls, right, not boys?"

Scott just glared up at Mal.

"I mean some of those little girls are cute. Maybe even hot, what do you say, Mike?" She turned to her partner again.

"Well, yeah, I mean it's only natural, right? A pretty girl is a pretty girl."

"It's *not* sexual. Artists have painted and photographed children for centuries. Have you never been to a bookstore or art gallery?"

"Apparently not the bookstores and galleries you go to. How about you, Mike? You ever see shit like this in the places you go?"

"No, I must be going to the wrong places."

"What do you do with these photos, Mr. Isaacson?"

"I'm making a photo book."

"That it?"

"I sell prints on my website."

"Ah, to other appreciators of *art*, right?"

Snidely: "Yeah."

"And you don't think any of your customers are getting off on this art?"

"And you wonder why I ran from you. *This* is the problem with people like you. You see the world through a disgusting filter. There is no innocence. Only filth. You assume the worst of everyone."

"That's because I *see* the worst of everyone day after day after day," Mal said. "But please, go on."

"Well, I'm not the worst of people. I find something beautiful in the innocence of youth. Something incorruptible. I weep that you can't see it."

"Then you won't have any problem giving us the key to your encrypted hard drives, if it's just *art*, right?"

"I know my rights. And I don't have to give you anything."

"Okay, fair enough. Listen, I don't give a damn about your little hobby. Really. If parents are dumb enough to let you take pics of their kids and sell 'em to perverts online, whatever. I just want to find the person that killed Chloe Conlan."

"It wasn't me."

"Okay, so help me clear your name by giving us the key to your encrypted drives."

Scott said nothing.

"Were you friends with Chloe?"

He met her eyes, his brow wrinkling as if she'd accused him of something inappropriate.

"*Friends?* No. We weren't friends. I ran into her now and then. I did some portrait work for her mother. But friends? No."

"What was she like?"

"She was quiet. Nice."

"Did she have other friends?"

"I don't know. I guess, she played with a few kids. And sometimes I'd see her with that retarded guy."

"What guy?"

"I don't know his name. He used to hang out at the park with the kids, then he flashed 'em or something last year, and they put him on the sex offenders list."

Mal turned to Mike and nodded, wanting him to take note. They'd gotten a list of people on the sex offenders list, and a few had been interviewed by other detectives. But she hadn't heard about anyone mentally challenged.

"And when was the last time you saw her with him?"

"I don't know. A few months ago, maybe longer?"

"When's the last time you saw Chloe?"

"A few weeks ago?"

"And where did you see her?"

"Hanging out downstairs near the pool, reading a book I think."

"And was she with anyone?"

"No. I don't think so."

"Do you know anyone who might have wanted to hurt her? Or maybe anyone who'd looked at her inappropriately?"

"No."

"And did you ever take *artistic* photos of her?"

"No. I only did portrait work that her mother commissioned. I only recently started doing nudes, and strictly at nude beaches."

Mal nodded, trying to conceal her disgust at least partially. She'd love to get a list of his customers and search *their* homes. She leaned forward, folding one hand over the other as she met his eyes. "What can you tell me about Megan Hudson?"

Scott let out a long sigh and shook his head. "I knew

this would come up. The cops already cleared me. Her mother even apologized."

"Tell me what happened. I wasn't there."

"Nothing! She lives in my complex. I've been friends with the family for years. I did portraits for them a few times at a discounted rate. One day Megan's mom wasn't home, and her grandmother wasn't home yet either. The girl had lost her key and knocked on my door asking if she could use my bathroom.

"I didn't think anything of it at the time. Sure, I said. But I'd forgotten that the knob in the guest bathroom gets stuck sometimes. Anyway, she was all done and trying to get out. I tried telling her to hold on, that I'd get a key and open it from the outside."

"A key?" Mal asked.

"Yeah, those little skinny picks they give you when you move in? Anyway, I couldn't find it, and she started freaking out, banging on the door, screaming."

"I told her to hold on. And at this point, I was starting to freak out, too. Getting worried that one of the neighbors would hear through our paper thin walls and think I was doing something to this kid. So I might have yelled at her a bit more angrily than I should have, to just hold on.

"Anyway, I found the key, opened the door, and she came tumbling out, crying. Then she ran from my house. I tried to follow her out to explain what happened, but she was gone by the time I got out there. Apparently, she went to another of our neighbors, that nosy old fart, Art Adleman. She told him that I'd locked her in the bathroom and that I'd tried to touch her on the way out. But I didn't *touch* her. I only tried to keep her from running out of my house screaming.

"A little bit later, two cops show up at my door wanting to talk. I told them what happened. They checked the door and saw that I wasn't lying. Then they went back to Megan's mom, and that's the last I heard of it. A day or two later, I approached her mom and apologized, saying that I swear, I didn't lock her in the bathroom. And she apologized right back. I didn't lock that girl in my bathroom, I didn't *touch* her, and I didn't do anything to Chloe."

Mal nodded. "Okay, let me check on some things."

She got up and started toward the door.

"How long are you all going to keep me here?"

Mal turned, hiding her annoyance. "As soon as we can rule you out. You can help speed this up by giving us the encryption key."

Scott said nothing.

Mal shook her head, then followed Mike out of the room.

"So, what do you think?" He asked.

"I don't know. Doesn't feel like him, but hell if he doesn't seem like he's hiding *something*."

Chapter 10 - Mallory Black

MAL WAS EXHAUSTED by the time she left the station and headed back to her hotel. Her back was a raw and throbbing nerve.

They'd ended their interview with Isaacson until they could get more information. He wasn't going anywhere. They could keep him on ice for a while on the resisting arrest charge alone.

Mal opened her hotel room door and saw the message light flashing on the phone. She called the front desk. "You have a message for me?"

"Yes, we have a package for you. Shall I send it up?"

"Yes, please."

Mal grabbed a beer from the fridge, popped open her laptop, and started browsing her LiveLyfe page while waiting for the package to arrive.

She scrolled through updates from the few people on her friends list —fifteen of them, most of whom she barely spoke to. Sometimes she wondered why she even went on the site. Mal tried to tell herself that she wasn't checking in on her ex-husband, Ray. But there were only so many cute kitten and puppy videos she could watch before admitting the truth — she was pretty much stalking him.

Ray's LiveLyfe posts were frequent and consisted of three types: the political rant, the cute animal video, and photos he took — both ones that the newspaper didn't use and those captured on his dime.

She clicked onto his photos page and scrolled down, unearthing pictures from a few years ago, back when they were still a family. And Ashley was alive.

She clicked on an old favorite, her and Ashley sitting on a bench on the beachside boardwalk. Ashley had been drinking a vanilla shake. Mal had tipped the bottom of the cup up, mashing whipped cream all over her daughter's nose.

Ray's photo caught the exact moment after, with Ashley's eyes wide in shock, Mal's mouth wide open as she laughed at Ashley's expression.

A knock on the door yanked her from the moment. Mal closed her laptop, stood, and answered the door. Then she traded five dollars and a *thank you* for a large padded envelope.

Mal closed the door, looking at the FROM address: her home.

What the hell?

A chill ran through her as she wondered who the hell would send her something from her address.

Mal opened the package.

There was a tablet inside. A cheap knock-off with no brand name.

A sticky note on the outside read: PASSWORD IS ASHLEY'S B-DAY.

The chill turned to ice, numbing her body and spiking her heart.

She pressed the power button, typed in the month and

day of Ashley's birthday. The screen started up, displaying a desktop clear of everything except for a yellow folder:

PLAYME

Inside, a .MOV file named Ashley_1_of_50.

One of fifty?

Mal swallowed and pressed play.

A man's voice spoke. Paul Dodd. The man who had kidnapped, raped, and murdered her daughter just before her tenth birthday. The man who took another girl, Jessi Price, whom Mallory put her own life on the line to save.

The man who was in jail awaiting trial for his crimes.

The man she sometimes wished she'd murdered instead of arresting.

"What do you want to say to your mommy?"

The camera turned, focusing on Ashley and her beautiful smile.

Mal pressed pause, unable to continue with the tears in her eyes.

Ashley was actually *smiling* in that secret room made to look like a princess's hideaway in Dodd's basement.

She must not have yet realized that he was holding her captive. This must've been when he'd first taken her under the pretense that he was a friend of her mom's, a fellow sheriff's deputy.

Mal wondered what sorts of lies he'd used to trick her out of his car and into a strange house. Her stomach turned, imagining Ashley's innocence being taken advantage of.

She'd failed as a mother. She'd taught her things like stranger danger, to look both ways when crossing, and how to be safe online, as well as some simple life-saving techniques such as CPR. Being a detective, Mal was prone to seeing the worst in people, and she'd actively tried not to pass that onto her daughter. She didn't want her to be paranoid. She wanted Ashley to enjoy life without constantly looking over her shoulder.

Every day Mal wished she could go back in time and tell Ashley not to trust *anyone*. Because monsters wear disguises.

Ashley might still be alive today if Mal hadn't been so afraid to scare her. She and her friend Rebecca wouldn't have trusted the man pretending to be a deputy. They would never have gotten into his car.

Mal pressed PLAY.

Ashley was smiling. "Hi, Mommy. I can't wait to see you. I love you."

Paul turned the camera on himself. "See you soon, Mal."

His smile was acid, blue eyes glimmering with a sadism that she'd experience firsthand.

Mal wanted to throw the tablet, but it was evidence.

Why the hell had he sent this?

She looked in the envelope and saw a slip of paper she'd missed.

She pulled it out.

I've got 50 more videos of Ashley's final days. If you come and see me in jail, I'll send you more.

She put the paper down, got up, and ran to the bathroom.

She fell in front of the toilet and emptied her stomach into it.

Her heart hurt.

Ashley's smile reverberated through her mind.

Hi, Mommy. I can't wait to see you. I love you.

She was so happy in the video. She wondered how long that lasted. How long Dodd duped her. How long before he revealed himself as a monster? Before she realized she was trapped? Before she knew she was going to die and that Mommy couldn't save her?

Mal screamed, tears streaming down her cheeks.

Dodd was in prison. Why did he want to see her? She couldn't imagine that he was going to apologize. He was surely hoping to hurt Mal, just as he'd done with the package he'd sent her on the anniversary of Ashley's birthday.

He was a sick fuck who got off on inflicting pain. Dodd couldn't hurt any children from prison, but he could still torment his victims' families.

She wondered if Jessi Price's parents or any of his other victims' families had received anything?

She played the video again, killing it before Paul's vile face appeared.

Fifty videos?

As much as she hated to play his game, there was a deep void in her that hated to think there were unseen messages from Ashley.

Not only did Mal long to see her little girl again, but she also wanted to know whatever Ashley had to say. Even if the messages were part of Dodd's sick tools to inflict damage, they were innocent to Ashley, right? She meant whatever she'd said.

And there were more.

Mal froze the screen on Ashley's smile as she waved to her mommy.

"Oh, baby, I'm so sorry."

Chapter 11 - Jasper Parish

FOR AS DARK and gloomy as yesterday evening's rain was, Ophelia and her three friends, Kimmi, Francis, and Taylor were playing Frisbee after lunch under a blue and brilliant sky.

It was a Sunday. The first two parks were filled with baseball and soccer teams using the fields. The third was one of the oldest around, and its baseball diamond was in desperate need of repairs. There was no one there most weekends, giving the girls plenty of space to throw the Frisbee.

Jasper sat on the metal bleachers with Alicia and Karen, shooting the shit, and laughing.

"Is Frisbee a *thing* here?" Karen asked after a while.

"No," Alicia said. "Ophelia and her friends like to do things that nobody else does, things so geeky that they're almost cool."

"Ah, so you're raising a little hipster."

"Yeah, her group is decidedly hipster, but they're good kids. And I like their families."

"Well, that's good. As long as they're having fun and staying out of trouble. You need to watch out, though. Ophelia is gonna be a head turner. You're going to have to be beating guys off with—" Karen smacked her face, correcting herself through a fit of laughter. "I mean beating them *away, AWAY* with a stick!"

Alicia laughed. "Well, that might be quite a way off. She doesn't even seem to notice boys. And the ones she hangs out with, like Francis, are either gay or dorky, so I'm not too worried."

"Which is Francis?" Karen asked, looking out at the tall, awkward kid wearing fake eyeglasses and a trendy beret, in skinny jeans and a colorful tee shirt.

Alicia shrugged. "I'm not sure. Maybe both? Maybe neither? Hell, maybe that's what's super trendy. I can't keep up with these kids."

"Me, either," Jasper said. "Things were easier when I was growing up. Maybe that's because I wasn't a teenage girl. My daughter used to make retching sounds when I said something about her looking pretty. She acted like she hated fashion, yet spent half her time picking out outfits to prove it."

"Yeah," Karen said, "that's hipster chic! A fashion in itself. Where's your daughter now?"

"She passed away a few years ago," Jasper said, hoping that Karen wouldn't ask how.

"Oh, I'm so sorry."

"Thank you."

He wasn't sure how much Alicia knew, but ever since last night, the memories kept coming. He remembered conversations they'd had, things they'd done together. He remembered laughing hard while playing laser tag with her.

He also remembered his cover story — that he'd lost his wife and daughter in an accident. He hadn't wanted to settle down since. That, coupled with his job as a "travel writer" gave him an excuse for not being around all that often. Things were working out alright so far. Alicia hadn't been pressing him to move or anything. Though, given how much affection she and her daughter obviously had for him, Jasper wasn't sure how long this could go on like it was before he was forced to make a decision.

But he couldn't get serious with them until he stopped seeing ghosts. Until he stopped feeling the compulsion to kill. Until he had *something* resembling a normal life.

In other words, probably never.

Ophelia and her friends ran to grab drinks from their cooler. Jasper watched them joke with one another. Seeing Ophelia with her friends made him miss Jordyn.

Not just the Jordyn who might have been if she'd not taken her own life, but the Jordyn that had stopped visiting him after he killed the person responsible. The Jordyn that might never return.

The kids were running back onto the field while Karen was talking about possibilities for her new life. The sound of motorcycles was like gunshots ripping through their peaceful afternoon.

Jasper looked up at the parking lot and saw four bikers in leather, denim, and enough ink among them to cover an elephant.

"Oh fuck," Karen barely squeaked.

Her eyes were wide. She was visibly shaking.

The men rolled up to the parking lot, about ten yards behind the bleachers.

"Which one is him?" Jasper asked.

"The one getting off his bike."

Clay Barlow wasn't particularly tall or muscular. He

was thin and wiry and on the short side. But what he lacked in size or brawn, he made up for in a menacing demeanor.

His hair was bright and fiery, his face an alcoholic red, his beard pointed and ugly, and his eyes cold and dark, despite being blue. Nazi symbols and twisted iconography lined his arms, at least what Jasper could see beneath his black tee and denim vest.

And the way he walked, staring straight at them, Jasper had seen that gait a million times, the strut of someone with no fucks to give and no regard for their life, or anyone else's. A Molotov cocktail of hate in motion.

He approached quickly, his three friends, all big, muscular, and ugly, following behind him.

He smiled, his teeth small and sharp like he spent his days chewing on rocks.

"Karen, Karen, Karen," he said, approaching with a disingenuous smile, his arms open for a hug. "You didn't tell me you were visiting your family."

Jasper held his ground. Clay wasn't looking at Jasper, but his men were.

No doubt they'd all sized him up, and at least one of them, if not all, were packing heat.

So was Jasper, not that he wanted to engage in a gunfight, particularly at a park where Ophelia and her friends were playing. He'd worked enough accidental shootings and drive-bys to know that innocents paid the price for hyper-masculine beefs.

"How did you find me?" Karen asked, not at all disguising the fact that she'd left, like a weaker person might have. *Oh, honey, sorry I didn't tell you. I'll be home soon!*

He smiled, though there was no warmth in that maw. "Oh, baby, you know I got eyes everywhere. I like to look out for my girl, make sure she's not associating with any unsavory types."

Clay glanced his way, but Jasper wasn't ready to give him the satisfaction of his response.

"Clay," the repugnant man said, introducing his hand to Alicia. "I've heard so much about you, Alicia."

Jasper wondered how he'd gotten her name. Had Karen lied when she said she didn't give her scumbag boyfriend details or had he done his homework? Did he, in fact, have eyes everywhere, or at least in this town?

"Pleased to meet you," she said, shaking his hand. Her tight lips and worried expression couldn't mask her true feelings.

"And who might you be?" Clay said, turning to Jasper.

Jasper — arms at this side — didn't accept the man's hand.

"Ah, the strong silent type! Gotta love it!" Clay looked out at the field, "And which one of those little ones is the lovely Ophelia?"

"What do you want, Clay? Why are you here?" Karen's voice was high-pitched, arms crossed over her chest.

"What? I can't visit my woman?" He pulled her toward him, trying to kiss her.

She pulled away.

His smile retreated.

His face turned red with embarrassment or anger. Probably both.

"I'm leaving you, Clay. Don't act like we were happy. We fought night and day. This is the best thing for both of us."

"I think we ought to talk 'bout this when you get home."

"No, I'm not coming *home*. It's over."

He stared at her.

Jasper could see the wheels spinning behind those icy eyes. He wanted to hit her, right here in front of everyone. Show his ownership, prove to his men that he didn't take shit from his woman.

But something was holding him back.

Did he hope to charm her back? Was he not yet desperate enough? Or was he afraid of Jasper, even with those thugs standing behind him?

Stupid people were driven by fear. But idiots were also impulsive and didn't always know when to back down. They were just as likely to blow everything to bits if it meant spiting their enemy.

What Clay did next would tell Jasper if he was cunning or a dumbass.

Clay looked at her, then at Alicia and finally at Jasper. "Okay, I get it. You need to think. Take your time, baby. And then, when you're ready, we can talk."

So, cunning it was.

"Goodbye," Karen said, not agreeing, nor disagreeing, but clearly wanting him gone.

Clay nodded, then turned and walked toward his motorcycle.

Jasper stared Clay's men down as they retreated, walking backward, as if expecting his charge.

Jasper held his calm, but also kept ready, as he saw them off.

As they drove off, he finally sighed.

Karen turned to her sister, and they hugged. "I'm so sorry," Karen kept repeating, her tears finally free.

Alicia cried too.

And the kids came up asking, "Who was that?"

Jasper stared, watching the bikers disappear down the road.

Alicia had been wrong when she'd said trouble was at her door.

But now it was.

And fuck if Jasper wanted any of this attention.

Still, he wasn't about to back down and leave this family on their own.

Chapter 12 - Mallory Black

MAL WOKE to the sound of her buzzing phone.

She fumbled for it in the darkness and brought the screen to her face. "Mike?"

"Where are you? The press conference is about to start, and Gloria's looking for you."

"Shit, what time is it?" She glanced at the alarm clock. 9:05 AM. "Oh fuck, I'm sorry. I'm on the way."

A long pause, then, "No, if you haven't left yet, don't worry. I got it. I'll see you after. I'll tell the boss that your back was hurting. It is still hurting, right?"

"Yeah." And it was. Just not as bad. "Thank you."

But Mike was already gone.

"Fuck," she sighed, hanging up. Her head pounded, thanks to the cocktail of pills and booze that had helped coax her to sleep.

The world was foggy.

She looked across the room at the small dinner table in her suite, where Dodd's envelope sat with his "gift."

But Mal couldn't think about that now.

She flipped on the TV to the local cable news and saw

that sure enough, they were coming live from The Creek County Sheriff's Office Communications Center, where Public Information Officer Felicia Day was speaking at the lectern. Behind her were Sheriff Gloria Bell and Mike, on hand for questions.

Mal couldn't see the rest of the room, but she figured it was packed with local and national reporters and cameras. Because a pretty dead white girl who also happened to be the granddaughter of a prominent city councilman was Big News to media vultures.

Mal cranked the volume as she hopped in the shower, listening to Felicia's latest update. It wasn't much of one. We have a dead girl. She's been identified as Chloe Conlan, yes Councilman Conlan's granddaughter. We're talking to people of interest, but have no suspect at this time. The investigation is ongoing. Please call us if you have any information regarding the crime.

When questions poured in from reporters, Felicia was ready with variations of the usual stock responses: we're not releasing the cause of death yet, nor are we commenting if there was any sexual nature to the crime. No, we've not named Kelly Conlan as a suspect.

Mal dried off and was getting dressed when a voice from someone who couldn't possibly be there tickled her ears. She didn't catch the name, and only heard the moniker of an unfamiliar publication, the Creek County Confidential.

She stopped and turned to the TV. She must be hearing things.

No way he's there. No way.

It had been two years since she'd heard from Cameron Ford, a reporter at The Chronicle, where her ex-husband Ray worked. He had published crime scene photos of Ashley's body on his Twitter account before getting fired.

The local news didn't show the reporters asking questions, so Mal couldn't see the weasel for herself, but there was no mistaking the sound of his ugly, uncaring voice.

Last she'd heard, he'd left town, finding some gig at a small rag in Wisconsin. When did he come back, and what the hell was the *Creek County Confidential?*

How the hell did he find another job?

"Hi, I'd like to ask Sheriff Bell if she has any qualms about Detective Mallory Black working this case given what happened to her daughter?"

Felicia was mid-response when Gloria took the bait and approached the mic. "Yes, Mister Ford, we have the utmost confidence in Detective Black. While she is not the lead here, she was instrumental in a successful resolution in the Jessi Price case and ensuring the girl's safety."

"Yeah, about that, wasn't it a conflict of interest to have Mallory Black working on the Jessi Price case when the suspect was the same man who allegedly raped and murdered her daughter? How is that fair?"

Mal wanted to throw something at the television. Why was this asshole back, and asking these questions? Was he still pissed about losing his job? Did he blame Mal for the blowback on *his* idiot decision to post pictures of a dead child on Twitter? Did he think any deputy would give him a single scoop after that pile of bullshit?

Don't take the bait, Gloria. Move on.

"Detective Black was a *consultant* on the Paul Dodd investigation, an investigation run by a task force with many agencies, with everything aboveboard. Thank you."

Gloria walked away from the lectern, visibly agitated.

Felicia stepped back up, ignoring Ford's attempts at follow-up questions, and called on Mandy Harrison from the local CBS station.

Harrison, a professional, ignored the shit that Ford was

NOLON KING & DAVID WRIGHT

trying to stir, and asked whether there was any connection to a recent missing girl case in Miami, to which Felicia said that there seemed to be no connections at this time, though the investigation was still early.

Mal finished getting dressed and was about to head out the door, when she stopped, went to her laptop and Googled Creek County Confidential. She found a local news site that promised to "deliver the truth THEY don't want you to know."

A quick scan of the articles and forums showed Mal a website that trafficked in gossip disguised as news. They fired shots at a broad range of targets from Pine Harbour's "Nazi" code enforcement board, to the "people lurking in the shadows who REALLY control everything," to this country's "escalating crime rate."

The articles were mostly written by Ford, supplemented with a handful of sourced to usernames like Nthe-Know or simply ADMIN. A glorified blog she'd be quick to dismiss if not for the sheer number of active commenters below the articles and in the forums.

So, was this Ford's blog, or was he hired by someone else? And if so, who was the owner? Some basement dwelling troll, or a political operative looking to screw things up for enemies while paving a path for friends?

As far as she could tell, the Confidential had been in existence for just six months.

Just in time for election season. What a surprise.

The website had developed a large following, despite its limited time online. Mal was surprised she'd not yet heard of it — many deputies read the local forums and secretly posted there with anonymous handles like high schoolers trading in gossip.

Maybe the deputies *were* talking about the Confidential, and she was unaware. Perhaps it just hadn't reached the detectives. Though, after today's presser, that would surely change.

Mal headed to work, pissed and wanting to break things. She tucked a couple of pain pills into her pocket, just in case.

Chapter 13 - Mallory Black

"WELL, look who the fuck decided to show up," Wilson barked as Mal headed to her cubicle. He was standing outside his office next to Detective Duncan O'Reilly, both of them holding coffees, shooting the shit.

"Sorry, boss, won't happen again," she said, not bothering with excuses. For one, Wilson hated excuses more than tardiness. For two, Mal was never late, so she figured she'd earned one pass.

"I don't need to buy you an alarm clock, right?"

"No, sir," she said as she took a seat at her desk.

Wilson returned to his conversation. Mike, sitting at the desk next to Mal's, rolled his chair over, and asked, "So, what happened?"

"Not now," she said. "What did I miss?"

"Still waiting on the DNA we pulled from the mom and the neighbor. I put in a call to Isaacson's girlfriend, Michelle Bolan. She's gonna swing by here at noon. I got Skippy visiting people on the sex offender and predator lists to see if there's anyone we need to bring in. I figured we'd check up on the mentally disabled man Scott said was friends with Chloe. Name is Terrance Burridge, thirty-five-years-old. He got into trouble a year ago for flashing his pecker at the playground. His mom, Dorothea says it was innocent fun. He's a big kid that doesn't know any better. He didn't do time but was put on the sex offenders list. He's on parole now, not allowed anywhere near kids or the park."

"I think I remember seeing that on the news," Mal said. "You think he was innocent?"

"I didn't get the call, so I dunno. Guess we'll find out soon enough."

DOROTHEA AND TERRANCE BURRIDGE lived at the end of a cul-de-sac, in an older house, with faded paint and an over-grown weed-infested lawn with plenty of brown splotches and bald patches of dirt. The house was the only eyesore on a block of homes and yards that were well-maintained; the kind of home Mal figured was routinely targeted by zealous code enforcement officials.

A run-down station wagon sat in the driveway. The garage door rotted from the bottom. The only thing missing was a second vehicle on blocks.

Mike and Mal got out of their car and approached the house.

Before they even reached the cracked path leading to the front door, a deep bark erupted in front of them.

Mike jumped before realizing that the dog, a black Rottweiler, was inside the home. The Burridge's windows were wide open, despite the August heat.

The dog kept barking while Mal knocked.

"Yeah?" a woman's voice said from the other side.

"Creek County Sheriff's Office, we'd like to talk to Terrance, please."

"He didn't do anything," the woman said, sounding like she had three cigarettes in her mouth.

Mike and Mal traded glances.

"All the same, ma'am, we'd like to speak to him." Mike didn't mention that they could come back with his parole officer. He would have to talk then, *and* have to let them inside.

"Hold on a sec," she said. Then, to the dog. "Shut up you fucking mutt!"

She struggled to bring the dog into a room in the rear of the house and lock it up before slamming the door and yelling at it again to shut up.

They watched through the window. Mike raised his eyebrows: *Lovely lady.* Moments later, they heard the security chain and bolt slide.

A heavyset dirty blonde in her late fifties opened the door all the way and stepped aside, looking at both Mike and Mal in suspicion.

"Come on in."

She was wearing pale blue sweatpants, a large shirt with a bedazzled bulldog, and flip-flops.

Mal followed Mike into the dark house. It reeked of smoke and despair, every surface and shelf littered with tchotchkes.

Terrance Burridge sat on a cracked leather recliner watching *Win, Lose, or Draw* blasting from the TV in the rear of the house, oblivious to the presence of company. Bowls of junk food sat on a table next to the chair, along with a giant plastic mug half-filled with still fizzing soda. Though he was sitting, Terrance was enormous. Around 6' 5" and well over three hundred fifty pounds. He had close-cropped dirty-blond hair like his mom, and a unibrow.

Dorothea stopped Mike and Mal before they got too far inside. "This about the dead girl?"

"Yes," Mal said.

"He didn't do it. He was home with me all day."

"We just want to ask him some questions."

"Please, don't upset him. He was friends with her. He doesn't know she's dead," Dorothea said, then led them into the living room.

She muted the TV. Terrance looked at her confused, then turned his attention to Mike and Mal, his brow furrowing.

"Have a seat," she said.

Mike and Mal sat on the plastic-covered green and brown couch.

Dorothea stood next to her son. "These folks are from the sheriff's department. They just want to talk to you for a few minutes."

"Hello." Terrance waved.

"Hi," Mal said, standing and offering her hand.

He shook it, his palms damp.

Mike also offered his hand.

They sat back down. Mal said, "Terrance, we'd like to ask you where you were yesterday."

"I was home."

"And what were you doing?"

"I dunno. Watching TV, playing Nintendo. I went for a walk with Ma."

"Yeah? Where did you walk?"

Terrance looked at his mother.

She said, "Just around the block a few times. He likes to get out."

Mal reached into her coat and pulled out her phone, finding a school photo of Chloe from last year, supplied by her mother.

Mal showed Terrance her screen. "Do you know this girl, Terrance?"

"Yeah!" His face lit up. "That's my friend, Chloe."

"Yeah? When's the last time you saw Chloe?"

"Yesterday."

"No, you didn't," Dorothea said. "You were home."

"Oh yeah."

Mal, annoyed, asked, "Do you remember when you did see her last?"

"Um … yesterday?"

"He gets confused with time."

"Please," Mal interrupted, "let him answer."

Dorothea's lips stretched thin across her teeth. She grabbed a pack of cigarettes off the table and popped one in her mouth. Then she lit it, fingers trembling as she held the lighter.

Mal asked, "So, where did you see Chloe last?"

"I saw her at the park."

"Yesterday?" Mike asked.

"Yeah. I think."

"And what were you doing?"

"We were just talking." He frowned. "I'm not allowed to play with the kids anymore."

"So, you were just talking to her?" Mal said. "Do you remember what you talked about?"

"She was telling me about school."

"What about school?"

"I don't remember."

"Okay, did she seem happy?"

"Oh yeah. She said she liked her teacher this year."

"Do you remember what time you saw her?"

"I dunno. Yesterday."

"Do you remember if it was before or after lunch?"

"Um, I dunno. After?" he looked at his mother, puffing away on her cigarette, and glaring at Mal.

"And was Chloe with anyone else?"

"No. She was by herself."

"And where was this?"

"At the park."

"So, you went into the park?"

"No. I just go up to the fence. I'm not allowed in the park."

"And did Chloe come outside the fence?"

"Yeah."

"And did you two go anywhere else?"

"Um, I don't remember."

"Do you ever go anywhere other than the park with Chloe?"

"Sometimes we play in the woods."

"And did you play in the woods yesterday?"

Terrance looked confused. Again, he looked at his mother.

Dorothea asked, "Terrance, when was your birthday?"

"Yesterday!" he said with a big grin.

Then she asked, "And when did you get in trouble at the park for showing your privates?"

"Yesterday," he said, looking down, ashamed.

Dorothea glared at the officers. "His birthday was in March. And I'm sure you already know how long ago you all arrested him."

Mal sighed. "Okay, Mrs. Burridge. Can you tell me the last time that Terrance saw Chloe?"

"Probably before he got in trouble?"

"Not since?"

"I dunno. Sometimes I'd walk him by the park because he misses the kids. And he gets sad. I tell him he can't go in, but we can walk by. What? Should I bring a measuring tape to make sure we don't get too close?"

"Does he ever go to the park alone?"

"I dunno. I can't watch him all the time. I have to work, ya' know?"

"Where do you work, Mrs. Burridge?"

"I work for the Wheatfield Retirement Community."

"So, you're saying that there are times that Terrance is unsupervised?"

"Yes, but not yesterday. I was off, and we were both home. All day and night."

Mike stood. "Do you mind if I look in Terrance's room?"

"What for?" Terrance asked, his face nervous.

"I just need to check on some things." Mike turned to Dorothea. "You know I don't *need* to ask. Right?"

She nodded. "Go ahead. Second door on the left. Don't go in the other one unless you want the dog to bite ya."

"Don't break any of my collectibles!" Terrance called out as Mike headed toward the bedroom.

"It's okay, honey," Dorothea said. "He won't."

Chapter 14 - Mike Cortez

MIKE OPENED THE BEDROOM DOOR. It was like stepping into a teenager's room, maybe a child's. Not a 35-year-old man. He pulled a pair of gloves from his jacket pocket and put them on.

The queen-sized bed had a twin-sized *Frozen* blanket atop it. The walls were plastered with posters of sports stars like any teenage boy, but Terrance also had My Little Pony, Disney's Cinderella, and a few female singers that Mike wasn't familiar with. If Terrance wasn't the way he was, Mike would've thought he was entering a creepy pedophile's lair.

Toys lined the shelves, some still in their boxes. Disney toys, Star Wars action figures, Lightning McQueen and Mater from Cars, and what looked like a full family of My Little Ponies.

There were also at least three dozen lunch boxes with the same cartoon characters on them.

Are these his collectibles?

A bookshelf was filled with children's titles, mostly

picture books. Mike wondered if Terrance could read, or if these were books his mother read to him.

There was no computer, though there was an iPad sitting on his bed.

Mike picked it up, but the battery was dead.

He lifted the blanket and spotted a large gray plastic container under the bed.

He pulled it out.

Inside was a scrapbook and nothing else.

Mike braced himself, unsure of what he'd find, but figuring it would be ugly, whatever it was.

Mike opened the scrapbook and saw pictures of several kids, including some of Chloe, most of them taken at the park. Some were from far away, like shots from a creeper. Others were close up, of Terrance and the kids, smiling, obviously taken by Terrance, maybe even with his iPad.

None of the photos were salacious, and even the far away creeper shots didn't indicate a sexual interest, but rather that of a lonely man-child unable to visit his friends.

Mike felt a flush of guilt for assuming the worst.

He took out his phone and snapped pictures of the photo album's contents, flipping the pages as he did. He reached the end and found something that made his heart skip a beat — a friendship bracelet just like the one that Chloe was wearing when her body was found.

Mike took photos, put the bracelet in an evidence bag, stuffed the bag into his jacket pocket, then replaced the book and the container under the bed.

Mike was giving the room a last look around when a man screamed.

He ran toward the living room. The dog was barking, clawing behind one of the hallway doors to get out.

In the living room, Terrance was throwing his food and drink everywhere, screaming, "Go, go, go, go!!"

Mike looked at Mal, but she just seemed confused.

Dorothea went to her son, trying to comfort him, saying, "It's okay, honey."

Mike mouthed *What the hell?*

"She's dead!" Terrance screamed. "Chloe is dead!"

Dorothea yelled, "Are you going to arrest my son or not?"

"I'm sorry," Mal said, then grabbed Mike by the arm and pulled him out of the house.

"What the hell happened in there?" Mike asked.

"I was talking to Dorothea, trying to get a better answer as to when Terrance last saw Chloe, when a commercial came on teasing the news. They showed Chloe's picture and talked about her being found dead."

"Damn it," Mike sighed on their way to the car.

"Did you find anything in his room?"

"Yeah." He dug into his pocket, grabbed the evidence bag with the bracelet and tossed it to Mal. "This."

Chapter 15 - Mallory Black

MALLORY SAT across from Michelle Bolan, Scott Isaacson's fiancée, in the same room where she interviewed him the night before.

Michelle was a middle school math teacher. Five foot five. Long brown hair and about twenty-five pounds overweight. She wore black tights and a long pink button-down dress shirt. She used a lot of makeup but took the time not to show it. Her nails were well manicured and recently painted, though Mal could see the gnawed ends.

"Hi," Mal said, introducing herself and Mike. "Thank you for coming in."

"Why are you holding him?" she asked, not bothering with pleasantries.

"We're talking to Scott regarding the death of Chloe Conlan."

"Is he a suspect?"

"It's early in the investigation," Mal said. "We're talking to as many leads as we can."

"But you think he did it?"

"As I said, it's early. How long have you been engaged?"

Michelle shifted in her chair. "Six months. The wedding is set for January."

"Congratulations, that's a good time of year. Not too hot, and travel is always easier after the holidays are behind us. Got a lot of people coming in?"

"No, it's a small wedding," Michelle said, clearly thrown off kilter by Mal's small talk. "A few friends and family. But yeah, they'll be coming in."

"From where?"

"New Jersey mostly."

"Ah, Jersey. Never been," Mal lied. "So, we asked you down here because we want to get your take on what happened with the whole bathroom incident."

"Again? That girl, Megan, locked herself in there and then she got scared. Is *that* why you're holding Scott?" Michelle glared, like someone who has had to defend her man a number of times over something she obviously didn't consider a big deal.

"No, we're holding him because when I asked him about blood on his sneakers and the cut on his hand, he took off running instead of explaining. In our experience, innocent people don't usually run."

Michelle looked down at her hands. "He gets terrible anxiety sometimes. He doesn't handle stress well. I'm guessing he got nervous, thinking you'd all think he did it."

"Why would he think that, though? I mean, he cut his hand on the washing machine. Pretty simple explanation, right?"

Mal waited to see if Michelle would challenge the lie and explain that he'd cut his hand making food. She sighed. "I don't know. I haven't seen him since Tuesday."

"So, why do you think he ran?"

"Because maybe the police wouldn't understand his art. A grown man taking pictures of naked kids is not exactly the thing a lot of people can easily understand."

"How about you? Do *you* understand it?"

"At first, I thought it was odd. Sure. But Scott photographs other things. The kids are new. But whatever I thought in the beginning doesn't matter, because my opinion changed the second I saw what he'd done. His photos are beautiful. Not perverted at all. They're innocent." Michelle laughed nervously. "I know, it sounds weird, saying nude photos are innocent, but it's all in the context."

Mal nodded. "Was he friends with Chloe Conlan?"

"He knew her and her mom, yeah, but I'm not sure I'd call them friends. Scott laid low after that whole bathroom thing. He used to work with Victoria Sutherland who lives in the neighborhood. She runs a wedding business. But, after the whole bathroom thing, she cut him loose, even though the girl's mom said it was only a misunderstanding."

"And how did Scott take it? Being fired?"

"He wasn't happy, obviously. It's not like it's easy to get photography work. At least not the kind that pays the rent. Scott decided to spend more time doing these passion projects, and taking side work when it comes."

She stopped talking, tears welling up in the corner of her eyes.

Mal leaned in, putting a hand on Michelle's. Her fingers were icy and trembling. "What is it?" Her voice was soft and understanding. Mal could almost feel Mike melting into the door behind her, not wanting to ruin the moment by shining a light on himself.

"I don't want to get him into trouble."

Mal squeezed the woman's hand. "What is it, Michelle?"

"It's nothing to do with the photos or the kids."

"Okay," Mal said, waiting, not asking for more. Sitting back and letting the silence work for you was often the most effective way to mine for details. Most people, whether guilty or aggrieved, wanted to be understood.

Michelle began to cry.

Mal let go of her hand, grabbed the tissue box and slid it to her.

She wiped at the tears and blew her nose, crumpling the tissue and clutching it in her hand.

"I went over there on Tuesday to break up with him."

"Oh?" Mal said. "Why?"

"His ex-girlfriend, Roslyn."

"What about her?"

"I saw him chatting with her a week ago when I showed up at his place unannounced."

"Chatting how? Like online?"

"Yeah, Skype. He got off, quickly. Like he was hiding something."

"Were they naked?" Mal asked.

"No. Though, she was in a revealing dress, showing off her cleavage."

"And you broke it off over that?"

"Not *just* that. He's been different lately. It's hard to explain why. Moody, distant. And I had a feeling he'd been talking to her and had even asked about it before I walked in on them chatting. He told me that he hadn't talked to her in more than a year. But I had a feeling. And then, after I saw them on Skype, he admitted that they'd been talking for a few months."

"Why did you have a feeling that they were talking?"

Michelle wiped at her eyes again, then took a deep

breath and said, "The sex was different. For a while, it was almost non-existent. And then, around the time I started suspecting they were talking, he suddenly wanted it all the time. And it was rough. Which was how Roz liked it."

Mal nodded. "So, what made you break up?"

"I just had a bad feeling that things weren't headed where I wanted them to be. After he admitted they'd been talking, I started wondering what else he wasn't telling me."

"So, did you ask?"

"No. I went over on Tuesday meaning to. I wasn't *positive* that I'd break up with him, I mostly wanted to see how things went. Anyway, I started to ask him about Roz. He freaked out, started yelling. He called me a cow."

"Oh," Mal said. "Fuck."

"Yeah, fuck indeed."

"So, then what?"

"I left. And he didn't even bother chasing me. I was so pissed. Here I was willing to give him the benefit of the doubt, but he didn't even bother to give me a lousy excuse. He just let me go."

"So, do you think he's seeing Roz?"

"I don't know."

"You said that Roz liked it rough. How do you know?"

"Because he tried to get me to do some of the same stuff he used to do with her."

"Like what?"

She blushed. "I dunno, like bondage. And we tried it once, but no, thank you."

"Didn't enjoy it?" Mal asked.

"No."

"Did he?"

"Yeah."

"What exactly did he do?"

"I ... I don't want to talk about it. If you want to know more about his sex life, I suggest you find Roz."

"What's her last name?"

"Blum. She's a server at Captain Jack's Alehouse. Can't miss her. She looks like a fifteen-year-old Goth Barbie, super skinny."

~

MAL AND MIKE sat outside the parking lot of Captain Jack's Alehouse waiting for Roz to show. They'd already called the manager for her hours. She was ten minutes late.

"She must be on Mal Time," Mike joked.

"Ha-ha. I'm late one fucking time, and you're gonna give me shit too?"

"Oh, relax. You got off lucky. In my rookie year, I was working long hours, lots of overtime, and I slept in until noon one day. Supposed to be in at six in the morning. I got a bit of shit from my captain, Martinez, but it was the next day that I really heard it."

"What happened?"

"I went out to my patrol car because back then we didn't have take-home cars, and I opened the door, and there were like twenty alarm clocks with bows on them from the guys. Fuckers!"

Mal laughed. "I bet you were never late again."

"No, I wasn't. So, you gonna tell me why you were late? Or do I not wanna know?"

"I wasn't partying if that's what you're asking."

"No, wasn't asking that, but good to know. So, what was it?"

"Paul Dodd."

"What?"

NOLON KING & DAVID WRIGHT

"He sent me a video of Ashley, taken while he had her."

"Shit. What kind of video?"

"Her talking to me. It was sweet. Sad. He must've lied to her, told her something to make her think I'd be there."

"He did that with Jessi Price, remember?"

"Yeah. So, he also sent a note saying if I visit him, he'll give me more videos. He's got like fifty of them."

"Fifty? Shit. Are you—"

"I don't know. I'm not sure I *can* face the guy without wanting to kill him."

"You … you don't think he's feeling remorse? That he wants to apologize, do you?"

Mal shook her head, remembering the evil in the man's eyes as he held her in the bedroom, threatening to rape and murder little Jessi Price right in front of her.

"No, no way he's changed. I think this is him wanting to get off, relive what he did to Ashley through me. Hell, maybe he recorded the whole thing. Oh, God, I don't think I could live through that. My head and heart might both explode. It's one thing to *know* what he did to her. But to *see* it? To see my daughter suffering? No, I think I might kill myself."

"Did you tell Gloria?"

"Not yet. Figured it could wait until after we solve this Chloe Conlan case. Right?"

"Probably," Mike said. "Do you want me to go see what Dodd wants?"

She met his eyes. They were dark and serious. She liked him better as a puppy. She hated that her torment triggered his pain.

"No. I'm a big girl. If I decide to see him, I'll do it. Until then, he can fucking rot while he waits for his trial."

Mike pointed. "That look like Goth Barbie to you?"

Mal followed his finger to a woman getting out of a neon purple VW Beetle, wearing a short red skirt, a cleavage-revealing white pirate shirt, fishnet stockings, and thigh-high leather boots.

"Sure does. Let's go and have ourselves a chat."

Chapter 16 - Mallory Black

"Hey, Roz," Mal called out.

She turned, eyeing them as if trying to place them. "Hi."

Roz had bleached white hair, wore dark, caked on eyeliner, and black lipstick. Despite the heavy make-up, she did look young enough to be a recent high school graduate. And gnawing on a wad of bubblegum definitely didn't add any years.

"Hi," Mal said. "We're with Creek County Sheriff's Office. We just wanted to talk to you for a minute."

"Um …" Roz looked toward the restaurant as if she didn't want to be seen talking to cops. She stepped behind a van, obviously obscuring herself. Mal wondered who she was hiding from. Someone at her work? Or was Goth Barbie dealing drugs? Mal could give a shit about some bottom rung dealer. She wanted to solve Chloe's murder.

"Okay, yeah," Roz finally said. "How can I help you?"

"We want to talk to you about your boyfriend, Scott Isaacson." Mal intentionally used the word *boyfriend* to gauge her response.

She laughed, her thin, almost non-existent blonde left eyebrow arched. "Excuse me? My *boyfriend?*"

"Yeah. Is … is he *not* your boyfriend?"

"Um, no. We fooled around a bit, but it was never anything serious. So, what about him?"

"Do you still talk to him?"

"He swings by now and then, or he'll Skype me. Guy can't seem to take the hint, and believe me I've left plenty. But then again, he's also the kind of guy you don't wanna blow off completely, because …" She brought a finger to her ear and twirled it: *loco*.

"What do you mean?" Mike asked.

"Dude is a few fries short of a Happy Meal. I don't want him walking in here with an AR-15."

"Was he violent with you?" Mal asked.

"No, well, not exactly. But the way he talked about other women he'd dated before was scary. Bitch this, cunt that. Really low self-esteem and always blaming women for his problems."

"Yet you fooled around with him?" Mal never understood why women went out with crazy guys. She could maybe understand if the guy went nuts over time, but there were usually warning signs with the genuine psychos. Some women always found reasons to stay.

"Yeah, for a few months. This was over a year or so ago. He used to come in here all the time. And he always tipped well. He seemed nice at first. He showed me his photos, and they were good. He appealed to my artistic side, plus I'd always wanted to model, and he said he could help me with my portfolio."

"I'll bet," Mike said under his breath.

"When I asked you if he was violent, you said *not exactly,*" Mal met her eyes. "What did you mean by that?"

She looked away. "Well, he was violent in bed."

"How so?"

She looked back and took a breath. "Bondage, choking, stuff like that. But that wasn't the part that creeped me out."

"What was?"

"He liked to roleplay, a whole school girl thing. But not like a college, or even a high school girl thing. He made me pretend I was in middle school, or younger. And he'd get *really* excited when I acted like he was hurting me. And he made me beg him, and say creepy things."

"Like what?" Mal asked.

"He made me beg him not to tear my little pussy. And sometimes, he'd hold a knife to my neck, and make me beg him not to cut it."

Chapter 17 - Mallory Black

MALLORY SLAMMED the door to the interview room where Isaacson was waiting, head in his arms as if the asshole was taking a little nap.

He snapped to immediately.

Mal glared at him, not bothering to hide her disgust. She flipped on the recorder. "So, you like little girls, eh?"

She took the opposite chair. Mike stood behind her, leaning against a wall, checking his nails, and looking bored.

"No," he said incredulously. "My photos are *art!* There's nothing even remotely sexual about them."

"I'm not talking about your photos," Mal said, specifically not revealing what she was talking about. Letting a suspect think you knew more than you did was an excellent tactic, especially with some of the dumber suspects. "You're a sick fuck."

"What are you talking about?"

"It's okay, Scott. We know."

"Know what?"

But now Mal was sure she could see doubt creeping

into his eyes, as he wondered exactly what she knew. Maybe he wondered if they'd cracked the encryption on his hard drives, and his sick little secrets were now laid bare for all to see.

She leaned back and smiled. "Way I see it, we don't even need to talk to you. Better you stay quiet. That way you don't get your side down."

"What are you talking about?"

"Yeah, just keep playing dumb," Mal said, standing. "God, I'm gonna love watching the jury make McNuggets outta you."

She turned and left, laughing.

Mal slammed the door, then made a beeline toward the observation room. She closed the door, and joined Chief Wilson in the dark, watching as Mike took the ball.

Chapter 18 - Mike Cortez

Mike stood in the corner, staring at Scott.

Scott stared back. "What's her problem?"

Mike took Mal's chair and let out a long sigh. "Let me tell ya' brother, if you ever become a cop, don't ever partner with a woman."

Scott stared at him suspiciously.

Mike went over to the video recorder and turned it off. There was still another one running in the observation room on the other side of the one-way mirror. He leaned in and whispered, "Moody as hell, I tell you."

Scott laughed.

Good.

"Why is she accusing me of liking little girls? That's not all I take pictures of. There are adults. And boys."

He stopped talking as if the latest confession might lead Mike to some very wrong conclusions.

"She's all worked up over the photos," Mike said. "I get it. It's art. Might not be my cup of tea, but hell, you can go to a bookstore and see worse than what you have."

"*Exactly*," Scott said, seeming to relax a bit.

"Hey, you want a drink or something?"

"She's not going to come back in here," Scott asked. "Is she?"

"No, I think she's good and pissed. She gets like this from time to time. Ask me," Mike laughed. "I think she needs to get laid."

Scott laughed, but he still seemed guarded, or not as stupid as Mike hoped he might be.

"Coke? Coffee? Whiskey? Just kidding on that last one, man. It's Coke, Diet Coke, or coffee, I'm afraid. Or water. I forgot about water."

"A Coke, please."

"You got it. Hold tight."

Mike left for the break room where he got a cold Coke from the dispenser, then headed back into the viewing room. He whispered, "So, keep this up and see what we can get?"

"Yeah," Wilson said. "If you don't get something soon, I don't want you two BFFs planning a camping trip. I'll send Mal back in, full-beast."

Mal smiled, raising a claw and slashing the air.

"You are such a dork," Mike teased, leaving her and Wilson to their spying.

He headed back into the room and slid the Coke can to Scott. His hands were chained at the wrist, though he wasn't secured to the table.

He popped the top and started drinking, slow at first, then chugging.

"Thank you," he said, his eyes practically watering. That was one thing about the Good Cop/Bad Cop thing. It didn't take much to win over most criminals. You show the slightest bit of kindness, like a cold drink, and some of them will start spilling their guts onto the floor.

Mike hoped to get this pervert singing.

"Okay, reason she's pissed, we were talking to your girlfriend."

"Oh, Jesus. What did she say? Does she think I had anything to do with that poor girl's death?"

"No, I don't think so. But she did bitch about you a bit, saying how you cheated on her or something. And, just between you and me, that's what happened with my partner. Her ex left her for a younger bitch."

Scott nodded, "Ah, that *does* explain things. But what does that mean for me? Do I have to stay in here because your partner has it out for men?"

"Well, I dunno. She can be pretty persuasive to the bosses."

"Fuck."

"Yeah. It pays to get her on your good side."

"How do I do that? She doesn't believe me. She thinks I'm a pervert."

"That she does. Even more so after she talked to … um, what's her name … Roz. Yeah, Roz! Oh boy, did she have a few things to say!"

"Like what?" Scott said, now clearly worried, his fingers clutching the Coke.

"Oh, she said you were super freaky."

"Fuck," Scott said, putting the can down and sighing into his hands before running them through his hair.

Mike leaned forward. "But hey, a fine ass bitch like that, I'd get freaky, too."

Scott looked up, not quite taking the bait.

"Come on. We're only human right? A girl that hot, and that kinky, she was asking for it, right? Was she the sub, or you?"

Scott looked down, not sure he wanted to engage.

Mike kept going. "Hey, I'm not judging. But man, if I

had that fine piece of ass in my place? Oh, the things I'd do to her."

Mike feigned an apologetic expression. "Oh, shit, I'm sorry, man. I didn't mean to … with your girl and stuff. Or your ex. Sorry, that was unprofessional."

"It's okay," Scott shrugged. "She is hot. And yes, she was into some kinky stuff."

"I knew it!" Mike slapped the table. "You can tell. She has those eyes that scream, *Slap me around! Be a man and take me.*"

"What did she say?"

"She said you were into some real kinky shit, like scat and piss."

"What? No way, man. No, just the usual bondage stuff. I mean, maybe we got a bit out of hand at times, but that was both of us, not just me. She used to beg me to do some kinky shit to her."

Scott's eyes practically lit up as he talked about her.

"Like what?" Mike asked, leaning forward, hands crossed. "C'mon, you can tell me."

"Nah, that's okay," Scott said, sitting up straight, that twinkle in his eyes dimming to a dull caution. "Besides, it doesn't matter."

"Well, one thing she said kinda stuck out more than others, at least to my partner."

"What's that?"

"That you liked her to pretend she was Chloe. And you'd run a knife across her neck?"

"That's bullshit! I never had her pretend she was Chloe. A schoolgirl, yeah, but not Chloe! That's just fucking sick."

"What about the knife thing?"

Scott stared.

Mike smiled. "Man, what two consenting adults do in

their own place, ain't nothing we can do about it. And hell, I ain't judging. A girl like that, I'd do whatever she wanted."

"She liked to cut herself. Sometimes she'd make me watch. It didn't do anything for me, and when that wasn't enough, she'd make me pretend I was breaking into her house and holding a knife to her neck. But I never cut her. It was roleplaying. And she was way more into it than I ever was!"

"Man, I knew she was kinky," Mike laughed again. "Shit. So, what happened between you two?"

"I dunno. I didn't want to cheat on Michelle. But Roz kept throwing herself at me. And she was younger, and a model. Roz was just more interesting. I felt like Michelle and I had run out of stuff to talk about. We stopped having things in common. Hell, maybe we never did. But then this young model comes around, gives me some attention, and ... you saw her, right? Can you blame me?"

"Not one fucking bit."

"Exactly," Scott said.

Mike leaned closer and pulled out his phone. Then he scrolled through photos they'd grabbed from Kelly's Live-Lyfe page of Chloe. He found one where Chloe wore a cheerleader outfit.

"Did you take this one?"

Scott looked at the picture, and his eyes showed a familiarity. He'd seen the photo before. Given that he wasn't friends with Kelly on LiveLyfe, he either took the picture or was stalking her page.

"No," he said. "I did some school shots."

"Was she a cheerleader?"

"No, I don't think so."

Mike stared at the photo for several uncomfortable

moments. He flipped to another, Chloe in a bikini. "And this one. You could tell she was gonna be a hottie, right?"

"Um, I guess …"

Mike smiled. "I'm not a pedophile or anything, but, hell, it's only natural, right? I mean back in the old days, people got married when they were twelve and thirteen, right?"

"Yeah," Scott said. "I mean, I think I read something like that."

"Oh, yeah. Then they come along and change the age of consent to some bullshit arbitrary eighteen. As if a girl is suddenly interested in sex at *that* age and never before, right? I mean, they get tits and hair around eight or nine, some of these girls. You're gonna try and tell me that they don't have sexual feelings? That they don't touch themselves? Explore a little, ya' know?"

Scott sighed. He had to know that Mike was playing him, but a part of him was still nodding along like he knew every word to this sick little song.

Mike flicked to another photo — Chloe in the bathtub. She was in a bubble bath, but you could see her from the chest up.

He slid the phone over to Scott, feeling disgusted for using a dead girl's photo as a prop, but if it helped nail this sick fuck to the wall for her murder, Mike would swallow the revulsion with a smile.

"Now that is just adorable, right? I mean, I couldn't blame you if …"

"I didn't touch her," Scott said, looking away from the photo.

"Not even a little? I mean, maybe she came onto you. That happens a lot, believe me. I see it more times than I can count, and we wind up having to let guys go because the girl entrapped them. Is that what happened here? Did she entrap you?"

"I didn't touch her," he repeated.

Mike continued, sensing he was getting close to something. "Maybe she came on to you, but you were strong. You told her no. Because you knew it wasn't right. But she just kept throwing herself at you like a little whore. And maybe she got physical, and you pushed her away, and maybe she hit her head or something. I mean, if that's what happened, or something like that, shouldn't you get your story out there before my partner puts something else together. Something that makes you look like a monster. I mean, I know you're not a monster, but …"

"I didn't touch her. And I didn't kill her," Scott said, tears streaming down his cheeks.

Mike was losing him. He was so close and … boom, Scott was done.

"Listen, Scott. I'm a guy. I get how this can happen. But my partner doesn't. And she *can't* understand because she isn't a guy. She doesn't get the same impulses that *we* do. She'll never understand. But you tell me what happened, and I can put it down in a way that people will understand. They'll know what happened, and that you didn't mean for it to get out of hand."

Scott met his eyes, and for the longest moment, Mike thought he'd opened a door — a sympathetic ear, and an offer at something other than condemnation. While Mike didn't say he'd get Scott off, the man could draw his own conclusions.

Come on, Scott, just step right in. Say it.

Say it.

"I want a lawyer."

Damn it! Don't say that!

Mike tried not to let Scott see his disappointment.

"Okay, do you have a lot of money, or are you gonna take your chances with one of those public defenders. I mean, it's your right to be represented. Not that I ever saw someone in your situation get off on something like this, at least not by a public defender. But I'm sure you have a nest egg, right?"

"I'm not saying another word other than I want a lawyer."

"Fine," Mike said, getting up and walking to the door, defeated.

Chapter 19 - Mallory Black

"Sorry," Mike said. "I thought I had him there."

Mal shrugged. "Let him lawyer up. He'll be begging us for a deal once the evidence comes back."

"No," Wilson said, hanging up from a phone call. "The evidence is back from the lab. The skin under the girl's nails isn't his. But the blood on his shoes *is*. We got nothing."

"We have his hard drives," Mal argued.

"Well, unless Tech can break the encryption, we've got dick there, too."

"Fuck," Mal said, wanting to punch something.

She turned to the room and glared at the monster. She wanted to go in and punch that smug grin off his stupid face.

"Gotta cut him loose," Wilson said.

"What, we can't charge him for running from us?"

"Yeah, you can," Wilson said. "But he's still gonna be out on bail. The best thing you can do right now is to get back to the investigation."

Mal sighed, frustrated, but the captain was right. Just

because Scott seemed guilty, and was likely a creepy pedophile with murderous fetishes, that didn't mean he killed the girl. And justice for Chloe meant finding the person that did kill her, not trying to force the crime on another sick bastard.

"Okay, boss."

Mal couldn't stand to see Scott going free, and needed a break.

She went to the restroom, dug into her pants pocket and pulled out her small plastic bottle. She tapped a pill into her palm. Just one, to dull the edge.

She popped it in her mouth, lapped up some water from her palms, and swallowed.

Chapter 20 - Jasper Parish

JASPER PULLED himself up with one final grunt, counting off the last pull-up of his third set at the park near Alicia's place. He'd been training since six in the morning.

As he let go of the bar and dropped to the ground, Jasper heard clapping behind him.

He spun around, expecting danger.

Instead, it was his mentor, Lenny. "Not bad. Not bad at all, for an old man."

"*Old man?* You want to give it a go, Pops?" Jasper teased.

"Nah, I'm still tired after a long night out with my lady friend."

"Braggart."

Lenny smiled as he approached a bench still wet with morning dew. "So, how's it going?"

"Hold up," Jasper said, unzipping his hoodie and throwing it down for the man to sit on so he wouldn't get his ass wet from the bench.

"Thank you, kind sir," Lenny said as he sat. "So, you enjoying your vacation?"

"I was, until some meth-dealing bikers showed up."

Jasper told Lenny all about Alicia's sister, and the drama she brought into town.

"Man," Lenny said with a long sigh, "trouble does seem to follow you."

"I know, right? So, what do I do? I mean this could get ugly fast. And I don't want Alicia and Ophelia caught in the crossfire."

"No, that wouldn't be good. Any chance Karen will go back with him?"

"I dunno. I mean, her car is packed with her stuff, so that tells me she's serious about getting away from him, right?"

"Maybe. Way I see it, you can't protect someone from themselves or their decisions. But, if she's making the right choice, she should be free to leave him. Not frightened into accepting her old life."

"I've seen shit like this go south a hundred times, Lenny. Women trying to leave shitty men and dying for the effort. What kind of man would rather kill a woman than let her go? That ain't love."

"No, no it isn't. That's a weak ass man. And nothing's more dangerous than someone weak acting strong. A man like that's liable to do all sorts of stupid."

"So, I need to kill him?"

"Only if you can do it in a way that doesn't come back to hurt the people you're trying to protect."

Jasper nodded, his wheels already turning, trying to figure the best way to take care of business.

"The problem is, he's already in town. Anything I do will attract attention. Maybe I can find out where he's staying, and go get him."

"You said he had friends? You planning to take them

out, too? You ain't ever taken care of that many at once, Jasper. You sure you're up to it?"

Jasper grinned. "You doubting my ability?"

"Not at all, son. But taking care of four people at once? You're not exactly getting younger."

"I'm fine."

"If you say so."

"I do," Jasper said, not wanting to come off terse, nor willing to debate.

Lenny sighed.

"What?"

"Well," Lenny said. "I was just thinking, maybe ride this one out a little, see where it goes. Maybe the problem will take care of itself. And then you don't have to spoil your vacation."

"Since when has a problem ever taken care of itself? Are you suggesting I let Karen go back to this scumbag?"

"I'm just saying that some people will always be drawn to the fire. Maybe it's better to let her go, so Alicia and Ophelia don't suffer the fallout. So *you* don't suffer the fallout."

Jasper shook his head. "That's the coward's way. Since when did Lenny Barnes advocate the coward's way?"

"I'm not saying to be a coward, Jasper. But sometimes when you fight for people like Karen, you invite pain upon the innocent. When I was running the gym, there was this pimp who went by the name of Curtis S. Hopkins, the meanest son of a bitch I ever saw. He ran the streets with a vicious fist, and the cops wouldn't, or couldn't, touch him."

"One night, it's raining real bad, and I'm closing up, taking the trash out in the alley behind the gym when all of a sudden, I hear crying. I look around and don't see anything. Then I check behind the dumpster, and I see this girl, couldn't have been more than fourteen. She was beat up, bloody and soaking wet. I took her inside and called Old Doc G over to heal her up 'cuz she was afraid to go to one of the clinics or a hospital."

"Her name was Josephina, though she hated the name and asked me to call her Josie. Never gave me a last name. She stayed in the spare room above the gym, same one you stayed in when you were having your troubles. She was there a few days before she finally told me what happened. She was a runaway, got caught up with Curtis and his crew. Josie felt stuck. She was hooked on H and trying to put money aside so she could get out of town. But Curtis beat the hell out of her when he found out. You don't short Curtis, and you sure as hell don't leave if you're still earning."

"A week or so later, a few of his boys started sniffing around, asking about Josie, knowing I had her upstairs, asking when she was gonna get back to work. I stepped in. Me and a few of my guys went to visit Curtis. I had some pull, as I knew most of the men that ran with Curtis since they was kids, and back then, even criminals respected me. I was planning on telling Curtis to back off, to let Josie be."

"At first he agreed. But then people around me started getting hurt. Curtis wouldn't come at me directly, so he left a few of my people in terrible shape. But you know me, Jasper. I was a stubborn mule even then. I wasn't gonna let that greasy little fucker win. I got the money together and gave it to Josie. Told her to start over. Put her on a bus to Baltimore where she had family, and that was that."

"Until three months later, I saw her working the streets, back with Curtis. I went up to her and asked if Curtis had kidnapped her or something. But no, Josie went back on her own. Why? She didn't know. She just did. About six months later, cops found her dead in a motel room, OD'd and pregnant, the baby dead inside her."

"God," Jasper said.

"Point is, you can't save everyone, Jasper. Some people, trouble is all they know. And no matter what you do to try and keep them from it, they gonna find it. Drawn like a moth to the flame. Don't let Karen pull you into the fire, Jasper."

MAL AND MIKE

Chapter 21 - Mallory Black

MAL AND MIKE were about to leave the station, headed back to the apartment complex for additional interviews, when Gloria found them and ushered Mal into her office.

Mike teased, "She heard you were late."

Mal flipped Mike off, then followed the sheriff.

They were sitting across from each other at Gloria's desk with the door closed behind Mal and the blinds all drawn shut.

"Where are you with the Jasper Parish investigation?"

Mal blinked, surprised. "Haven't found anything. And it's not like we can exhume the body. His will called for his remains to be scattered at sea."

"And you haven't found anything from old friends of his, family?"

"There is no family. His only friends are former cops he worked with, and not a single one has seen him. They all think he's dead. To be honest, I've hit a wall. What makes you ask? Do you have something?"

"No, but Dodd's lawyer is sniffing around. He won't have access to anything until the discovery phase, but he says that Paul is talking about a 'man in black' and the lawyer's asking questions, asking if we're even looking for the guy. I don't want this thing muddying up the trial."

"We're not charging him with the murder of Wes Richardson, so it shouldn't affect anything. That's an open case as far as anyone else is concerned."

"An open murder that we like a ghost for. You know how this will look when it gets out, right?"

"Well, it's not like Jasper's name is out there. Nobody knows we like him for this. That's why you wanted me on it, right? To keep things quiet. He doesn't know that we know. Maybe he'll slip up and show his face somewhere. He'll run if he sees himself on the news, and then we'll have nothing."

"How do we know he hasn't already run?"

"I don't *know,*" Mal said. "It's just a hunch."

Mal didn't dare divulge her theory, that Jasper might also be responsible for the disappearance of Calum Kozack. The sheriff's office was already getting hell from Oliver Kozack for not doing enough to find his son. If Oliver knew that Jasper Parish was suspected to be living, he'd raise holy hell for the sheriff to find him. And that sort of attention this close to the November election could spell disaster for Gloria's chances to hold off the former sheriff, Claude Barry, who somehow won the Republican primary last spring.

"Well, I'm not sure how much longer we can sit on this," Gloria said. "Who's lead on the Conlan case?"

"Mike."

"Okay, if you get any downtime from this, I want you looking into Jasper."

"Yes, ma'am," Mal said.

"After that, we're putting his name out there."

"Okay."

Mal *could* tell the sheriff about her suspicions, but doing so would only force the sheriff to put Jasper's name out there faster, to get in front of the ball before it crushed her.

"Okay, that's it for now," Gloria said, dismissing Mal.

Mal left with a twisted stomach. The time to catch Jasper was running out. Every lead had gone nowhere so far. She wasn't sure an extra week or few would change that. Jasper's name would be on the TV soon enough, and then he'd be in the wind.

An ex-cop like him could fall off the radar without much hassle. Hell, he'd somehow managed to fake his own death, and gotten away with it. That wasn't an easy task. Mal's only advantage right now was Jasper believing that he was still operating anonymously.

Her phone buzzed with a text from Mike telling her to meet him in the parking lot. She walked to the car, still thinking about Parish.

He was clearly a vigilante, but he also knew things that nobody else did. Like that her daughter was going to be taken by Dodd. And that the monster had managed to kidnap her and Jessi Price, before bringing them to Mal's house where he planned to kill them both. He knew about Jeff Brown targeting his wife and her fiancé. Vigilantes didn't typically know about crimes before they happened. The man would almost have to be psychic.

She laughed.

But then Mal remembered something else he'd said after she'd asked how he knew. Jasper said that she wouldn't believe him.

Was he psychic?

The thought was preposterous. While the department, under the last administration, had used psychics a few times to try and find missing kids, they'd never had any success. And the only psychics Mal had ever run into were charlatans looking to separate vulnerable, gullible people from their earnings.

She shook off the thought of Jasper being a psychic.

The only thing she knew about him that wasn't on some file somewhere was that the man was bonkers enough to believe that his daughter was still alive. She wasn't even sure what kind of delusion that might be.

Mal pulled out her phone and made an audio note. Maybe she could ask one of the psychology experts she knew and do some cross reference to find possible doctors or pharmacies that may have treated Jasper. But two things made that idea seem shitty before she even turned off the recorder. Patient privacy laws might make it difficult to search, and Jasper's actions likely meant he was off whatever meds he may have been prescribed.

Which left Mal back where she began: with nothing.

She pushed through the doorway and out into the late afternoon sun where Mike was sitting in his idling car just outside the door.

Mal got in and buckled up.

"So, what'd the boss want?"

"To see what was up with the Parish case."

"Ah. And?"

"I told her I have nothing. Gloria said she might need to go public just in case it somehow gets out that we had a name but didn't release it."

"It's an ongoing investigation, though. We don't have to."

"Yeah, but she's afraid Claude Barry might find out, leak it, and make it into an election issue. I can't say I blame her. That man will do anything to get elected again."

"God help us all."

~

MAL SAID, "Any word on Conlan's boyfriend?"

Mike shook his head. "We're looking for him. He supposedly works at Fancies, that new strip club right near the county line, but the staff all seemed to have come down with the same case of amnesia by the time I got there. He's probably in the wind, figuring we'll grab him for possession or intent to sell or something. We put out some feelers, bribed a few people to tip us off if they spot him."

"And Kelly? Anything new on her?"

"No. I tried to get another interview, but the lawyer is playing hard to get, too. We have a councilman's pampered princess of a daughter and a drug-dealing scumbag. They don't respect the law, let alone understand how it works. I don't expect much from either of them."

They got out of the car and headed to the apartment of Art Adleman, the old man Megan Hudson ran to after she claimed that Scott locked her in his bathroom.

Art lived on the first floor of the building directly across from Scott, and diagonally across from Kelly's apartment, giving a good view of both neighbors' entrances.

Mal spotted a mezuzah on the right side of the door frame, tilted inward. She touched it with two fingers, then kissed her digits.

Mike looked at her. "You're Jewish now? I thought you were a heathen that didn't believe in anything."

"Still a heathen," she teased, "but I figured we could use some divine help. You know, if it's out there."

Mike, a Catholic who somehow kept his faith despite the horrors of his job, smiled. "I knew you'd come around eventually."

She glared at him playfully.

"Hello?" an old man's voice said from the other side.

"Hello, Mr. Adleman," Mike said. "We're with Creek County Sheriff's Office and would like to talk with you about Chloe Conlan."

He unlocked the door and opened it wide.

Art was a short, balding man in his late seventies, with wisps of white hair over each ear, giant glasses that made his eyes look five times their natural size. The only thing louder than the man's checkered shorts was his screaming blue polo. His gait was slow, and movements careful.

"Hello, officers. Come on in."

Mal followed Mike inside, giving the little old man a friendly smile on her way.

The apartment smelled faintly of mothballs, but it was extremely tidy, with a small table in the kitchen. There was a salad plate with an apple and a knife. Beside it, a book on early 19th-century life in Europe.

Art led them to the living room, where a fat gray cat lay in the window. The television blasted MSNBC.

"Have a seat." He gestured toward a blue couch, probably ancient though it still looked fairly new. Art sat in a well-worn recliner opposite them. He grabbed the remote from the coffee table and muted the TV.

"How can I help you?"

"How long have you lived here, Mr. Adleman?" Mike asked.

"Oh, gosh, I don't know. I think we moved here in '95. It was the year before Martha passed. More than twenty years."

"How well did you know Chloe and her mother?"

"Ah, Chloe, she was such a sweetheart. She'd come and talk to me at the park sometimes during my walk. She'd help me feed the birds. Back before I fell a few months ago, anyway. Had to get shoulder surgery. It's okay now, but damned if my back hasn't been all wrong ever since. Anyway, Chloe was a sweet kid, and incredibly lonely."

"Why do you say that?" Mal asked.

"She was always wandering around the neighborhood looking for someone to play with or talk to. Her mother wasn't around all that much. And when she was, well, she had some rather unsavory types around."

He whispered "unsavory" as if saying it too loud might bring retribution from the accused.

Mal raised her eyebrows. "What kinds of unsavory people?"

"Men. Lots of men. Some of them looked like druggies. Others looked like, I don't know, gangsters. And always different men. Kelly would give Chloe a few bucks and tell her to go to the store, keep herself busy. Imagine that, giving an eight-year-old money and kicking her out of the house so you can spend time with men. That poor kid deserved better."

"Wow," Mal said. "How often did she do this?"

"I don't know. Seemed like every weekend there for a while. But then there would be entire weeks where it looked like she was spending time with her kid. And you should've seen Chloe's face when she'd tell me about the places she went with her mom. The girl was so happy just to do anything with her, even if it was only going to the store together. That girl loved her."

"What about Kelly's boyfriend? Are you familiar with him?"

"Which one?" Art asked with a sad laugh.

"Eddie Dixon."

"Ah, Eddie. Yeah, I'm familiar with him. He always gave me dirty looks and would do a little 'Heil Hitler' salute sometimes when he'd pass my place. Chloe didn't much like him. Said he was always taking money from her mom, and that he was mean to her."

"Lovely," Mal said. "So, was he around a lot? When's the last time you saw him?"

"He was around off and on, kinda like most things with Kelly. As to the last time I saw him, maybe Thursday?"

"The day before Chloe was found?" Mike asked.

"Yes."

"And what was he doing when you saw him?"

"He and Kelly were fighting in the parking lot. I'm not sure where Chloe was at the time."

"Did you hear what the fight was about?" Mike asked.

"Something about money, I'm not sure. I just know he wasn't very happy. He tore out of here. Kelly flipped him off when he left. Then she started crying."

Mal asked, "Do you remember the last time you saw Chloe?"

"That morning. The morning she passed."

"Where?"

"Waiting for the bus to come. The stop is just inside the main gate. I was out front getting the paper, and she came over and got it for me, so I didn't have to bend down. She said, 'Here, Mr. Adleman' with the biggest smile. That was the thing about Chloe, even though she had such an awful life, a negligent mom who didn't seem to want her, and kids picking on her, she still found a way to smile."

Art stopped to raise his glasses and wipe the tears welling up.

Mal looked down, blinking herself.

"Sorry," Art said. "Anyway, Chloe asked if she could come by after school and see Oskar."

"Oskar?" Mike asked.

"That lazy guy over there." Art pointed to the cat, still

NOLON KING & DAVID WRIGHT

stretched out beneath the window sleeping. "She never did show up. Around five or so, I got up and went outside to see if maybe she was playing with one of the kids who weren't so mean to her. That's when I saw people gathering, everyone looking toward the woods. Part of me knew before anyone told me, Chloe was dead."

Mike leaned forward, his brow furrowed. "Why would you think that, Mr. Adleman?"

"I don't know." The old man shrugged, looking truly lost. "You know how some people just seem destined for tragedy? As much as I hate to say it, Chloe's mom always reminded me of one of those mothers you see on TV who report their kid missing. Then you find out they did it."

"So, you think her mother killed her?" Mike asked.

Art looked away as if realizing the seriousness of his accusation. He swallowed. "I don't know. Let's just say I wouldn't be surprised."

Mike asked for more details about Kelly, but Art didn't have much more to say. They asked him to go over what happened with Megan Hudson being locked in the bathroom, so he told that story in detail, which aligned nicely with the official record.

"Do you think Scott locked that girl in his bathroom?" Mal asked.

"I honestly don't know. But I wouldn't be surprised. The way he looks at kids when he thinks no one's watching."

"How is that?"

"Like a pervert."

"What exactly does he do?" Mike asked.

"Oh, he's not doing anything. It's all in the eyes. Hell, it's probably why he got fired by Vicky Sutherland. He used to do wedding photography for her, but then all of a sudden he stopped. I asked her about it, and she said it was just creative differences. But I could tell it was something else."

"Did this happen after the bathroom incident?"

"A few weeks after, yes."

"What about other neighbors? Do they think he's a creep?"

"He's still got a few friends, but anyone with kids pretty much ostracized him after that. Even if they didn't believe the accusation, who's going to take a chance?"

"Do you know why Megan's mother rescinded the accusation?"

"Well, apparently Megan was making up stories a lot for attention because at the time her parents were going through a divorce. And she couldn't be sure. Plus, she said that the police told her that the doorknob was prone to locking and getting stuck."

"What do you think?" Mal asked.

He turned to her, "I don't know. As I said, the way he looks at kids, boys and girls, it just seems off."

Mal circled back. "You said there were a few people who weren't mean to Chloe? She had friends?"

"Yes, a few of the kids."

"Can you give me names?"

"Sure. It's only three. Hector Vargas, a good kid; and Lucas and John Sutherland. Lucas is the same age as Chloe, and they'd sometimes walk to the bus stop together. Lucas got picked on too. He's chubby."

"Sutherland, as in Vicky Sutherland's sons?" Mal asked.

"Yes."

"And did Chloe go to the bus stop with Lucas that last day you saw her, on Friday?"

"No. Lucas's mom was taking both the kids to school after the older brother, John, got into a fight with a couple of older boys who were picking on Lucas last week. But he did come downstairs for a few minutes and was talking with her before his mom and brother came down and got in their car."

"Did you hear what they talked about?"

"Not really, my hearing isn't so good these days, and I never remember to put my hearing aid in."

Mal made a note then said, "Do you know the names of the kids he got into a fight with?"

"Not their last names, but yes, Landon and Hunter. A couple of bullies."

"Did they pick on Chloe too?"

"Yeah, they picked on pretty much every kid smaller than them. Tell you what, parents these days don't give a damn. If I were a kid, I'd put those two punks on their asses."

"What did they do to Chloe?"

"They teased her. Made fun of her for being autistic. Made some crude remarks about her body."

"Like what?" Mal asked.

"She didn't say, other than they said naughty things, and it made her sad."

Mal made a mental note to bring the two bullies in for questioning, maybe asking Kelly if she knew anything about the bullying.

Mike thanked Art for everything. On their way out, the old man said, "Oh, yeah, I forgot about one other friend she had."

"Who?"

"Terrance Burridge. Are you familiar with him?"

"Yes," Mike said.

"Anyway, I always thought he was harmless, even after he got into that trouble at the park. Seemed like a big misunderstanding. But, all the same, he was supposed to stay away from the park and from kids, right?"

"Yes," Mike said. "Why?"

"He still saw Chloe. They used to meet up in the woods. In secret."

Chapter 22 - Mallory Black

MIKE AND MAL sat in the Interview Room Three's observation area, watching Dorothea comfort her visibly shaken son. There were three chairs at the table rather than two, and she was holding Terrance's arm tightly as he cried.

They'd called and asked her to come down with him "just to talk," figuring it was better to have her in the room than risk trying to question him on his own and her calling a lawyer or having one attempt to throw out whatever he said.

Mal and Mike waited for Captain Wilson, knowing he'd want to watch the interview.

He showed up just after seven, and griped, "Whatever happened to detectives clocking out at a decent hour?"

"Sorry," Mike said. "We're workaholics like that. Plus, we had to make up for Mal being late."

Wilson rolled his eyes and sighed. "Alright, let's get on with this."

For the most part, Wilson's grousing was an exaggeration. Deep down, he wasn't too bad. But when you made him late for dinner, he got grumpy — especially when it was something that could wait, like interviewing a mentally disabled man with zero flight risk.

Mal and Mike left Wilson, walked down the hall, around a corner, and entered the interview room.

"Thank you for coming down," Mal said as she sat.

Mike rooted himself to a spot in the far corner, away from the door, behind Mal.

Dorothea's eyes were red, just like her son's. "Do we need to call a lawyer? Aren't you supposed to read us our rights?"

Mal said, "I'm not arresting you. This is merely a formality. You're free to leave at any time."

Dorothea nodded, looking only slightly more relaxed. She cracked her knuckles, her knee bouncing as though fueled by a gallon of coffee. It could be nerves, fear for her son, or a simple craving for a cigarette.

"Hi, Terrance," she said. "It's going to be okay. I just want to talk to you about Chloe some more."

"She's dead," he said, not meeting her eyes.

"How do you know she's dead?" Mal was hoping he might slip up and confess.

"The TV told me."

"Yes. She's dead, and I'd like your help to find out what happened. Can you do that? Can you help me?"

"I dunno," he said, looking nervously up at Mal.

"Well, let's try and see what happens, okay?"

"Okay."

"Can you tell me about the last time you saw Chloe?"

"I dunno," he said, then whispered, not softly at all, to his mother, "I'm not supposed to say, am I?"

Dorothea shook her head, knowing how guilty Terrance must look. "It's okay, honey. Just tell them the truth, and you'll be okay. They're here to help Chloe."

Dorothea was remarkably soothing in speaking to her son, convincing him that the officers weren't there to harm him, though her eyes said differently. She didn't trust them and did not attempt to hide her suspicion.

"I saw her yesterday, in the woods. We was playing."

"Yesterday?" Mal repeated.

"Obviously, it wasn't yesterday," Dorothea said. "He means on Wednesday."

"It was yesterday!" Terrance shouted.

Dorothea sighed.

"Okay," Mal said. "Do you remember if it was morning or night?"

"Morning. I would walk to the park before anyone was there, so I wouldn't get in trouble. And sometimes she'd talk to me before her bus came."

"In the park?" Mal asked.

Terrance shook his head. "No, in the woods. She didn't want anyone to see us. She said I'd get in trouble. Am I in trouble?"

"No, Terrance, we're not looking to punish you for talking to her. We just want to find out what happened."

Dorothea continued to glare at Mal, likely figuring that the minute the interview was over, Mal would report Terrance to his parole officer for violation of the terms. In which case, Terrance could be locked up.

"So, the last time you saw her, was she alone?"

"Yes."

"And what did the two of you do?"

"We talked, like usual."

"What did you talk about?"

"She was sad. Her mom yelled at her."

"Do you know why?"

"I don't remember."

"What else did you all talk about?"

"I dunno. I told her about a baseball game I watched yesterday."

"What game?" Mal asked.

"The Rays. They won eleven to two. Chloe didn't watch baseball, but she listened to me talk about it because she was my friend."

Mal would have to check the Tampa Bay Ray's schedule to see what night they won by that amount. "Do you watch the Rays every day?"

"Every game. But most of them are at night. Not the day."

Mal decided to test a theory. She pulled up the Rays' schedule on her phone, then read dates and games, asking the scores. She went back with Terrance for the last seven games. He remembered the score for each one. So, while he thought of days as "yesterday" when it came to his own life, he somehow recalled dates and scores with perfect clarity.

"He loves baseball," Dorothea said, smiling proudly, likely deducing what Mal was already understanding.

"Okay," Mal said, "so the last time you saw her was the morning after the Rays won eleven to two?"

"Yes."

"That was Friday morning," Mal said. "Yesterday."

Dorothea sighed, then swallowed. She looked like she was going to say something, but she stopped herself, waiting to see where Mal would take this.

"Did you like Chloe?"

"Yes, she was my best friend. She was the only one who still talked to me after I got in trouble at the park for showing my privates." Terrance stared at the table, avoiding Mal's eyes.

"Did you think Chloe was pretty?"

"Yes."

"Did you ever touch her?" Mal asked.

Dorothea scoffed, "No, he didn't *touch* her!"

"Please, Mrs. Burridge. Let Terrance answer. Did you ever touch Chloe?"

"Yes," he said.

Dorothea opened her mouth, but Mal held a hand up to silence her.

"Where did you touch her?" Mal asked.

"I dunno. Her hair. Her hands. Sometimes we'd play hide and seek, and I'd tag her."

"And did you ever touch her privates?"

Dorothea looked like she wanted to punch Mal but somehow managed to keep her cool, her leg bouncing even faster as tears filled her eyes. She looked at her son, waiting to see what he'd say.

"No," he shook his head fast. "No, no, that's naughty."

"Okay." Mal was calm, trying not to trigger a freakout.

"Did you ever see her privates?"

"No," he said, still shaking his head, now almost violently.

"And did she ever see yours?"

"No, she wasn't at the park when I did it."

"And when did you do that?"

"Yesterday. But I said I was sorry. I was just trying to make people laugh."

"Okay," Mal said. "And did you ever hurt Chloe?"

Terrance kept staring down at the table.

Mal looked at Dorothea. She looked at her son, her face confused when he didn't answer. The silence stretched, so deep that Mal could hear her heart racing.

"Terrance?" Mal said calmly. "Did you ever hurt Chloe? Even accidentally?"

"I don't want to say," he said, tears streaming down his

red cheeks as he grabbed either side of his chair tight, his thick knuckles turning white.

Mal turned to Mike. He was staring at Terrance along with Dorothea.

"It's okay if you did," Mal said. "Sometimes accidents happen. If you tell us, we can make this better."

"Can you bring her back to life?"

"No, I'm afraid we can't do that."

"Then you can't make it better!" Terrance started to rock back and forth.

"What happened?" Mal asked.

"I don't want to get in trouble," he said, his voice a low whine, snot leaking from his nostrils.

Dorothea held a napkin to his nose and told him to blow.

Mal waited until he finished, then asked again, "Terrance, we just want to find out what happened to Chloe. If it was an accident, we can tell the judge."

"I think we should go," Dorothea said, starting to stand.

"Please," Mal urged. "Just tell me, Terrance."

"You don't have to say anything. Come on, honey."

Mal raised her voice, startling him. "Chloe would want you to tell us, Terrance."

He looked at Mal, his eyes wet, nose red, and head tilted ever so slightly. "We were playing hide and seek, and—"

"You don't have to—" Dorothea tried to pull her son from the room, but he refused to budge, or shut up.

"I was hiding real good. And she kept walking back and forth, looking for me. I jumped out to scare her, and she slipped, and she fell down, and she hit her head. She was hurt."

"And then what?" Mal asked.

Dorothea continued to glare at Mal.

"She cried. And I helped her up and said I was sorry. And she was mad at me, and she ran away, crying. Did I scare her to death?"

"When did this happen?" Mal asked. "What baseball game was on?"

"The Rays played the Yankees. And they won four to three."

Mal looked at her phone. If Terrance was remembering correctly, and not lying, then this happened two weeks ago.

"Did you see her after that?"

"I dunno," Terrance said.

"Did you see her the day after the Rays one eleven to two?"

"Yes," he said.

"And was she still hurt or mad at you?"

"I don't think so," he said. "She didn't say."

Dorothea took Terrance's arm and yanked. This time, he followed.

"If you want to harass us anymore, I'm calling my lawyer." She stormed past Mike, opened the door, and marched out with Terrance.

Mike and Mal stared at one another. The interview had turned to shit, and the partners were no closer to the truth.

Captain Wilson appeared in the hallway, then whistled and motioned for them to follow.

INSIDE WILSON'S OFFICE, the captain handed Mike a manila folder with the medical examiner's results.

Mike looked through the folder, while Wilson summarized.

"Time of death was around 4:00 PM. Cause of death, blunt force trauma to the head. Judging from the size and force, we're thinking an aluminum bat, weapon not yet found. The slit throat was post-mortem. No sign of rape. DNA under her fingernails, possibly that of her attacker, but hard to say just yet. Nothing in her vagina or anus, despite the fact that her underclothing was removed. However, there were signs that she might have been sexually abused in the past. The primary crime scene was a tree house about thirty yards from where her body was dumped. Blood found there matches the victim. She was likely moved to the secondary scene shortly after her death. There were no signs of semen or anything at either crime scene."

"So, you think this retarded guy did it?" Wilson asked.

"I don't think so," Mike said.

"It's possible that it was an accident," Mal suggested, "which was where I thought this might go. But the last time he saw her was in the morning, and she was in school on Friday. She took the bus home. And I'm thinking that there was no way Terrance would approach her late in the afternoon when more kids were around."

Mike's phone rang. He took the call, then, after a couple of minutes of listening intently, hung up.

"Aanya was just going through Dorothea's LiveLyfe. She was at a park in St. Augustine at four in the afternoon. Then at a restaurant in Jacksonville at five-thirty."

"A park in St. Augustine?" Wilson said. "Do you think she brought Terrance?"

"I'm thinking he was so sad that he was ordered to stay away from parks in town that she took him somewhere he wasn't as known."

"I'll call the restaurant and see if they remember them."

Mal sighed. "I think Terrance is a dead end. If the girl has signs of prior sexual assault, we need to find Kelly's boyfriend, Eddie Dixon."

"Well, that can wait until Monday," Wilson said. "Take tomorrow off and get some rest."

"Goodnight, Captain," Mal said, turning to leave.

Chapter 23 - Mallory Black

It was nine in the morning, and Mal needed at least another five hours of sleep, but her phone wouldn't stop buzzing. She looked at the screen. Mike. *Again.*

"What the hell? We're supposed to be off today. Didn't you get the memo?"

"Yeah, well my wife is out of town visiting her dad. He fell and hurt himself. Now he's in the hospital. I figured I'd make myself useful."

"Sorry about your wife's dad, but fuck you for waking me up."

"Sorry, partner. But I couldn't hold onto this. You wouldn't want me to, and I've been sitting on it since last night."

"Last night? What?"

"Well, I couldn't sleep, so I went to The Boat Yard Cafe where Kelly used to work, to see if I could find anyone who remembers her."

"And?"

"Oh, yeah. One bartender in particular does. Woman named Erica Ramos. Said she was friends with Kelly because at first, she seemed like a decent person. And Erica, who at the time was a single mom but has since married, also had a young daughter so she could relate. But after a while, she said that money started disappearing from the register, and Kelly would come to work all coked up."

"Did they fire her?"

"That part's a bit hazy. Erica reported her to management, but she's not sure what happened, only that Kelly was gone the next day. And she never saw her since."

"Okay, anything else?"

"I thought you'd never ask."

"Come on, bastard, I'm barely awake, get to the good shit."

"Well, Kelly partied a lot. And she'd come to work hungover and barely awake. For a while, she left Chloe with her mom on the weekends, but sometimes when her mom was busy, Kelly would just leave the girl at home. She was around six or seven at this time. When Erica asked if she was worried at all about leaving Chloe alone, Kelly would joke about giving the girl enough Benadryl to make sure she was out all day. Other times, she'd say, 'Please it's not like someone's gonna kidnap her. And if they did, they'd return her in less than twenty-four hours.'"

"Nice," Mal said.

"There's more."

"One time her boyfriend Eddie was hanging around, waiting for her to get off. And he was drinking, a lot. Erica overheard them talking, and it was clear that Eddie liked being with Kelly, but hated the girl being around. And rather than tell this guy to get lost, she'd apologize, trying to appease him, saying she'd make sure they had alone time, not to worry. One time she said she ought to just leave Chloe with her mom, but she didn't think her mom could handle the girl. She could barely handle Kelly. Another time, she said, and I quote, 'Believe me, Eddie, there's not a day that goes by that I don't wish I got an abortion.'"

"Fuck that bitch."

"I'm going to call Aanya to see if we got anything new. She said there was nothing incriminating on Kelly's computer, but her phone's browser had zero history. So Aanya's put in a call to her provider."

"Good work, detective. And thank you for waking me up."

"No problem."

Mal looked at the clock, "Want to grab lunch later?"

"Can I get back to you? Danny called earlier and asked me to come over for the game."

Danny was Mike's neighbor, one of his few non-cop relationships, who got together sometimes with him to watch sports in Danny's garage. Sometimes, Mal found herself jealous of how easily guys could make friends, and how undemanding male friendships were. You like sports? You like to drink or play ball? Let's hang out! It was far harder, at least for Mal, to find a female companion who she had anything in common with, and didn't demand too much of a commitment.

That was another thing Mal admired about male friendships. They didn't seem to get bent out of shape if they didn't see each other for five months. When they did get together, it was like they'd lost no time at all. They'd talk sports, drink, and have a good time. Women Mal had been friends with got offended when she didn't check in on them regularly, or drop everything to hear all about their current problem.

Too much drama.

"Okay," Mal said, secretly wishing that Mike would

invite her over to hang out, too. She could get into a game and was definitely down with the drinking. Just not enough to drop any hints. "Alright, see you tomorrow if not."

Mal hung up, then looked at the clock, wondering if she could get back to sleep. But then her phone buzzed again. This time with a number she didn't expect: Colleen Price, Jessi's mom.

"Hello?"

"Hi, Detective Black?" She sounded harried. "Can we talk?"

"Sure, what is it?"

"Can we meet?"

Mal got a sinking feeling in her gut. "Is Jessi okay?"

"Yes, she's fine."

Mal sighed with relief. Mal wanted to ask if Jessi's shrink was still helping, but Mal had paid for the help anonymously and didn't want any credit from her mother.

"Okay, I need to shower, but I can swing by your house in about forty minutes. Does that work?"

"Yes. Thank you."

Mal hung up, and got in the shower, wishing she could also wash away the gnawing in her gut insisting that something was wrong.

She thought about the terror that Dodd had subjected Jessi to. How he had nearly destroyed the child's life and planned on forcing Mal to watch her destruction.

He was a monster, and though she hated to admit it, there were times when she wished she'd let Jasper kill him. She hated the idea of the man not paying for his crimes, but there was another factor that Mal hadn't considered when Jasper tried convincing her to finish Dodd, or let him do it for her. And that was the psychological cost of allowing the monster to live.

How much hell did Jessi Price and her mother go

through knowing that he was still alive? Sure, Dodd was locked away, but he was out there, and there was some chance, as slim as it might be, that he might someday be free. And if that knowledge kept Mal awake some nights, it was surely a nightmare for Jessi and her mother.

Chapter 24 - Mallory Black

MAL PULLED up in front of a small home on a quiet street with several old oaks standing proudly in well-manicured yards.

She got out and approached the house, remembering the last time she saw Jessi in a fast food joint a few months ago. How she seemed triggered by the sight of Mal. They'd gone through hell together at the hands of Paul Dodd, so perhaps the girl could never see Mal and think of anything but the monster who raped and nearly killed her.

Mal knocked on the door, her stomach doing somersaults as the door swung open to Colleen and Jessi.

"Hi, Officer Mallory," Jessi said, smiling, not crying, nor scared. She seemed genuinely happy to see Mal.

"Hi, Jessi," Mal said, entering with her very best smile. "How are you?"

"Good."

"How's school this year?"

"Good so far. They were going to hold me back because I didn't go back last year, but they gave me a test and decided I could be in fifth grade, anyway."

"That's great. And you like your teacher?"

"Yes, her name is Ms. Freeman, and we have a class hamster."

"A hamster?"

"Yes, he's sooooo cute. His name is Roland, and he's really fat! He shoves food in his mouth, and his cheeks get super big like this!"

She put her hands to her mouth and puffed her cheeks.

Mal laughed. She'd talked to many victims over the years and was always amazed when someone managed to bounce back to something resembling normalcy after suffering at a predator's hands. She wondered if Jessi was normally this happy now, or if she went through phases. She doubted that the girl could be free from residual pain.

Colleen put a hand on her daughter's back. "Why don't you go upstairs and play for a bit."

"But I want to show Officer Mallory my drawings."

"I'll call you down after we're done talking adult stuff."

"Okay," Jessi pouted as she turned, her short blonde ponytail bouncing as she bounded up the stairs.

The moment Jessi was out of sight, Colleen's mask faded. Her eyes were concerned, hands twisting over one another in knots.

"Come," she said, leading Mal out of the living room and into the kitchen. "He sent me a package."

"Who?" Mal asked, even though she already knew.

"*Him.* Paul Dodd."

"Did you open it?"

"Yes. It came without a return address. I didn't think anything of it until I played the video."

"A video? On a tablet?"

"Yes, how did you know?"

"What was on it?"

"A video of Jessi when he had her."

"What was on the video?"

"Jessi talking about her daddy coming soon, and how he was a friend of Officer Bob, which is what he told her his name was at first. She was so happy in the video." Colleen wiped at her tears. "Anyway, he said he'd send more videos, worse ones, if I didn't give you a message."

Mal braced for what was coming.

"He said he wants you to visit him in jail."

That fucker!

"I'm so sorry that he sent that."

Colleen looked at the stairway to make sure that Jessi wasn't nearby, and then reached into a high cabinet over the refrigerator, pulled out a bubble envelope similar to the one that Mal had received, and handed it to her.

"Please, take this. I don't want it. And I don't want him sending any other videos to my house. God! Jessi is just starting to sleep through the night. If she finds one of these tablets, or if he sends it to her somehow, and it's one of the bad videos, I don't know what I'll do."

Mal took the envelope. "I'll take care of this."

"Why does he want you to visit him in jail?"

"I have no idea."

"He's a monster."

"He can't hurt you anymore. He's locked away."

"Is he even allowed to send this stuff? I mean, how does he do it when he's locked up?"

Mal looked at the envelope. There was nothing indicating it came from the jail. Paul must have someone on the outside sending these packages on his behalf. And if they were willing to help him do this, what else might they help him do? Exact revenge?

"Hold on a minute, okay?"

Colleen nodded.

Mal headed outside to her car, tossed the envelope on the passenger seat, then called Wilson's cell. Four rings later he said, "This had better be a call inviting me to come watch the game with you."

"Nope. Sorry, not watching the game."

"Are you working, Mal? I didn't approve any overtime. And in fact, I explicitly told you to rest. If Jesus can take Sunday, so can we."

"I got a call from Colleen Price."

Captain Wilson was on vacation during the whole Dodd thing but was up to speed enough to listen when Mal dropped the name. "And?"

She explained the situation, including the envelope that both she and Colleen received, and how Paul wanted a prison visit from Mal.

"What the hell does that fucker want?"

"No idea, but who knows how many more envelopes he'll send out to victims' families if I don't go."

"This isn't a good idea."

"You think most ideas are bad. And what I do off duty is my business."

"So, why are you calling me on a Sunday?"

"I want a unit on Jessi and her mother."

"How long?"

"I don't know. But if Dodd has someone working with him, what else might they do?"

"Jesus, Mal. You really know how to ruin a fella's Sunday."

"Well, I'd rather ruin it with a request than calling you over two more bodies."

"Yeah, yeah, text me the details, and I'll set it up."

Mal texted him, then went back inside and told Colleen what she did.

"Do you think I need to be worried?"

"I don't think so. But I would be cautious."

"Like I'm not already. Ever since she came back, we're always together, except when she's at school. At first, she was too scared to sleep in her room. But now, I feel better when she's in my bed."

Mal nodded. Colleen was a stark contrast to Kelly, a woman who couldn't stand being around her child, regretted having her, joked that she wished someone would kidnap her. Mal hadn't seen Kelly since her interview and wondered if she missed her little girl yet. If the woman felt guilty for being a horrible mother, over her culpability in Chloe's death.

Jessi came down the stairs, holding a giant art pad. "Are you leaving?"

"Not before I see your art!"

Jessi smiled then ran the rest of the way. "Thank you, Officer Black!"

"You can call me Mal or Mallory."

She sat next to the girl whose life she had helped to save.

Jessi showed Mal colorful drawings of her life, including many of Roland, the fat hamster. Mal thought back to when Ashley would bring her drawings, and felt sad and nostalgic. But there was also joy in sharing this moment with Jessi. The girl would have died if not for Mal and Jasper. But she was alive, despite the fiend who tried to finish her.

Mal thought of that monster, embracing the inevitable confrontation they were about to have. There was no way on earth she would have ever gone to see him if he'd not pulled Jessi and her mother into this. It pissed her off to no end that he could still pull her strings even behind bars.

And again, a part of Mal — a part that was only growing bigger as she sat next to this precious little girl whom she longed to protect — wished she had let Jasper butcher the beast.

Chapter 25 - Jasper Parish

JASPER HAD to get out of the house.

It felt weird being in Alicia's place. She was at work, showing a house, while Ophelia was at school. Karen was driving Jasper nuts with her incessant chatter. She meant well enough, trying to make small talk since they were stuck together until the others got home. But she was the sort of person who felt compelled to fill every silence with too many words.

Karen loved to tell stories, *lots* of them. Stories about her life, stories about Alicia, stories about people Jasper didn't know and never would — all matter of minutia that made Jasper feel as though the walls were closing in.

Jasper needed solitude and quiet to think, especially when he was trying to figure out how to solve Karen's problem — Clay Barlow.

He humored her for a while, then said, "I need to run some errands." And after that, he left without giving her a chance to invite herself along.

Only after he got in the car did Jasper finally realize

that he'd been a bit antisocial, but he wasn't about to go back in and apologize.

He drove, trying to figure out how to get Karen out of her sticky situation without having the whole thing end in violence that might splash back on Alicia and Ophelia.

The solution came after a light lunch at a sports bar where Jasper read the paper while watching the locals. It was a quiet, seaside town comprised of mostly wealthy retirees. Not many crimes. It seemed like a good place for golden years, and far more relaxing than Creek County. The kind of place he could see himself settling.

Carissa's ghost appeared across from Jasper. "She's nice," said his dead wife, staring at him from across the booth. She wasn't smiling but didn't seem mad. Judging from the few times he'd seen that expression during their marriage, it was to be feared more than her wrath.

"She's not you," he said.

"Please."

"What?"

"You don't need to act like you don't like her. I can tell that you do."

Jasper wondered if Carissa had been in Alicia's bedroom while they were making love.

"And her daughter is sweet. She reminds me of her."

"You can say her name."

"I didn't know if you wanted me to since she's not talking to you."

"Have you seen her?"

"From time to time."

"How does it work? Do you talk to each other?"

"Sometimes. It's sort of like a dream, though. One minute I'm here, and the next I'm at our old house. Then I'm at some other place from my life. I don't control any of it. Sometimes she's there. Sometimes, I get to visit you."

Great. My delusions are creating complicated rules for their existence.

Jasper looked into his satchel, found his pills, popped one into his mouth, and swallowed some ice water.

"So, you're taking your meds now, eh? What? To get rid of me? Do I complicate things, Jasper?"

"I just want a normal life. I—"

"Are you okay?" a woman's voice asked.

Jasper turned to see Natsuko, his server, standing there, looking at him, then the chair opposite him.

He smiled. "I'm not crazy."

Her eyes widened.

Great, I'm gonna scare the hell outta this college kid, then she'll call the cops.

He held up an index finger, and explained, "It's this new therapy I heard about on NPR, where you talk to people from your past who you've had a falling out with. Well, you don't talk to them, but you have a conversation with an imagined version of them. It's supposed to help you work through your issues so you can talk them out in real life later."

"Ah," she said, not looking especially convinced.

He laughed, "Except, *I think* you're supposed to do it in your head, not in a crowded restaurant. Sorry about that."

She visibly relaxed. "It's okay. My Oba used to talk to people that weren't there all the time. She said she saw ghosts."

"Do you think she did?"

Natsuko smiled. "When I was little, I thought so. She would tell us things that she had no way on earth of knowing. But I dunno. Maybe that's just the sort of stuff you believe as a kid."

Jasper nodded. "Sometimes, I think back to when I was

growing up. Everything seemed so mysterious. I'd make up these things in my head to make sense of the unknown. Kind of like early man invented myths to explain the world. Weird as it may seem, sometimes I feel like I understood the world better as a kid."

"You're so right. Sometimes I wish my Oba was still alive so I could ask her all the things I never thought about asking her then."

"Maybe you can ask her, anyway," Jasper suggested. "Just don't to it out loud in a crowded restaurant."

Natsuko laughed and set his check on the table. "Here you go. No rush. I'll take it whenever you're ready."

Jasper sat there, considering childhood's simplicity. He wished he could tap into some of that creativity now, use it to solve some very adult problems. To maybe find the life he was meant to have, instead of being a bitter widow, and a mourning father seeking vengeance on a world gone rotten.

Carissa would be disappointed in what he'd become. What he'd allowed the bad world to turn him into.

There were many moments Jasper wished he could have back. But wishing only made him more miserable.

The biggest two were also the most obvious. Jasper would go back to warn Carissa of the cancer she didn't know was eating her insides. He'd go back and be there for Jordyn in her time of need, to prevent her from feeling so hopeless that she saw suicide as her only way out.

And now he had a third moment for the list. Jasper wouldn't have abducted Calum Kozack. He'd let the bastard live out his life, perhaps drink or drug himself into an early grave. Who knows, maybe in time guilt would eat at him, same as Carissa's cancer.

But even the best lives never offered a single do-over.

And Jasper would only get one shot to resolve Karen's issue.

An idea so simple, so perfect, and seemingly flawless appeared from nowhere. Jasper had the one thing Karen required to start her life over, and it didn't involve him going to war with her ex-boyfriend or his thug crew.

Chapter 26 - Mallory Black

MAL ARRIVED at the prison just before three o'clock. She checked in at the front, surrendered her weapon, and sat while waiting for the prisoner to be led to the phone bank.

As she waited, her back began to hurt again. And her heart raced.

She'd left her pills in the car, and wished she'd thought to take one earlier. It would help while she waited for the monster. The last time she saw him was the worst night of her life.

Mal had always known she'd see Dodd's evil eyes again. She would be in court to testify against him, whenever the hell the trial finally started.

Murder cases, especially big ones like his, could be drawn out for years. And during that time, there was this anxious need for closure among the victims' families. Detectives had found the bodies of five other children and two adults near his secret forest bunker. And those families would likely also be watching and waiting for some sense of closure.

Despite knowing she would have to face him again,

Mal felt herself shrinking as the moment approached. She felt a volatile mix of hate, fear, and shame that he'd managed to put her in such a vulnerable position. That she'd almost gotten herself, and Jessi, killed.

Hate wasn't a strong enough word. This was something even deeper. Something she never knew she could feel until her child was murdered.

A door opened on the other side of the Plexiglass divider, and the monster appeared, ushered in by a tall, black prison guard who looked like he bench pressed dump trucks for exercise.

Mal tried not to flinch, though she was startled. Dodd's head was shaved, and he looked even more sinister than he had before.

His blue eyes were practically beaming as he sat with cuffed hands.

He reached up and grabbed the phone as the guard left him to his meeting.

Mal didn't pick up her line. She simply stared at Dodd, trying to bleach her face of emotion. Whatever he wanted, she didn't want to give it.

She buried the hate and the fear and the disgust behind an expression so vacant, one might wonder if Mal were sleeping with her eyes open.

He smiled, not evil or threatening. His expression seemed genuine, like an old friend excited to see her. He nodded toward her phone, silently requesting that she pick it up.

She did so, but kept her mouth closed.

"Hello, Mallory."

Mal said nothing.

"I see you got my package." This time his smile shifted ever so slightly. A predator's smile, toying with his prey.

"I'm here. What do you want?"

"I wanted to tell you that I'm sorry."

Of all the things she thought he might say, that wasn't on the list. Not that she thought for a moment that he meant it. Or cared if he did. You don't get to rape and murder someone's child and then apologize. No matter what horrible things made him into the monster he was, there was no excusing his actions. He couldn't say anything that would make her forgive him.

"Why?" Her response widened his eyes. "Sorry you killed my little girl or sorry that you got caught before you could kill another?"

"Sorry that I killed Ashley. I truly did love her, more than the others."

Mal shook her head, struggling to keep from yelling. "No. You did not love her. Don't you dare claim that you loved her."

"But I did. She was by far the sweetest child. She was curious, caring, and innocent."

"And then you took that from her, you sick fuck."

So much for keeping her emotions in check.

Dodd lowered his head, the smile fading. "I want you to have the rest of the videos."

"I don't want them. And neither does Jessi's mother."

He blinked. Something about it made Mal wonder if maybe Jessi wasn't meant to get her video yet. Perhaps whoever was helping him shipped too soon, not giving Mal enough time to respond.

"Don't you want to know your daughter's final moments? Aren't you curious?"

She fought the tears, desperate to break free. She shook her head, biting her lip, before saying, "Why would I want to when they were with you? When she was scared out of her mind? When she knew she was going to die and her mommy couldn't save her. Why on earth would I want to experience *that?*"

"If you don't see her last words to you, then they were uttered in vain, were they not? Are you truly that selfish that you'd deny your daughter's final wishes?"

Mal closed her eyes and put the phone on the receiver.

She was done.

Paul screamed on the other side of the glass. It was muffled, but she could still hear it.

Mal ignored him, anyway. She stood and turned.

He banged on the Plexiglass with the phone, screaming more. The guard would get him any second. All she had to do was walk out of the room, and that was it. He would suffer. Whatever he brought her here for, she refused to give it to him.

Mal turned back, saw the guard putting the phone on the table, then shoving Dodd against the wall, one hand against his neck, as another guard came in for back-up.

Mal held her badge to the window and tapped it to get the guard's attention. Then she pointed to the phone.

The guard picked it up, "Yes?"

"Give me another second."

"Okay." He handed the phone to Dodd with a *Don't-Fuck-With-Me* glare.

Mal said, "If you ever fuck with Jessi Price's family ever again. If you so much as wave in their general direction, or send one of your buddies to deliver a message, I will make it my mission to find new and inventive ways to make you wish I'd let you die. Nod if you understand me."

Dodd nodded, no smile on his face, nor gleam in his eye.

Mal hung up.

Chapter 27 - Mallory Black

MAL WAS TREMBLING when she left. Her heart raced, sweat beaded her brow, her breathing was too shallow. She had to get the hell out of the prison, *now*, before the walls finished closing in.

She rushed through the halls, retrieved her gun, then practically ran to her car, hoping she wouldn't pass out from a panic attack.

Once inside, she grabbed her pills from the center console, popped two into her mouth, and washed them down with a warm bottle of water.

She keyed the ignition, turned the air conditioning on, closed her eyes, and lay back in her seat, waiting for something approaching calm.

As she tried to focus on slowing her heart, she kept thinking of Dodd staring back at her, insisting that he loved her daughter.

Loved!

It was bad enough that he had violated her, that he had ended her life. Him saying he loved her seemed like yet another violation, an offense against her very soul.

Then she realized — that was why he had asked her to come. Dodd couldn't brutalize Ashley anymore, nor any other child as long as he was locked away, so he decided to do the next best thing by assaulting her memory.

She imagined the joy he must be feeling as he returned to his cell. Hell, the fucker was probably masturbating.

She grabbed her cell, then checked to see if Mike had texted her back. She didn't want to be alone and wasn't sure what she might do if left to her own devices.

No messages from Mike.

She pulled up her contacts and thought about calling Ray.

Her finger hovered over his name as she remembered their awkwardness a few months ago. Clearly, they still had feelings for one another, but he was with Julie now, and Mal wasn't a home wrecker.

She cycled through her contacts, coming to the sad realization that when it came right down to it, Mal didn't have any friends. Mike was her partner. He was also married and usually busy in the few hours a week he wasn't already working. There were a few people she was friendly with on the force, but nobody she could consider a friend, no one she could just call and commiserate with.

She considered calling Mary, her sponsor, but Mal had barely kept in touch with her at all. It seemed like she hadn't been to a meeting in forever, so calling now would be shitty.

Mal dialed Mike, got his voice mail, and said, "Hey, just checking in to see what you're up to."

She hung up, feeling desperate and stupid for calling him when he said he'd text her later.

Mal dropped her phone on the seat and stared out the window, waiting for the pills to cut into her anxiety.

She wished it would rain, but even the sun refused to cooperate, shining big and far too bright in the sky.

"Fucking sun!" Mal growled.

She put her car in reverse and started driving, not sure where she was going, just away from Dodd and the venom he'd worked into her soul.

The pills kicked in as she drove. Mal laughed at her miserable self, cursing at the sun of all things.

She was almost back at the hotel when her phone rang. She put the call through to her car speakers. "Hey, Mike."

"Hey, my buddy had something come up, so you wanna grab lunch?"

Mal agreed to meet at Gator Jack's, a sports bar along the beachside.

GATOR JACK'S was a popular place, always packed, decent food, attractive servers, and a TV at every booth that you could tune to any number of games. Mal arrived before Mike, so she chose a national news station where a pair of anchors were discussing yet *another* tropical storm raging across the Atlantic.

The server, a tall, athletic college kid with blond hair and blue eyes set a pitcher of beer on the table just as Mike was taking his seat.

"Thanks, Finn," Mal said.

"Sure thing." He turned to Mike. "Need a minute to look at the menu?"

"Nah," he said, turning to Mal. "Wanna do wings?"

"Yeah, can we get a plate of 50 wings?"

"Mild, medium, hot, or blazing?"

Mal looked at Mike. She was fine with anything, but he had a more sensitive stomach.

"Let's do half mild, and half whatever she wants."

"I'll go with hot," Mal said.

As Finn left, a tiny brunette server in ass-hugging shorts, a low scoop black Gator Jack's tee, and a pushup bra shoving her implants onto full display approached their table. She gave Mike a flirty smile and touched his arm. "Hey, Detective, how are you?"

"I'm doing well," Mal said. "And you?"

The server turned and gave Mal an artificial smile, either not getting Mal's joke or not caring. She turned back to Mike. "Haven't seen you and the other guys around in a while."

"Yeah, been real busy at work."

Mal tried to see the girl's name, but her badge was too near her ample cleavage.

"Ah, well hope to see you soon," she said, giving his arm another squeeze before leaving.

Mal laughed.

"What?" Mike said, innocently.

"So pathetic."

"*What?* She's usually on Sunday nights when a couple of the guys and I come in to watch baseball."

"Wow, she could not be any more obvious," Mal said, reaching over and squeezing Mike's arm, just like the server. "*Oooh*, you have such big muscles, Detective. Have you been working out?"

Mike blushed and gave her the finger. "She's just nice to get a good tip."

"Just the tip or the whole thing?" Mal laughed.

Mal found it hilarious that law enforcement attracted such rabid groupies, especially with young women in the service industry. It wasn't uncommon for detectives, single and married, to sleep around. Not that Mal had room to criticize. While she didn't have groupies — *thank God* —

she'd had more than a few one-night stands since her marriage went to hell and she lost her daughter.

But she hated the idea of Mike, such a nice guy, and happily married to a wonderful woman, being weak and falling for a groupie.

"So," Mal said, "there's nothing going on with you and her?"

"Sheesh, Mal, come on. I'm happily married, thank you."

"Okay, okay. I believe you. So, you find anything on Eddie Dixon?"

"I went to a pool hall where he hangs out sometimes and got in touch with one of his cousins. I told him that we wanted to talk. That we just need some help catching Chloe's killer, and that he can come in voluntarily, or we can bring him in. Obviously, that wouldn't be as fun for him."

"Think he'll bite?"

"Hell if I know."

Mal told Mike about her day, starting with her visit to Jessi Price and ending face-to-face with Dodd.

"Oh, wow. What a bastard. You think he'll stop?"

"Hell if I know." she echoed. "I'd love to find out who delivered the packages for him. He hasn't been in prison long enough to gain any respect or favors, right? Makes me wonder if he had someone working with him. And if so, is this another rapist-slash-killer?"

"Maybe groupies? Did you ask for visitor logs?"

"Shit. No. I was in such a rush to get out of there; I didn't even think to."

Mal made a note in her phone to do that tomorrow.

"Did you put someone on Price's house?"

"Yeah, Wilson said he would."

"What about you? You going to station someone at the hotel, since he knows where you are?"

"No. Fuck that. If his buddy wants to come at me, I'm ready. But I doubt he'll do anything. Way I'm thinking, Dodd wants me alive if only to have this … whatever it is … between us. It's like he's getting off on our shared history."

"You're his souvenir," Mike suggested, "his best way of reliving his crime now that he's locked up."

She shuddered. "I need a shower."

Finn appeared and set their wings on the table. He smiled at Mal. "Anything else I can get you?"

"No, we're good. Thank you."

Mal watched him walk away, admiring his shoulders before fixing her eyes on his ass. Then she looked up to see Mike staring.

He laughed. "You hypocrite!"

"Hey, I'm not married. I can look. And besides, he's not all touchy flirty like what's her face."

"Brooklynne."

Mal shook her head. "So, you know her name? You're such a dog."

"What?" He laughed. "She's an excellent server."

She bit into a wing as something caught her attention — a video of Kelly Conlan in lingerie. A red graphic read *EXCLUSIVE* beneath it.

She turned up the TV to hear a commercial for the notorious exploiter of kidnapped and murdered women and children, Molly Grant. "Tonight, on *Exposed With Molly Grant* we reveal Florida Councilman's daughter, Kelly Conlan's secret side as a cam prostitute, selling herself online as her child is murdered right outside her door in a cozy bedroom community. Could this murder have been prevented? And what role does online porn have in an innocent child's death? Only tonight on *Exposed With Molly Grant*."

"Fuck," Mal said as the commercial ended.

Mal looked around to how many TVs were tuned to the same channel. Most of the other TVs were showing sports, but a few tables had the same channel on, and she could already see people staring and whispering.

She sighed. "And this is how the media circus begins."

Grant was a parasite. As a former prosecutor, her show started off as an advocate for victims of crimes, many unsolved. But somewhere along the line, ratings became more important than the lives of the people she was shoving under the spotlight. Grant routinely went after people with little to no evidence, shared graphic murder photos and videos online, and had driven one innocent mother of a missing child to suicide.

Grant showcasing Conlan meant that a white-hot spotlight was now turning its attention onto Creek County, its denizens, and, of course, the Sheriff's Office. Eventually, the light would shine on Mallory herself.

Grant had done a few stories on Mal when Ashley was found dead and did another after Jessi was saved. Mal had turned down interview requests both times but didn't think she'd be so lucky as to avoid her a third time.

Storm clouds gathered, in her gut and the sky.

Mike steered the lunchtime conversation toward jokes and humorous work stories whenever Mal got too deep into discussing their current case. The check came, and Mike picked it up, despite her efforts to pay.

Mal realized something. "Hey, your buddy Danny didn't change plans on you today, did he?"

"What?" Mike pulled out his credit card and set it on the little plastic tray.

"You … you're trying to cheer me up."

"Why would you say that?"

"Because you're so fucking obvious, with all these Best Of Work stories every time I try to bitch about anything."

Finn grabbed the bill, then brought it back.

As they stood from the table, Mike took the leftover wings and said, "Fine. Yeah, I lied. I could tell by your voicemail that you weren't in a good place. And you might need a shoulder to lean on."

"Thanks," Mal said, tearing up.

Brooklynne walked by and waved at Mike on their way to the exit. "Bye, Detective Mikey."

Mikey? Oh, she is such a groupie!

As they pushed through the door, Mal laughed one last time.

Chapter 28 - Mallory Black

MAL SAT IN HER CUBICLE, scanning the archived history of Kelly Conlan's LiveLyfe account, searching for anything that might be useful, and noting any relevant friends which they'd not yet interviewed.

She kept commenting to Mike as she scrolled, about the lack of depth in her postings. The majority of Kelly's entries were photos or videos, mostly selfies, taken at parties, many late at night and out of town.

Mal wondered if Kelly's mother, Gayle, always watched Chloe, or if she was bringing her daughter to the parties. Maybe she was dosing her kid with Benadryl and leaving her alone.

"Have we heard from Gayle yet?"

"No," Mike said. "She's in France and hasn't returned any of my calls."

"What's she doing in France?"

"Her mother is sick, so she went to be with her."

"She must've heard about Chloe by now, right? Why the hell isn't she back? Or at least calling us?"

Mike leaned back in his chair, sipping his iced coffee. He shrugged. "Hell if I know; the whole damned family is odd."

And as if on cue, Councilman Conlan shouted in the halls outside the bullpen demanding an audience with Sheriff Bell. When someone in the hallway told him that she wasn't in, he asked for the person in charge of his granddaughter's investigation.

Deputy Harrison led Conlan into the room and pointed to Mike and Mal. "You want to talk to Mike Cortez."

Mike sighed as Conlan approached, red-faced and fists balled. Normally on weekdays, the councilman wore fine suits, silk ties, and nary a hair of his greased back hair out of place. This morning he was in suit pants and a dress shirt, nice for sure, but they looked slept in.

"Who leaked this sleaze about my daughter?"

Mike stood, raising his hands. "We didn't leak anything, Mr. Conlan. Videos of your daughter's cam sessions were all over Reddit and NonAMus within hours of Chloe's death hitting the news. It was only a matter of time before the media picked up on it."

"Bullshit! This is you all trying to get back at me over the budget bullshit. I knew Gloria was vicious, but hell, I never thought she'd politicize a child's death."

"If you have a problem with how we're doing our job, talk to the sheriff, or …" Mike looked back and saw Wilson coming from the break room with a fresh giant mug of coffee. "Or talk to Captain Wilson."

Wilson went into his office, set his drink down, and returned. "How can I help you, Councilman?"

"Where's the sheriff?"

"She's not in yet, but I'd be happy to help you."

"I want to know who leaked that bullshit to Molly Grant."

"I'm not sure what you think we do here all day, but believe me, we're not calling Molly Fucking Grant and giving her shit on your daughter. We're doing exactly one thing — trying to find out who murdered your granddaughter, something which would be a little bit easier if you didn't lawyer your daughter up during a routine interview."

"Is *that* what this is all about? You're pissed because I'm looking out for my daughter? Sorry, but I know how you all do your business, and I'm not letting you railroad my daughter so that you can get to me."

Wilson was about to respond, likely taking a moment to filter out his more vulgar impulses, when Conlan looked past Mal's shoulder and onto her computer screen.

"What the hell are you looking through my daughter's LiveLyfe for? That's on private."

"I'd like you to leave now, Mr. Conlan," Wilson said before Mal could respond.

"Excuse me? I want to talk to the sheriff."

"Well, she's not here yet. I'll let her know that you stopped by and voiced your concerns."

"I'm not done here."

"I think you are. Listen, I know it may seem difficult to believe, but we are working a murder case, trying to find the person who killed your granddaughter. We don't give a good goddamn who your daughter showed her tits to. Now, if you don't mind, please get the *fuck* out of my office before I lose my best manners."

Mal and Mike traded glances. She wasn't sure if she wanted to burst out laughing or worry for Wilson's job.

Conlan looked around, seeing all the office eyes upon him. Then he lowered his voice to a whisper that only the four of them could hear, and leaned forward, his musky cologne making Mal want to gag.

"You all want to play dirty, eh? Well, I can roll around in the mud with the best of you pigs."

Then threat delivered, Conlan turned and left.

Chapter 29 - Mallory Black

MIKE AND MAL avoided the break room for most of the morning, knowing that if they went in there, other deputies and detectives would ask what Councilman Conlan whispered. Neither of them wanted to fuel the fires of gossip, especially when Wilson might very well get the riot act read to him once word got back to the sheriff.

They also both actively avoided calls and emails from Cameron Ford, figuring he was following up on the salacious story of Kelly's cam girl history.

They walked around the block to get some fresh air. Mal waited until they were at least half a block from the sheriff's office when she finally burst out laughing.

"Oh my God, did you see Conlan's face?"

"See it? I got a picture."

"No, you didn't."

"Yeah, I turned my webcam on the moment he came in."

Mal laughed again. "Why would you do that?"

"I dunno, insurance. You never know what a politician

is likely to do. I don't trust any of them, but particularly him."

"Why?" Mal asked.

"I get a bad vibe from him. Plus, as you know, he and Claude Barry were tight. And when you're friends with a racist asshole, that doesn't say much for you."

"You think Conlan's a racist asshole, too?"

"Oh, I don't know. Maybe he's just an opportunistic asshole, willing to throw in with the racists if it gets him what he wants. And, I'm not sure what's worse these days. At least you know where racists stand. They hate who they hate for whatever stupid reason. But an opportunistic politician? They're a special kind of dangerous."

Mal's phone buzzed. A text from Ray.

Need to talk when you're able.

She read the text to Mike then said, "What the hell? I hate when people leave vague messages like that. Let me know *why* you need to talk so I can decide if I should call you right back or if it can truly wait."

"What's going on with him?"

While Mal told Mike most things, for some reason she'd omitted any mention of their awkward moment at the hotel a few months ago. Maybe because it didn't paint Ray in a flattering light, him wanting to cheat on his girlfriend with Mal, and she didn't like to trash him. Their divorce had been difficult enough, but it was sad more than acrimonious, and a part of her did still love him. They were, technically, friends. Hell, at the moment, Ray was her only friend other than Mike.

"I don't know. We haven't talked in a while. I think he's doing okay."

"And yet you're annoyed by his text?"

"Well, yeah. I'm working. I don't know if he's calling just to shoot the shit or if something's wrong. And I don't want to call him and be stuck on the phone if he just wants to talk about nothing."

"Just tell him you're working," Mike said as if it were that simple.

"I can't. He gets pissy if I blow him off. He can be so sensitive."

Mike laughed. "Man, you are such a dude."

"Fuck you, pal," Mal laughed. "By the way, where is Gloria? She's not usually *this* late."

"I think she had some training in Jacksonville or something."

"Ah," Mal said. "So, I guess Wilson's job is safe for one more day."

"She won't get rid of him. Not for that. Hell, she might make him undersheriff."

The current undersheriff, a man named John Bunker, had spent the better half of the past year in and out of hospitals being treated for prostate cancer. Gloria probably should have replaced him, but she was loyal to Bunker, as he was one of the few Good Ol' Boys from the former administration that helped get deputies on her side after she won the election. He also came from one of the county's original families on the west side, where he helped her secure a number of votes from people who typically wouldn't vote for a Democrat, let alone a black female. Much of Bunker's work fell on Sheriff Bell, and to some of the captains heading the departments.

They were almost back at the office when Captain Wilson texted a link to a news story on *The Creek County Confidential.*

"Fuck," Mal said as she began reading a hit piece from Cameron Ford: *Sex Offender Last Seen With Chloe Conlan, Yet Sheriff's Office Lets Him Walk.*

The story quoted several "reliable inside sources"

inside Creek County Sheriff's Office who claimed that Mike and Mallory were using the investigation to target the Conlan family while ignoring evidence that pointed at Terrance Burridge. The story ended with, *Calls to Detectives at CCSO for comments on this story were not returned by press time.* It wasn't just the standard line a reporter would write when they couldn't get comments in time for publication, but it was also a subtle dig at the story's targets. A way of saying, "Hey, they're refusing to comment because they have something to hide!"

Mike's face burned red. "Well, I guess this is what Conlan meant when he said he was going to play dirty. Cameron Ford must be his personal lapdog to get a story out this quickly."

"Well, I guess now we know who is pulling the editorial strings of this website."

Mal and Mike picked up their pace to get back, figuring Wilson would be on the warpath, but not knowing what he might want in response.

Mike's phone rang.

Mal, not able to see who it was, figured it was either Wilson wanting to know where the hell his detectives were, or the sheriff asking what the hell happened while she was gone.

"No shit. Okay, send a copy to both me and Mal. Thank you, Aanya." Mike hung up, smiling from ear to ear.

"What is it?"

"Aanya got a hold of Kelly's deleted phone browser history."

"And?"

"There are Google searches."

"For what?" Mal asked, "Spit it out, man!"

"About untraceable poisons, and about how much

Benadryl would kill a child. There's more, but that's the big stuff."

"No fucking way," Mal said.

"We need to get her back in the room."

"Yes, we do," Mike said, putting in a call to his ex-partner, Skippy. "Hey, can you go pick up Kelly Conlan? She's staying at her mom's. I'll text you the details when I hang up."

They arrived back at the station, surprised to find that somebody else was already waiting for his interview — Kelly's boyfriend, Eddie Dixon.

Chapter 30 - Jasper Parish

KAREN LOOKED DOWN at the envelope, confused. She glanced from the kitchen counter where she was cutting cheeses and fruits to place on a plate for Ophelia and Alicia when they got home, back to the envelope, then finally to Jasper. "What's this, and why did you give it to me?"

"Five thousand dollars to get you on your feet in New York."

"What?" she said, staring, her eyes wide. "You're kidding."

"No, I'm not. It's yours. And you don't need to pay me back."

"Why are you doing this?" she asked, her eyes watering. "You don't even know me."

"Because I love your sister, and she loves you, and I want you to be happy. I want you to have the best chance possible, away from that loser."

Karen ran around the counter and threw her arms around Jasper, jumping up and down like she'd just won a prize. Maybe she had.

But then she pulled away, shaking her head. "No. I can't. I mean, that is a *lot* of money."

"You can and you will," Jasper said, smiling. "And if you need more, let me know."

She looked at him like he was crazy.

"Damn, Alicia didn't tell me you were a millionaire, Dennis."

"Nothing like that," he said. "But I'm doing okay for myself. And I hate to see something like money be the only thing standing in your way to having the life you want. So, please, take it, my gift to you."

"Wow, I … I don't know what to say."

"Just say yes."

She hugged him again, crying, and thanking him over and over.

Jasper smiled, wondering if this was the sort of joy that Mallory Black felt after discovering the winning lottery ticket he'd planted in her living room. He'd never told her it was his numbers, *Jordyn's* numbers.

Of course, that wasn't entirely true, was it?

Jordyn had the vision, but if Jordyn was a manifestation of his imagination, then wasn't it his? He was the psychic, after all?

Jasper's phone rang.

He broke away from Karen's hug and saw a message from Alicia.

Running late. Can you pick Ophelia up from school? I already called and gave them your name. Sending a link to the address.

"Gotta pick Ophelia up from school."

"Thanks again," she said, kissing him on the cheek.

～

JASPER PUSHED through the doors of Elmhurst Elementary School, went to the front office, gave them his fake name, and waited for Ophelia.

"Dennis!" she yelled, still no less enthusiastic to see him than when he'd first come downstairs for breakfast a few days ago.

He hugged her, then looked at her backpack, which was nearly as big as she was.

"Wow, what all do you carry in that thing?" he said, lifting it, surprised by its bulk.

She started going down a list of everything in her backpack as they walked outside.

"Who's that by your car?" Ophelia asked.

Jasper looked across the parking lot and saw one of Clay's thugs seated on his motorcycle, right behind Jasper's car, blocking his exit.

"Nobody, Sweetie," Jasper said, picking up his pace, still walking toward the man, but keeping himself between Ophelia and the thug.

"Can I help you?" Jasper asked.

The man was big, both in stature and bulk. His face was long and broad, and he had shaggy blond hair. He reminded Jasper of a pro wrestler. He wore jeans, a white tank top, black leather boots and a vest.

"Clay says hi," said the man with a sneer.

The gun tucked into a holster under the man's vest got Jasper's heart. If he reacted poorly, this could spiral out of control.

Relax, he's just here to send a message.

Jasper's gun was in the glove compartment, but he was carrying a black carbon steel fixed blade knife sheathed to the belt in the small of his back. He didn't reach for it. Yet. "Okay. Tell him I said hi back."

Jasper walked Ophelia around to the passenger side of

the car, let her in, and closed the door. Then he walked around to the front of his car, while the thug continued to stare.

Jasper got into his car and closed the door.

He looked in the rearview and slipped on his seatbelt.

The man wasn't moving.

Shit.

Jasper couldn't go forward, because of the large parking stone in front of his car, and a lamppost beyond that. He considered getting out but instead honked his horn.

"Why isn't he moving?" Ophelia asked, turned halfway around, concern creeping onto her nine-year-old face.

"Don't worry. He'll move." Jasper honked again.

He kept his eyes on the rearview, and a hand on the gearshift, ready to kick the car into reverse if the fucker pulled out his pistol. The taste of copper coated his tongue.

Jasper watched, the man's beady eyes meeting his in the mirror.

Then the thug revved his motorcycle and drove away.

Jasper watched as the man left the lot.

"He was scary," Ophelia said.

Jasper glared at the man until he was a distant dot on the road. "There's nothing to be scared of, honey. Dennis is here."

Chapter 31 - Mallory Black

WILSON WATCHED the closed-circuit monitors along his left wall, focusing on the bottom row in particular, broadcasting a feed from the interview rooms.

Kelly Conlan sat in Room Three with her lawyer, waiting impatiently. In Room One Eddie Dixon sat alone, looking almost smug.

Wilson asked, "You think they know each other is here?"

Mike said, "Well, he might have called her to tell her he was going in, but I doubt he knows we've got her. Who should we interview first?"

Wilson looked at the lawyer, Jack Shapiro, and made an unpleasant face. "Make them wait. Interview Dixon."

≈

EDDIE DIXON WAS THIRTY-THREE, but with his blue mohawk, gaunt body with way too much ink, and a face full of modifications, he reminded Mal of a disaffected teenager trying too hard.

He leaned back in the chair trying to come off as casual, speaking in a slow slur. Mal couldn't tell if it was some sort of affectation or if the guy was high. Maybe both. Either way, he was calm, cool, and cocky while answering Mike's opening questions:

When's the last time you saw Kelly?

Thursday.

When's the last time you saw Chloe?

Also Thursday.

Where have you been since Thursday?

Chillin' with friends in South Florida, ya' know?

He was short with his responses as if he'd rehearsed them. Mal stood in the corner, watching, waiting for something she might be able to use, something she could pounce on.

A few times Eddie looked at her with a raised eyebrow and a slight nod, as if she just might go with him after this little interview was over.

She stifled a laugh.

Mike finished, and Mal started in, staying in the corner next to the door, arms folded over her chest.

"What did you think about Chloe?"

"I dunno," he shrugged. "She was 'aight, I 'spose. Didn't know her too well, ya' know?"

"Did she like you?"

"She was a weird kid. Off in her own lil' world, ya' know? But she ain't bother me if that's what you askin'."

"So, you never told Kelly that you hated Chloe being around?"

His demeanor shifted, slightly less relaxed, his smile slightly less confident.

"I dunno. I mean, I might'a said somethin' 'bout wantin' to have some alone time, 'n shit. But, it ain't mean nothin'."

"And did she tell you that there wasn't a day that went by that she wished she didn't get an abortion?"

He pursed his lips. "I dunno. I don't remember her sayin' anything like that. Why?"

"Do you think that Kelly Conlan wanted to kill her daughter?"

Dixon made an over-exaggerated show of distaste, sitting up, coming alive for the first time since they'd entered the room. "Hell, no. She loved that kid!"

"Even though there wasn't a day that went by that she wished she didn't get an abortion?"

"Man, you always be twistin' shit people say into somethin' else. Who hasn't wished they made dif'rent choices, eh? That ain't mean she didn't love Chloe."

"Okay. I guess I can understand that. Tell me, Eddie," Mal said, approaching the table smiling, working her charm, "did Kelly ever do drugs around Chloe?"

"I wouldn't know. I wasn't there all *that* often."

"So, she does do drugs, then?"

"I don't know."

"Come on, Eddie, don't play dumb. We know you deal coke, weed, pills, maybe a bit of heroin now and then?"

He crossed his arms, jaw clenching.

"And we don't care," Mal said. "This isn't narcotics. We just want to know what happened to Chloe. Was it murder or an accident? Maybe Kelly was high, and something terrible happened. Maybe she didn't mean for it to happen, but it did, and then she freaked, didn't know what to do, so she made up a story."

Eddie shook his head. "No, she wouldn't hurt that girl."

"Yeah, but what if it was an accident?" Mal suggested. "Accidents happen, right?"

Eddie shook his head, still staring at the table, wheels spinning.

"Would you like a drink?" Mal asked. "We're gonna get something from the break room."

"You got Mountain Dew?"

"I believe we do."

Mal left and met with Mike in the observation room.

"So," he said, "what do you think?"

"I dunno. I feel like he knows something, but at the same time, I don't think he thinks she did it."

"You think *he* did it?"

Mal shook her head. "No. I don't."

"Alright, let's talk to our Mother of the Year."

Chapter 32 - Mallory Black

MALLORY TOOK a seat opposite Kelly and Kelly's lawyer.

Three days removed from the death of her child, Kelly looked tired, maybe heavily medicated, but well put together, wearing a conservative dress and an almost naked make-up look. A stark contrast to the salaciously blurred clips that had run on *Exposed With Molly Grant*, then several other shows, last night and likely until the end of time — *especially* if Kelly was found guilty of her daughter's murder or the case went unsolved.

"That was some shady stuff," Shapiro said. "Tipping off Grant."

Mal didn't take the bait and moved into her opening salvo.

"We've got Eddie Dixon in the next room, and boy is he telling us some stories."

Kelly's eyes widened. She looked at Shapiro. He said, "And you're going to take the word of a felon over my client?"

"Your client who went out with said felon for two years? Yeah, I might listen to what he's got to say."

Shapiro laughed with a dismissive wave.

Mal continued, "Tell me, Kelly, do you love Eddie?"

She paused for a long moment, then shook her head. "No. I thought I did once, but he's trouble."

"What about Eddie is trouble exactly?"

"My client has no knowledge of any illegal activities that Mr. Dixon may or may not be engaged in."

"Of course." Mal nodded. "I'm sure he left the room whenever he bumped a few lines, shot a bit of H, eh?"

Kelly said nothing, keeping her eyes on Mal, likely coached by Shapiro.

"Did Eddie … *like* Chloe?"

Kelly looked at Shapiro. He nodded. "No, not really," she said.

"Why not?"

"He was very immature. He wanted me all to himself."

"And you never thought about, I don't know, maybe running off with Eddie and leaving Chloe with your mom?"

Kelly shifted in her seat and swallowed. "No."

"So, you never said this?"

"I … I dunno."

"Do you expect my client to remember everything she may have said in passing? She's been through a lot, and has barely slept."

Mal ignored him. "Did you also say that there wasn't a day that you didn't wish you'd aborted her when you had a chance?"

Kelly's eyes began to tear up. "I didn't mean that."

"But you *did* say it?"

"You don't need to answer things you might not recall, Kelly."

Kelly wiped at her eyes. "Yes, I said it, but I was in a bad place. I didn't mean it."

"That's not what Eddie says. He says that you told him you'd 'take care' of Chloe," Mal lied to gauge her response, to see if it was significantly more impassioned than her prior denials. Mal could usually measure a person's innocence by the might of their rebuttal. The guilty might put up some resistance, but innocents freaked the hell out when you accused them of something they didn't do.

"He's a liar!" Kelly spit. "I *never* said that! I would never say that!"

"But you'd *think* it, right? I mean, we can't help the horrible things we think, can we?"

Shapiro cut in as if objecting in court. "So, now you're going to harass my client for what she might think? Wow, *Minority Report*, anyone?"

"Except this isn't a thought crime. There's a dead child, and these are legitimate questions."

"Legitimate questions? Interesting coming from the detectives that freed a known sex offender. Come on, we all know what this is — a hit job, looking to ding my client's father, whom your sheriff has a beef with."

Mal smiled. "Funny how you all are trying to spin this conspiracy theory to smear us. We must be getting close to something that you don't want us to find."

Mal stood, then leaned down in front of Kelly, looking down at her, fists balled on the table. "Listen, Kelly. I get it. Being a single mother is difficult. Raising an autistic child is even more demanding. I understand. I also understand that Eddie might have pressured you to do something that you didn't want to do."

"He didn't pressure me to do anything! I didn't kill Chloe!"

"Do you think Eddie could have?"

She started to say something, but Shapiro interrupted. "She can't possibly know what's in his mind."

"What were you fighting about the other day?" Mal asked. "On Thursday?"

She paused, and Mal wondered if she was trying to remember or manufacture a lie.

"He wanted me to borrow money from my father to pay off a debt."

"What kind of debt?"

"I don't know. He owed some dangerous men and told me they'd hurt him if he didn't give them twenty grand."

"So that was *his* money and drugs in your house?" Mal asked.

"The money was mine. Money I'd saved up."

"And the drugs?"

"His. I mean, I smoked some weed now and then, but I didn't touch the hard stuff."

"My client has anxiety and needs medicinal marijuana to ease it."

Mike laughed in the corner, "Man, you've got an answer for everything, don't you, Jack?"

Shapiro smiled at Mike, then folded his hands on the table.

"Don't worry, Kelly," Mal said. "We're not looking to make a drug arrest. And believe me, if we wanted to cause problems for your father, we would be pursuing drug charges. You had enough there for us to hit you with intent to sell."

"Not my client's drugs."

"We both know that doesn't matter," Mal snapped back. "What I'm getting at here, *Kelly*, is that I want to find the person responsible for killing your little girl. I lost a girl of my own, and it took me two years to find the monster responsible.

And those two years were absolute hell for me. I don't want that for you. I want you to sleep at night, knowing that you did everything possible to help us find Chloe's killer. So, is there anything at all that you can think of that could help us?"

Kelly stared into her eyes, and Mal felt the woman's pain. That didn't make her innocent, but it also didn't make her a monster.

"I can't think of anything, unless …"

"What?" Mal asked. "Anything you can think of."

"What if the people who wanted money from Eddie came after her?"

"Do you think that could've happened?"

Mal carefully observed Kelly's responses, especially interested in whether she'd pursue the debt murder notion. If she were too eager, it would practically point a big neon sign toward her guilt, or at least her knowledge of what *did* happen.

Mal waited, hoping that Shapiro wouldn't butt in again and screw things up.

Finally, Kelly said, "I … I don't know. Eddie didn't say anything about us being in danger. Just him."

"Thank you," Mal said. "That's it for now."

Kelly stood, wiping her eyes.

Shapiro headed toward the door, not saying a word to either Mike or Mal.

Just as Kelly reached the threshold, Mal pulled the trigger on the question she'd been waiting to ask.

"Kelly?"

She turned and looked at Mal. Behind her, Shapiro did the same.

"I'm just wondering if you could tell me why you were Googling untraceable poisons and how much Benadryl it would take to kill a child."

Kelly's face went pale. Her eyes widened. A deer in

front of a roaring car in the black of night. Shapiro took Kelly by the arm and started to lead her out, saying, "We're done here."

Mal grabbed Kelly's hand. "She didn't answer yet."

Kelly shook her head. "I didn't search for anything like that."

"Are you certain?" Mal asked.

"Yes, I'm fucking certain. I never Googled anything like that! I swear. You've got my computer. It'll show the stupid shit I do look up and believe me, that's not on there."

"How about your phone?" Mal asked. "Interestingly, the history was wiped. But your service provider was kind enough to back up your searches so we could get them."

"I didn't," she said, shaking her head.

"Did anyone else have access to your phone?" Mal asked.

"Well, Chloe used it sometimes. And ..." her eyes widened again. "Eddie used it, a lot."

Shapiro glared at Mal. "Are we done here, *detectives?*"

Mal nodded. "For now."

Then she let go of Kelly's hand.

As Shapiro pulled her out of the room, Kelly no longer looked like a deer in headlights, but rather a doe that saw its entire family flattened by trucks.

Chapter 33 - Mallory Black

MIKE TOOK A SEAT OPPOSITE EDDIE, handed him a cold Mountain Dew, set a folder on the table between them, then placed a ballpoint pen atop the folder.

Mal stood behind Mike, arms across her chest.

Eddie popped open the drink and took a deep gulp, looking at the folder, but playing it cool, not asking what was inside.

"So, here's the deal, Eddie," Mike said. "We've got Kelly in the other interview room, telling her side of this story. But she's not alone. Oh, no, she has a fancy pants lawyer, paid for by Daddy. And wooh, boy, can this guy tell a story! If you think for one moment that that lawyer is looking out for you, then you're sadly mistaken. You know that, right? You know someone like him doesn't give a damn about someone like *you*."

Eddie shifted in his seat, knee bouncing as he digested this uncomfortable truth along with his Mountain Dew.

Mal leaned forward. "You familiar with internet searches for poisons that can't be traced, or how much Benadryl it'd take to kill a child, Eddie?"

His brow furrowed as he sat up. "No, why?"

"Because we found those searches on Kelly's phone. And she said you were the only other person to use it. I don't need to tell you what that's going to look like to a jury, do I?"

"I didn't search for that shit on her phone!"

Mal kept her voice calm as she explained exactly how this would play out. "What do you think the jury will think when they see you, then they see Kelly? I mean, yeah, she has tattoos and did the cam girl stuff, but she's a rich politician's daughter. She cleans up well, believe me. They're gonna see a poor, sweet innocent young woman with her daughter murdered, and then they're going to see you, with the blue mohawk, the questionable tattoos that can't be hidden by dress shirts, and a face full of metal. How do you think that's going to play out with a conservative jury, Eddie? You think they're going to believe you over her?"

"Is she saying *I* searched for that shit? It wasn't me!"

"Do you know who did?" Mike asked.

"No, man. I ain't keepin' track of her phone. All I can tell you is that one hundred percent, I had nothing to do with that girl getting killed!"

"Did you ask her to kill Chloe?" Mal asked.

"No, man. That's messed up shit right there. Did I joke around, did we *both* joke around from time to time and say shit that might'a come off mean? Yeah, but neither one of us wanted Chloe dead."

"Is there any way she could've interpreted some joke you made as a request?"

Eddie thought for a moment, his finger running a ring around the rim of the Mountain Dew can before he shook his head. "No. No, man. Besides, we ain't joked about that stuff in a long time. Things was goin' okay, ya' know? Once she started camming, the money started coming in, and it was easier for her to be home with Chloe."

Mal asked, "Did you ever touch Chloe?"

"What do you mean touch? Like diddled her or some shit?"

"Yes, that's exactly what I mean."

"Hell no. Kelly didn't say that shit, did she?"

"I'm just asking. Did you ever touch her in a sexual way?"

"Hell no. I ain't no fuckin' pedo!" This was the most pissed Mal had seen him. Eddie was more upset by the accusation that he touched the girl than killed her, and judging from her gut, the man wasn't lying.

Mal was about to ask a follow-up if he knew anyone who might have touched Chloe when he snapped, shedding whatever was left of his cool demeanor.

"Why don't you all ask that fucking retard if *he* touched her before you let him go, eh? Did you all ask him that? Fuckin' guy shows his dick to a playground full o' kids and y'all just let him walk outta here like nothin'. How the hell is he not in jail? Answer me that! Meanwhile, ya' harass me and Kelly like *we're* the bad guys. Seriously, what the hell is wrong with y'all?"

"We had him in here," Mal said, trying to calm him. "And he has an alibi for where he was during the time of Chloe's murder. He didn't do it."

Eddie looked at them like he wanted to keep ranting, but he was out of steam. His emotions had slammed into a hard wall of irrefutable facts.

Mike, trying to steer this back to Eddie, asked, "Who did you owe twenty grand to?"

Eddie shook his head, let out a long sigh, and shook his head. "Man, I ain't even talkin' 'bout that."

"If you don't, Kelly will," Mike prodded. "And I want to hear *your* side."

"That has nothin' to do with this."

"Tell us," Mal said.

"Is you all gonna give me, um, immunity? Like you ain't gonna use this shit to arrest me?"

"All we want is to find out who killed Chloe," Mike assured him. "We're not looking at anything else."

Eddie looked from Mike to Mal, and took a big swig of Dew. "I dunno. These are some bad people. I say shit, they might come after me."

Mike said, "Tell us who, Eddie. We can protect you."

He sighed, polished off the rest of his drink, then put the empty can on the table and crushed it. "Fine. I'm into this dude for 20 large for some coke he fronted me. But I got robbed before I could move it. Fuckers hit me on the way from the pickup. Had to be a set-up, ya' know? And I went to him, told him what happened, and he said I needed to get the money, or else."

"Or else what?" Mal asked.

"I didn't ask for specifics, but judging from his rep, I'm guessing I'd be chopped up and never found."

Mike asked, "So what happened next?"

"I went to Kelly and asked her for money. She offered what she had, but that wasn't enough. I told her to ask her dad. But she said no. She doesn't want anything to do with him."

"Why is that?"

Eddie looked at Mal and then shook his head. "That's somethin' you need to ask her. Anyways, I told her I'd ask her dad. And she got pissed, said if I did, she'd never talk to me again."

"So, *did* you ask him?" Mike asked.

"Naw, man. I skipped town, figured I'd lay low 'til I

could figure a way to scratch up some cash. Went down to South Florida, met up with some old friends, and, don't ask me how, but we came up with the money. I came back and paid the man. Then I heard you all was lookin' to talk to me."

Mike asked, "Can anyone corroborate where you were?"

"I dunno, man. These ain't exactly the kinda stand up people who is vouching n' shit."

"Did you have your phone with you when you went to South Florida?" Mal asked.

"Yeah, why?"

"No reason," Mal said, wondering if Eddie was actually unaware that cell towers were always checking your location. She made a mental note to check his phone records if Mike or Aanya hadn't already done so.

"So, what happened when you paid this man his twenty grand?" Mike asked.

"Nothin', I asked if we was good, he said we was, and that was that."

"Do you think he could have hurt Chloe, to send a message to pay up?"

Eddie shook his head. "Man, I dunno. If you is asking if I thought that before I left, then no. No, I didn't even think 'bout that shit. I was just concerned with gettin' the money. But if you're asking if I think he's capable of shit like that, then yeah. I do."

Mike opened the folder, revealing a neat stack of eight and a half by eleven printer paper. He slid it to Eddie. Then he clicked his pen and handed that to Eddie as well.

"I need a name."

"If I give you his name, you need to leave me out of it. You understand? He thinks I sent you all, he will kill me."

Mal met his eyes. "And if you don't give us his name,

you are our number one suspect in the murder of Chloe Conlan. And I don't know, but I'd say snitching against a drug dealer probably pales to the reputation you'd have in prison as a child rapist and killer."

The rapist part might not be true, but the threat was good enough.

Eddie took the pen and wrote the name of a drug dealer in Jacksonville that went by the name Raul Gonzalez.

Mal was making plans to call her Jacksonville narcotics contacts when her phone buzzed with a text from Dorothea Burridge: *LOOK WHAT THEY DID!!*

Chapter 34 - Mallory Black

MAL READ DOROTHEA'S TEXT. After *LOOK WHAT THEY DID*, there came a photo Dorothea's house, where someone had spray painted giant red letters reading *PEDO* on the side.

Mal stared at the photo, her mind racing over the events that had led to this. All signs pointed to the "article" on *The Confidential*. Cameron Ford's little story had mobilized a witch hunt targeting a handicapped man.

Mike advised Eddie to stay away from Kelly for the time being, and that he'd better answer his phone when they called, or they'd lock his ass up, and throw him in a cell with Raul Gonzalez's men.

After Eddie left, Mal showed Mike the photo and said, "We need to get over there."

Mike looked from his phone to Mal, his face solemn.

"*The Confidential* has another story. An interview with sources saying they saw Terrance and Chloe together in the woods the afternoon she was found, and that these sources told the sheriff's office. They were ignored, and Conlan called this a political witch hunt."

"Bullshit. We didn't get anyone saying he was with her that day, did we?"

"No," Mike confirmed. "Art is the only person that saw them, and he said it was in the morning. He also said that he didn't think Terrance did it."

Mike clicked on a link. "Oh, no. I didn't see this story. It ran just before the other one."

"What?"

He read the headline, "Parents Want to Know: How Many Kids Has Terrance Touched?"

"What?" Mal asked. "He's never been accused of touching anyone! What the hell?"

Mike read through the article, an opinion piece written by a "concerned parent" asking why the sheriff's office was protecting Terrance, why he'd not been put in jail when he flashed children at the park, and how many kids he's touched who have been too afraid to come forward. His piece ended with a plea for any parent whose child has been touched by Terrance Burridge, or who thought they might have, to contact The Confidential.

"My God," Mal said. "Now they're fabricating crimes that never happened. You just know some people are going to come forward for attention."

"Do you think it's possible that he has touched someone?"

"I don't know, but we sure as hell don't have any evidence that he has. And we can't prosecute him for something he *may have* done. You went in his room; you saw his collection of photos. You said there wasn't a lurid one in there, right? He's like a big innocent kid that they're turning into a beast."

Mal called Wilson and asked him to send a deputy to the house for a statement, and to ensure the harassment didn't escalate.

Rain fell lightly as Mike and Mal pulled onto Dorothea Burridge's street at 1:19 PM, and saw an army of news vehicles establishing camp up and down the street.

"Fuck me," Mal said as they passed a blue van with an *Exposed With Molly Grant* logo emblazoned on its side. The show's name was lettered next to a stern, bespectacled Molly Grant, in a suit with her arms crossed over her chest to prove she meant business and to rain justice on the bad guys.

"Fucking parasite," Mal hissed.

Every neighbor on the street, and seemingly from adjacent ones, was lined outside the home's perimeter which a CCSO deputy had erected.

"What the hell?" Mike said, blurting the siren and flashing their dash lights to cut through the crowd.

He pulled up to the Burridge house, and the deputy, one of two on scene decked out in rain slickers, pulled a traffic barricade erected in front of the driveway aside so Mike could drive in.

Mal stepped out of the car and saw the giant red *PEDO* spray painted on the garage. Her eyes then traveled to the broken front window, then to the growing mob on the street beyond the caution tape.

"Arrest him!" shouted a bearded man in all black.

"Pervert!" a woman yelled.

A few people held signs which read: *CASTRATE ALL PEDOS! and LOCK UP ALL PREDATORS! KEEP OUR KIDS SAFE!!*

Mal stared at the crowd, not quite believing how quickly the story had moved from nothing to lynch mob. Which of these neighbors had painted the message or thrown something through the window? Whoever it was,

Mal bet they were mighty proud of themselves, tormenting a disabled man and his mother without any proof that Terrance had done anything to anyone.

Several reporters rushed toward Mal, though staying their distance behind the tape, shouting questions:

Are you here to arrest Terrance Burridge?

Why is he not in custody?

Why did you ignore people who told you that Terrance was with Chloe before she died?

Is Terrance Burridge a suspect in the death of Chloe Conlan?

Mal ignored every question and turned to follow Mike to the front door. The dog kept barking from inside, likely freaking out at the crowd of strangers he perceived as a threat to his masters.

Mal knocked, waited for Dorothea to put the dog away, then greet them at the door, a cigarette dangling out of her mouth. She pointed to the garage. "You see that shit?"

"Yes, do you know who did it?"

"You'd see their balls hanging on my mailbox if I did," she yelled, loud enough for the closest of the horde to hear her. "Damned cowards! I've known these people goin' on twenty-five years, had these people over to my house, broke bread with them. Terrance has been nothing but nice to any of them, and this is how they treat me, treat *us*, now?"

A man shouted, "Pedo!!"

A bottle crashed behind Mal.

The dog kept barking, now slightly muffled.

"Let's get inside, Ms. Burridge," Mike said, ushering them away from the crowd.

As they went inside, Mal turned and glared at the crowd, wanting to snarl at the cameras recording every moment to create a narrative so far from the truth it may as well have been propaganda.

She wondered where Molly Grant and Cameron Ford

were; surely out there, hiding in the crowd, admiring the flames of a riot they were stoking.

She went inside, shut the door, and felt an immediate claustrophobia, hearing the people chanting outside, walls reeking of cigarettes closing in on them, while the dog continued to incessantly bark.

Mal was trapped in a madhouse, anxiety tightening like a band across her chest.

She needed to get the hell out of the house, and back in her car.

"Where's Terrance?" Mike asked.

"In my room, in the back, crying. Ever since the first brick came through the window. Fuckers!"

Dorothea inhaled her cigarette while lighting another, shaking her head, inches from tears. "What the hell am I supposed to do now?" Seeing a tough woman like this so near tears tugged at Mal's heart, and paused her swelling anxiety.

Mal had never had a panic attack until after her daughter vanished. She'd had two since then, one on the job that nearly got her and other deputies killed. But seeing Dorothea moved to tears forced Mal to set her feelings aside so she could be present for this woman and her son. Neither of them deserved any of this.

Mal collected her thoughts, then said, "I think we should get you and your son out of here, get you somewhere safe until this blows over."

"Can't you go outside and just tell them that he isn't a suspect?"

Mike shook his head. "I wish we could, but hell, they wouldn't even believe us. *The Confidential* is spinning some conspiracy theory about us going after the Conlan family, and these people are buying it."

"So, my son is caught in a political pissing match?"

"There's no match, ma'am. This is one side launching whatever they can to try and destroy the investigation, to undermine the sheriff's office."

"Fuckers ought to burn, every one of them," she said, peering at the mob through the drawn curtains.

Dorothea turned to meet Mal's eyes. "Did the mom do it? Is that why they're trying to put this on my Terrance?"

"We're still investigating."

"Oh, come on, what do you *think?* Did she do it?"

"We don't speculate, ma'am. We work with the facts we have."

Mike got on the phone to Wilson, told him what was happening, and asked him to send a van to the Burridge place so that they could put Terrance and his mother in protective custody.

As they waited, Dorothea sat in the back of the house, flipping from one news channel to another eventually settling on Molly Grant's show.

Molly was, of course, safely tucked away at studio headquarters, far from her damage, as a reporter stood outside the Burridge home interviewing neighbors.

One woman, identified on screen as Carol McCleary, told a reporter, "I never did trust that Terrance. He was always touching himself as he walked down the street."

"It wasn't sexual, you bitch," Dorothea said, turning to Mal, "you know how kids sometimes walk around cluelessly touching their privates? That's what he sometimes does, but damn, he's not walking around stroking it!"

Another neighbor, an unidentified young woman holding a toddler, was asked if she felt safe in the same neighborhood as a known sexual offender. She shook her head, "Lord no. They ought to lock that man up before he hurts someone else."

"You believe this bitch? Her boyfriend is a goddamned

drug dealer, and she's saying Terrance doesn't make her feel safe?" Dorothea laughed. "Fucking hypocrites, all of them!"

The dog kept barking.

Mal was wondering when the hell the van would show up when Mike's phone rang and a deputy told him it was there.

Dorothea coaxed Terrance out of her bedroom, saying they were going to get away from all the bad people.

He came out, a large quilt clutched tightly around him, "Hello," he said, recognizing Mike and Mal.

"Hi," Mal said. "We're going to get you out of here, and find a nice hotel for you all to stay at. Would you like that?"

"Yes," he said, eyes wet with tears.

"Is my momma coming?"

"Yes, honey, I'm coming too."

"Can Petey come?"

"Petey?" Mal asked.

"The dog," Dorothea said.

"No, we'll come back for him tomorrow after everything settles down. Your mother gave him plenty of food and water, so he'll be fine in the bathroom."

"He doesn't like it in the bathroom. He gets scared." Terrance started to cry.

"Tell you what, Terrance, when you all leave the house, I'll open the door and let him out into the living room, okay?"

He nodded at his mother. "Okay."

"Here," Dorothea grabbed a large duffle she'd prepared with their supplies. "Come on, honey."

Mal and Mike traded a glance, steeling themselves for the shouts that would accompany the open door. The crowd would probably throw debris at the van as they pulled away.

She was pleased to see that when she opened the door, three more deputies were staged outside, and another patrol car was at the end of the driveway, just outside the perimeter, lights flashing.

Mike led the way. Mal looked back at Terrance and said, "Come on, just a short walk."

He looked up, his eyes widening at the sheer number of people outside, his face practically ghost white in the flashing lights.

"I'm scared," he said, looking back for his mother, still inside the house and letting Petey out of the bathroom.

"Come on," Mal said, holding out a hand for Terrance to hold.

He didn't take it, keeping his hands inside the blanket, like a turtle in his shell.

"Pervert!" a man yelled, followed by more shouts from the mob.

Pedo.

Monster.

Retard.

Terrance turned around, crying, "I want to go back."

Shit!

Mal's heart raced as she went to get him.

The chants gathered steam.

Mal could practically feel the crowd pushing at the police tape and the barricades, threatening to spill over.

If they did, a few deputies wouldn't be able to hold them back.

Her chest constricted as she imagined everything spinning out of control, the crowd becoming a lynch mob, grabbing Terrance and dragging him away, throwing a rope around the tree and hanging the man, regardless of actual guilt.

Terrance made a beeline for his front door, and Mal thought she might lose him for good. Just then, Dorothea came out, pushing the dog back as she did, and locked the door.

She looked to Terrance, somehow ignoring the crowd. "What is it, honey?"

"I want to go back in."

"No, we're going to a nice hotel. Where it'll be nice and quiet. There'll be a nice restaurant, and I think it even has a pool, is that right, Ms. Black?"

Mal wasn't sure if the hotel had a pool, but at the moment, with her heart pounding and the crowd writhing just beyond the perimeter, she'd tell Terrance it had unicorn rides if it would get him in the fucking van.

"Yes, a big pool, and all the ice cream you can eat," Mal promised.

"Okay," he smiled.

Terrance slowly shuffled around, his feet getting tangled in the blanket before Dorothea helped him straighten the tangled fabric.

Mike waited in front of the open van door, smiling at Terrance, and holding out a hand.

Suddenly, something, a blur of movement, came flying toward them, striking Dorothea right in the face.

She fell in an instant. Time crawled as several things happened at once.

Mal spun to see who had thrown the bottle, but everyone was glaring, arms raised, many of them holding all matter of objects.

Two deputies shouted at the people to step back. One grabbed his baton.

Mike moved to get in front of Terrance.

And Terrance screamed as he dropped next to his mother. "Mommy!"

Mike and Mal got in front of Terrance like Secret Service protecting the President, arms up, ready to intercept anything else that might come flying.

Another object came, a bottle crashing just next to Dorothea.

"Hey!" Mal yelled at the person who threw it, a young man who couldn't have been more than sixteen.

He took off.

More objects came.

A few men broke past the police tape, charging one of the deputies.

Mal couldn't believe this was happening.

Mike moved to intercept the men before they could hurt the deputy, or Terrance and his mother.

And then, gunshots.

At first, Mal thought they were coming from the crowd.

Her hand went for her weapon, her head pivoting as if on a swivel, still everything in painfully slow motion, looking for the source.

Then she realized, the shots were coming from behind her.

She turned back to see Terrance crying out, a pistol in his hand, firing blindly into the crowd.

Where the hell did he get a gun?

Thwap-Thwap-Thwap-Thwap.

Shots rang like thunder as Terrance fired, screaming, "Stop, stop, stop!!"

Mal was frozen, heart in her throat as she watched him firing into the mob.

Finally, after what felt like forever, she managed to turn her gun on him.

He looked at her, crying, confused, and scared, holding

the gun pointed down at the ground, but he could just as easily raise it and fire again.

Screams behind her as the crowd dispersed.

More screams, of pain, the people Terrance had hit.

"Put the gun down, Terrance," Mal pled.

He cried, violently shaking his head, "No, no, no, no, no!"

Mal didn't think he was saying *no* to putting the gun down, but rather at what was happening.

Dorothea was coming to but she was behind Terrance and he couldn't see her.

"Please," Mal begged, hoping like hell that she wouldn't have to shoot him. "*Please*, put the gun down."

He looked back toward Mal, tears and snot running down his face.

Mal wondered where Mike was. Had he been among those hit? But she couldn't turn around; she had to keep her eye, and gun, on Terrance.

And time wasn't just crawling for Mal, but now also for Terrance, as she saw him look past her, realization creeping into his eyes. He had hurt people, badly.

He cried, "uh-oh, uh-oh, uh-oh," shaking his head slowly.

And then, time snapped like a rubber band, slowing movements into blurs, as Terrance raised the pistol.

Mal's finger froze on the trigger, unable to fire as Terrance brought the gun to his face and pulled the trigger.

Mal screamed as she rushed toward his collapsing body.

Chapter 35 - Mallory Black

As THE NIGHT rolled in outside, Mal sat at her cubicle next to Mike filling out paperwork for what was turning into one of the biggest clusterfucks she'd ever had the distinction of being an intimate part of.

Mike and Mal may as well have been alone. Everybody still at work in the detective division was giving them a wide berth, as if the storm clouds that hung over them might spread.

"You sure you want to leave that on?" Mike pointed to the iPad next to Mal's computer, tuned into a "special edition" of Molly Grant's show, which threatened to run all damned night what with all the "breaking exclusives from the Chloe Conlan case!"

"Hiding from the news won't make it go away," Mal said.

The day had gone to hell, now all that was left was to wait to see how bad the fallout would be.

Terrance Burridge was dead, his mother at the hospital being treated for shock and a head wound from the bottle.

Terrance managed to shoot two people; one of them, a

twenty-nine-year-old man, died at the scene. The other, a young woman who had brought her four-year-old daughter to the mob, was in critical condition. She was okay, but traumatized.

The news media was having a field day showing footage from every angle on repeat, from the moment Mal and Mike arrived to someone throwing the bottle at Dorothea, to Mal standing frozen for what felt like forever as Terrance shot into the crowd and she did nothing.

Grant was asking her audience, "Is this the sort of professionalism that the Creek County Sheriff's Office embodies?"

Molly dove into Mal's past, from the murder of her daughter to the incident that initially cost her her job — a panic attack during a hostage crisis that ended in tragedy.

Calls for her job were already starting. Soon those calls would spread to Mike, then up to the sheriff herself.

Local news media, including blogger Cameron Ford, demanded that Mal and Mike at least be removed from the Chloe Conlan case, with some even suggesting that the Feds ought to handle it.

Gloria was going to have a press conference at eight tonight, a presser that Mal and Mike had been told to steer clear of.

Captain Wilson, to his credit, didn't raise holy hell when Mal and Mike returned to the office. He merely told them to "write it up as it happened and we'll see what's what."

Mike finished his report and stood. "You want to take a break?"

"No," Mal said. "I just wanna finish this."

"Come on, take a break, you've been at that for hours."

"I don't need a break. Please, just let me finish."

Mike sighed then left. Mal continued typing her report.

Once finished, she sent a copy to Wilson for review before printing a second copy for the sheriff.

Mal's phone rang. Tim Brentwood who worked narcotics in Jacksonville. "Hello?"

"Hey, Mal, calling back on that thing you wanted me to look into with Raul Gonzalez."

"Yes?"

"He died earlier today, in a drive-by shooting."

"Of course," Mal said, deeply sighing, wondering if Eddie Dixon was somehow behind it, retaliation if he thought Raul had killed Chloe.

"Did you catch the killer?"

"Yeah, a couple of kids from a rival gang."

"No ties to an Eddie Dixon?"

Brentwood laughed. "Who?"

"Never mind," Mal said, figuring if Eddie Dixon wasn't on Brentwood's radar, he probably wasn't involved. Tim knew everyone who was anyone worth knowing in the northeast.

"Thank you," Mal said.

"Hey, you alright? I saw the shit show on TV."

"Yeah, just a fucked day gone sideways."

"Hang in there, okay?"

"Thanks," she said.

"If you need something to take your mind off it all, lemme know. I've got tomorrow off."

Mal smiled. She'd had a brief fling with Brentwood last year when he'd been in town following up on a case. They ran into each other at Paddy's Bar, and shit happened. Tim was young, incredibly good-looking, and just the right amount of arrogant to intrigue her. He was also fantastic in the sack.

She strongly considered the invitation. Every bit of her wanted to walk into Sheriff Bell's office, hand over her badge and leave again. This time before she could be let go.

The way Mal saw it, it could only end one way. Pressure from the media, and the way she froze on the spot, there was no way to come back from that.

Mal was a liability. She may as well leave and spare her bosses and partner the trouble that was sure to be coming. It would only take one person to discover her past drug use to trigger a drug test. She'd be out the door, jeopardizing the Conlan case and the sheriff's career.

"You know what? I *could* use a break. Know any good bars up there?"

"You familiar with StoneHouse Ale?"

"No, but send me the deets, and I'll meet you. What time you get off?"

He avoided the obvious innuendo, thankfully, and told Mal that he was already off duty.

"I'll see you in thirty minutes," Mal said, then headed out the rear exit to avoid running into Mike or anyone else.

The parking lot was divided into two sections, employee and general parking. As Mal got into her car, she spotted that general was crawling with reporters, and likely politicians. A veritable Who's Who of Creek County, all showing up for a front row seat to the Shit Show of the Century.

Mal headed out the rear exit, thankful for both it and the tinted windows as she quickly put the Creek County Sheriff's Office into her rearview.

Chapter 36 - Mallory Black

MAL CLOSED her eyes atop Tim, throwing her head back, riding him to an earth-shattering climax that, along with two pills and who knows how many shots of Jack, finally delivered pleasure to an otherwise hellish day.

She fell back on the bed, riding the euphoria as he lay beside her, caressing Mal's breasts in lazy half circles around her nipples.

"That was good. Thank you."

"Thank *you*," he said.

Mal lay in his cozy apartment wondering why she'd broken things off with him so quickly before.

Oh, well, it didn't matter.

For now, things were good.

And she'd just learn to enjoy the now.

He leaned over and kissed Mal on the mouth before standing. "You want to shower?"

Oh, yeah. He's a clean freak who has to shower a minute after sex.

"No, I'm good," she said, stretching in the silk sheets and down comforter, wishing she could stay in bed forever.

Outside of his second story bedroom window, rain pelted the glass and lightning streaked across the sky.

It was all *very* relaxing.

~

MAL WOKE to her phone buzzing and the bright sun coming through Tim's windows.

He wasn't in bed with her.

She picked up the phone and saw that it was Mike texting.

WHERE ARE YOU?

She texted back.

Sick. Not coming in today.

Then she silenced her phone and rolled over, trying to get back to sleep.

But lying in a practical stranger's bed when he wasn't there, made her uncomfortable.

She rolled out of bed, got dressed, and found Tim in the kitchen drinking a glass of orange juice and reading on his tablet.

"Hey," he said, "want anything to eat or drink?"

Her head was pounding, and she seriously considered asking for alcohol, but that probably wasn't a good idea. She needed to get back to her hotel room. That's where the pills were, and she was out.

"You got coffee?"

"Nope. Water, OJ, and milk. And wine."

"Water's fine. And a few Tylenol if you've got 'em."

"Ah," he smiled. "I thought you might regret that seventeenth shot of Jack."

"I did not drink seventeen shots," she said with a friendly laugh.

"No? I lost count after ten. Wow, you can hold your liquor."

"Thanks?" she said, unsure if that was a compliment or accusation.

"So," he said, handing her a cold glass of ice water and a bottle of Tylenol. "This is the first time one of us wasn't rushing out the door in the morning to get back to work or life or whatever."

"Yeah, way not to be awkward about it," she said swallowing three pills and downing them with water.

He laughed. "So, you want to do something?"

"I would, but I've gotta head back. I'm late for work."

"Oh, you're actually going in today? Shit, I'm sorry. I would've woken you up, but last night you said, and I believe your exact words were, 'fuck that place, I'm done.'"

Her face went red, not just embarrassed by that outburst, but whatever else she might've told him. She tried to remember, but couldn't.

Shit.

Mal hated not being able to remember the night before, or worse, what she might've said.

Well, at least he's not with Creek County. That would be way more awkward.

"So? You're not quitting the force and going to live on a private island?"

"Shit, I said that?"

"Yeah," he laughed.

"Wow, how obnoxious was I?"

"Well, you did go on a bit about Molly Grant, and some 'prick' named, um, Campton *Ford?*"

"Cameron," she corrected, laughing, but also worrying if she'd said anything she shouldn't have, stuff that could complicate her case or her life in general, especially if shit went south like she expected it to.

"I'm sorry, I don't usually drink that much."

"It's okay." Tim came over and kissed her.

She turned away. "Morning breath."

He kissed her forehead instead, then hugged her.

She looked around his apartment, not remembering many details from the other time she'd been there. It was small, but nice, with a modern style. He had a few choice paintings on the wall that seemed expensive, not that she'd know one artist from another, let alone their value.

He had a large TV, like most single guys, with cable and game consoles connected. But he also had a bookcase — rarity among the men Mal slept with.

She went over to the shelf and perused the titles, most of it non-fiction, an interesting mix of history, survival stuff, marketing, and science, with a specific interest in bioengineering and Artificial Intelligence.

Also, some large art books.

"Pretty eclectic taste you've got," she said.

"Thanks. I don't get as much time to read as I'd like, but now and then I'll go through two or three books in a week. What about you? What do you like to read?"

"Hmm," Mal said, feeling on the spot. "It's been a long time since I read for pleasure. I mostly read the news, and stuff related to the job, maybe a bit of psychology here and there. I read a lot more when my daughter was alive."

It felt odd bringing up Ashley with this man she barely knew, a guy who probably knew her from the news before they'd even met, as The Mother Of…

"What did you read then?"

"We read through the Harry Potter series. Well, the first three, anyway. The others, I wanted to wait until she was older. Now I guess she'll never read them."

Mal hadn't meant to sound so maudlin. "I should go."

She went back to his room, got her stuff, and headed for the front door, keys in hand.

He stopped her, extending their awkwardness. Was he going to try and cheer her up? She didn't need that. Was he going to kiss her goodbye? They weren't quite there yet.

"Hey," he said, putting his hands on her shoulders. "I know you're going through a rough time right, so I'm not going to ask when I'll see you again or anything. But I do want you to know that I'm here if you need anything. Even if it's just a friend or someone to talk to."

She smiled, trying not to get emotional. "Thank you. I will."

They stood frozen in the awkward moment. Did she kiss him goodbye or shake his hand? Why was he still standing there?

He laughed.

"What?"

"Sorry," he said, "but you left your car at the restaurant. So, unless you're up for a five-mile walk, you might want me to give you a ride."

And great, the awkwardness continues.

She laughed, at both herself and the situation as he went to grab his keys, wallet, and holstered gun. "Thank you."

Chapter 37 - Jasper Parish

ON TUESDAY, Jasper drove Ophelia to school and Alicia to work. With no showings that day, she was planning to put in a few hours at the office. He'd pick her up around lunchtime.

After dropping off Ophelia, Jasper updated Alicia on what had happened with the biker from Clay's crew. He'd wanted to tell her last night but didn't want to spoil the celebratory mood after Karen told her about Jasper's gift. The girls had all been so happy, and spent much of the evening baking cookies and planning Karen's new life.

Jasper had never seen five thousand dollars matter so much and was happy to use his cash to create such a possibility for change.

Later, Alicia showed her appreciation in the bedroom, so Jasper didn't want to spoil the mood *then*, either.

"Do you think he knows where we live?" Alicia asked.

"I have to assume he does."

"We need to get her to safety."

"Yeah, I didn't like how far off she seemed to be planning this last night. Way she's talking, she's looking to move next month. I think she needs to go now, as in tonight."

Alicia nodded. "I'll talk to her after you pick me up."

"That's a good idea. And I'll help in any way I can."

"Man, it's going to suck when you have to go back home."

Jasper said nothing. Saying what he was thinking would only set himself up for misery. Maybe he'd stay. Maybe he didn't have to go back home.

But it was too soon to do that.

First, he needed to eliminate this problem. Then, and only then, could Jasper hope to have a normal life.

He pulled up to her office, which was twenty-five minutes from her house, and kissed her goodbye.

"See ya at one," she said.

"See you."

Carissa appeared in the passenger seat. Startled, he slammed on the brakes just feet from the curb.

"Good morning, Jasper."

"Don't do that to me! Can't you wait until I'm sitting somewhere?"

"You *are* sitting," she teased.

"I meant not sitting in a moving vehicle!"

"You didn't take your pill today, did you?"

Jasper sighed, then pulled over. He reached into the back seat for his satchel, pulled it up front, unzipped the bag and took out the bottle. Then he popped off the top and swallowed his pill. "Thanks for reminding me."

She shook her head, frowning. "Do you hate seeing me that much?"

"You know that's not it. I love seeing you. But I can't see you and have a normal life. It's too hard."

She looked at him, eyes welling up. "It's okay. I under-stand. I want you to be happy."

Carissa had never been emotionally manipulative. She said what she was thinking, and that was that. You always knew where you stood with her. But Jasper wasn't sure if this version meant what she was saying, or if she were trying to take him on a guilt trip.

Of course, if that were true, it only meant that he'd bought the ticket himself. And that made a whole hell of a lot more sense than Carissa doing it.

"By the way …"

He looked at her. "Yes?"

And then she was gone.

"Damn it!"

She had to have done that on purpose. The pills didn't kick in *that* fast.

Jasper put the car back into drive and merged onto the road, heading back to Alicia's.

Karen's car was gone when he got there.

Something was wrong. He got out of the car, headed to the front door, telling himself that she went to the store or something. Nothing was wrong.

He went inside and looked for a note.

Nothing.

Jasper paced the living room, the same room they'd all had such a great time in just twelve hours earlier.

He went to Karen's room, opened the door, and searched for her cash.

He found it in the top drawer of the dresser, grabbed then opened it, and began counting.

A thousand dollars short.

Fuck!

He returned the money, shut the drawer, and went downstairs cursing, trying to still convince himself that nothing was wrong.

She went to the store, got some stuff she needed.

But then he heard Lenny's voice. *Some people can't help but be drawn to the flame.* He thought he was doing the right thing, giving her money to reboot her life. He'd not considered the flip side, which was that he was handing cash to someone with questionable judgment. Someone who may or may not be a junkie.

He went upstairs again, searched through her dresser, then other belongings. He found a heroin kit. No heroin, but the needle, spoon, a tourniquet, and matches were all there.

"Damn it!"

He went back downstairs, cursing himself for not having been better prepared. If he'd been planning ahead, he could have put a tracker on her car. He could've found Karen, and likely where her scumbag ex-boyfriend was staying. He could have gone back at night to eliminate the problem the only permanent way he knew how.

But Jasper hadn't been prepared. He hadn't even been the one to plan the trip to Alicia's. It was some alter ego whose existence he didn't even know about until a few days ago.

He pounded the kitchen counter, wanting to hit more.

"Fucking idiot," he said to himself over and again.

Chapter 38 - Mallory Black

TIM DROPPED Mal off at the restaurant. She got in her car, plugged her phone into the console to charge it, and checked her voicemails. She had three total, two from Mike and another from Gloria.

She drove back to Creek County, listening to the messages in order.

Mike asking where she was and if she was okay.

Mike again, asking her to call him, *please*.

And then Gloria.

"Hey, Mal. I don't know what's going on, but we need you to call into the office. Call me back on my personal phone if you want."

She gave Mal her number, which Mal committed to memory.

She called Mike first.

"So you are alive?" he said quietly.

"Yeah, I needed a mental health day. What's going on? Am I suspended yet?"

"No, and I don't think you're going to be."

"What?"

"You didn't watch the press conference last night?"

"No, I couldn't even deal with it."

"Gloria stood up for you."

"She did?" Mal was surprised. Gloria had not come to her defense when the shit hit the fan before, back when there wasn't even an election looming.

"She said there's no finer deputy than you, and told reporters to go ahead and put themselves in the situation and see how quickly *they* respond."

Mal laughed. "Oh, that's going to go over well."

"That wasn't it."

"No?"

"She scolded the reporters for creating a dangerous atmosphere that led to last night's events. She said, 'I won't name names, but you know who you are, and you've got the blood of two lives on your hands.'"

"Holy shit. Any response from the media yet? Or Conlan?"

"Media is divided, half loving her brashness for calling bullshit, the others saying she's just protecting her own, and trying to act like the sheriff's office didn't botch this whole thing."

"I'm sure Conlan and Cameron are working on a response right now."

"Maybe. For now, we've got a job to do. Starting with an interview."

"With who?" Mal asked.

"Two kids, Hunter and Landon, the bullies who chased that kid Hector into the woods when they all stumbled on Chloe. They were at Terrance's last night, among those throwing bottles. Deputy Simmons talked to the kids, asking why they were there. They said that Terrance was a pedo and that they'd even seen him touching kids in the woods. Simmons had their parents pick them up. They're coming in to give a statement."

"You think they were lying? Trying to get out of trouble?"

"I don't know. Guess we'll find out. They'll be here at noon."

"Let me shower, and I'll be there."

She hung up with Mike and called Gloria back.

"Mal?"

"You called?"

"You coming in today?"

"Yes," Mal said.

"Good. I was afraid I might've lost you last night."

"No. And … thank you. I heard what you did, defending me."

"Don't mention it. I should've done that before."

"It's okay. You did it now."

"Are you okay to work? You need time?"

"I'm good," Mal said. "I just froze. Even though he'd fired into the crowd, I didn't think he'd shoot anyone else. I couldn't pull the trigger. And then it all happened so quick, and I … I blanked. I'm sorry."

"Yes, I saw in the report. I also saw the video from three of the cameramen who didn't flee the minute Terrance took aim. And, you weren't frozen that long. I don't think there's anything you could've done differently, except maybe get yourself killed. Don't worry, Detective, I've got your back on this. So does Wilson."

"Thank you," Mal said, feeling relieved, and that perhaps she could still be of use in solving this crime.

Chapter 39 - Mallory Black

MAL MET UP WITH MIKE, Gloria, and Wilson in the main observation room which looked in on Interview Rooms One and Two, where Hunter and Landon sat, isolated from their parents. They went over the game plan, determined to see if there was any validity to last night's claims.

First, they went over the Deputy Simmons' report, stating that the boys had thrown bottles and fireworks at the house. Additionally, they were both streaming the whole thing on LiveLyfe, laughing and yelling insults such as "retard," "pedo," and "faggot," in addition to chanting "die, pedo!" All of this was prior to Terrance opening fire on the crowd, and some before Mal and Mike's arrival.

"Why didn't Simmons charge them with anything?" Mal asked.

"He made a judgment call," Wilson said. "Figured with the information they had maybe it was better to get them here without incident. If he arrested them, maybe we'd get more of a shit storm than we already have."

"I don't believe them." She hadn't even spoken to

them, but as she looked between the boys, Mal was sure they were full of shit.

Hunter Naismeth was tall and good-looking, with tanned skin and shaggy blond hair. He was the younger of the two at twelve, but remarkably calm as he sat patiently waiting for the detectives to enter.

Landon Bowman was older at thirteen, but the exact opposite in disposition. Fidgeting, biting his nails, and unable to sit still, the freckle-faced redhead couldn't hide his discomfort.

"Let's start with Red," Mal said as she led Mike to Interview Room One.

They entered together, with Mike taking the seat opposite Landon and Mal hanging back, watching.

"So, I understand you were at Terrance's yesterday."

"Yes, sir," he said, barely able to maintain eye contact for more than a few seconds.

"Why'd you go there?"

"Hunter saw the people on the news at Terrance's, and said we ought to go there and help expose the pedo creep."

"Expose him for what, exactly?"

"He was abusing kids in the woods. We saw him doing it."

"Okay," Mike said. "Tell me exactly what happened, and if you remember dates or kids' names, I'll need those too."

"I don't remember dates and stuff. But it was during the summer. Me and Hunter would be hanging out at the skate park near the playground. And we'd see that retard around the fence because he's not allowed in the park, ya' know. Anyway, he'd hang around, moping, and then eventually some kid or another would come over to him, and then they'd both disappear into the woods for a while."

"Okay," Mike said. "So, what happened after that?"

"Well, it happened a few times, a few different kids, mostly the little ones, like six or seven. And at first, we didn't think much of it. We'd seen him in the woods with that Chloe girl before, and they were just hanging out at the tree house, playing with Hector, John, and Lucas. We thought it was weird that anyone would want to hang out with him, but all three of those kids are weirdoes, anyway. Losers."

"What next?" Mike asked.

"One day Terrance came over to the fence, and a little girl went off with him into the woods, same as usual. A few of us joked about it, like, 'oh, here comes the pedo man,' but I don't think any of us thought he was doing anything to the kids. But it started raining, and Hunter and I decided to head home, but we took the path through the woods, just to see what was going on.

"And when we got to the treehouse, we didn't see anyone. So we called out to see if someone was in there. And then the girl comes running out of the treehouse, buttoning up her shirt and pants before she climbed down the ladder. A dark-haired girl wearing a white shirt with a unicorn on the front, and pink pants."

Mal's stomach sank. She didn't want to think of Terrance as a predator. He'd seemed so sweet. In the moments she had with him Mal honestly thought he was a child in a man's body who had been railroaded by overzealous or frightened parents into being labeled a sex offender. A sex offender who was so traumatized by the lynch mob that he shot into a crowd out of fear before ending his own life. It was a terrible tragedy. But if Landon's story was true, it meant that Mal's instincts were off. And it made it impossible to feel sympathy for Terrance even one second longer.

"What then?" Mike asked.

"We asked the girl what happened, but she just ran away. Then we look up at the tree house, and Terrance is up there, smiling his big stupid smile. He asked us if we wanted to play. We took off."

"Do you know the girl's name?" Mike asked.

"No. But I think Landon might."

"You said he abused multiple kids. Did you see him with any others? Did any of them tell you what happened in the tree house?"

"Not me personally, but Landon said he'd talked to a few of the kids, and they told him some crazy shit, ... er, sorry, I meant *stuff*."

"And did you tell anyone what happened?"

"Um. No," Landon said, looking down at the table.

"Why not? If you thought he was touching kids inappropriately why not go to the police or at least tell your parents?"

"I dunno. Hunter said we there was no point because the cops already let him go once, so obviously nobody cares, and nobody would believe us."

Mal wondered if Mike was going to press on that answer. It seemed like a flimsy excuse not to report what they believed to be multiple rapes. But Mike didn't pursue it, instead opting to take a break.

"Okay, we're gonna take a break and get you something to drink. Coke? Water? Something else?"

"Coke is fine," Landon said, "thank you."

"Okay, here's some paper and a pen. Just write down everything you told us so far, and if you can remember anything else you might have forgotten, add that too, okay?"

"Yes, sir."

They left and returned to the observation room.

"You think he's telling the truth?" Gloria asked.

Mike sighed, "I don't know. Seems like if they thought several kids were being molested, they might have done *something* about it."

Wilson shook his head. "I'm not buying it. Go talk to his buddy."

Mal looked in at Hunter, thumbing at his phone's screen, feet propped on the table like he was waiting for dinner.

As Mal and Mike left the room, Wilson barked, "And tell that little fucker to get his feet off the goddamned table."

Chapter 40 - Mallory Black

MAL AND MIKE entered the room. Hunter didn't divert his attention from the phone or his game. He kept his feet on the table and continued to lean back in his chair.

Mal, annoyed, cleared her throat.

"One second," he said, still playing the game, chair tipped back on two legs, for five full seconds as they stood there.

But Mal wasn't having it.

She reached out quickly, slapping his feet off the table, almost sending his ass and the chair to the floor.

He threw his arms out to regain his balance and dropped his phone.

"What the fuck?" he snapped, straightening himself out and sitting up, both feet on the ground, glaring at Mal like he wanted to hit her.

"This isn't your fucking house, so keep your feet off the table, and when detectives enter the room, you put your toys away."

He reached down, picked up his phone, and examined

it for a cracked screen, sulking as he reclaimed his seat. "You're lucky this didn't break!"

Mike, playing the role of good cop, raised his hands and said, "Hey, hey, calm down Mal. Let me talk to him. You go get yourself a drink or something, okay?"

"Fine," she said, glaring at Hunter. Then she stormed out, slamming the door and returned to the observation room.

Wilson and Gloria offered faux applause.

"Bravo," Wilson said, "that's some ace fucking acting right there. Hope it works better than with that Isaacson creep."

"He's got this." She sat on the bench in front of the one-way-mirror and watched Mike go to work.

The kid was no longer cool. He was riled up, glaring at the door. "What's *her* problem?"

"Sorry, she's still a bit shaken with all the stuff that went down last night. I mean, yeah, we're cops, and we see a lot of bad stuff, but it's never easy when someone shoots into a crowd then takes their own life, you know?"

Hunter nodded. "I guess. But who cares if he took his own life, right? He was a pedo. He deserved to die. I mean, I still don't know why he was walking around after he got busted showing his dick at the park!"

Instead of arguing the facts, Mike played sympathetic. "Yeah, I don't know what's up with the courts these days. We arrest them then they're back on the street in days. Sometimes, you wonder why even bother."

"Right?" Hunter said, engaging with Mike, animated.

"So," Mike said, "you told the officer last night that you had some dirt on the retard? You saw him touch some kids or something?"

"Yeah," Hunter said, continuing to recount the same

story that his buddy had told, almost word-for-word as if they'd rehearsed ahead of time.

Mal looked at Gloria who had taken a seat beside her on the bench, exchanging a glance that clearly said, *you believe this shit?*

Mike continued, playing friendly and understanding the entire time, writing in a pad as Hunter spun his tale.

As Hunter finished, Mike flipped back a page and looked at Hunter, confused. "Wait a second, that time you were walking in the woods, and you saw him and the kid coming from the treehouse, you said it was a boy?"

"No, a girl from the neighborhood."

"And what happened again? I thought I got it down, but I must've missed something."

Hunter repeated the details, the girl buttoning up her shirt and pants as she got out of the treehouse. A dark-haired girl wearing a white shirt with a unicorn on the front, and pink pants.

"Okay," Mike said, writing it down. "What was the girl's name? Did you recognize her?"

"Yeah, I've seen her around, but don't know her name."

"So, um … hold on," Mike said, flipping back a few pages, to notes he'd supposedly taken in his interview with Landon. "What about the blond boy?"

"*Who?*" Hunter asked.

"When I was talking to Landon, he said, um … lemme look here, … that it was a girl *and* a boy in the treehouse with the retard."

Hunter's brow furrowed. "Um, no, it was just the girl."

"Are you sure? I mean, I want to get this right, and Landon says there was a little blond boy, like six or so, with the girl. I mean he remembered the kid pretty well, too, said he was wearing a Spiderman shirt. None of this ringing a bell?"

Hunter stared, not sure what to say.

Mal smiled, loving that look when a liar has to decide which fib to claim, unsure of what his partner might have said.

Mike continued, "Anything?"

"I'm trying to remember …" Hunter looked up at the lights in the room as if they might hold an answer.

Mike leaned forward and lowered his voice.

"Listen, I just want to get this right. But if you two are both remembering the events differently, we're gonna be here a while. I'll need to go back and talk to him, then come back and talk to you, maybe get a couple other officers in here to go over the statements. I hate to keep you here all day, but it's important to get things right, do you understand?"

Hunter took the bait.

"Oh, yeah, there was a boy! Blond kid, yeah. I can't remember if it was a Spiderman shirt, but yeah, I remember him. Sorry."

Mal smiled. "Got you."

"Thanks," Mike said. "So, what then? Did you all do anything? Tell anyone?"

"Naw, man. We didn't. I mean, we *should* have, especially now with all this other stuff, what happened with Chloe and all, but no, we didn't. And, I wish we did, believe me. Maybe we could've saved Chloe."

"What do you mean?" Mike asked, leaning forward.

"Well, I saw Chloe with Terrance, in the tree house."

"When?"

"A few times."

"Did Landon see this?"

"No, just me. I was alone, riding through the woods, and I saw them together."

"Why didn't you tell anyone?"

"Well, I'm not sure if you know, but I've gotten into a lot of trouble at school. Suspended for fighting, other stuff. And I'm not used to adults listening to me or caring what I have to say. Figure it's easier just to keep my head down and stay out of trouble."

"I get it. I mean, adults, especially cops, can be intimidating, I know." Mike jabbed a thumb toward the door where Mal had left. "Trust me, *I know.*"

Hunter laughed.

Good, keep him on your side.

"But this wasn't about you. You saw kids being abused. You saw Terrance with Chloe, that seems like something you would've come forward with, especially after you all found Chloe dead."

"You're right," Hunter said, suddenly quiet and shy. "I wish I had."

Mike asked, "So, what were you doing in the woods that day you found her?"

"We were playing with Hector, and we all came up on Chloe right about the same time."

"Right, playing *with* Hector, and not chasing him to beat him up?"

"Is that what he said?"

"Come on," Mike said, "cut the shit. Just tell me what happened."

"Fine, we were chasing him. But we weren't going to beat him up. I just wanted to scare him."

"Why?"

"I don't like him," Hunter said, matter-of-factly, all the charm gone from his boyish face, leaving a tundra of emotion behind.

"Why not?"

"You wouldn't understand," Hunter said.

"Try me."

"No, you wouldn't understand because you're, what, Mexican?"

"Spanish. My grandfather came here from Spain. But what does that have to do with anything?"

"Listen, it's nothing personal, but kids like Hector, and his family, coming here, taking American jobs. It just ain't right. People ought to stay in their own country is all I'm saying."

Mike stared at the kid for a long moment, then, "So, you beat him up? What purpose does that serve?"

"I dunno. So he knows his place?"

Mike stood, looked in the one-way-mirror and widened his eyes, shook his head, and sighed. "I'll be right back."

"Jesus, that went south quick," Wilson said, once Mike was back in the observation room.

"Whatever," Mike laughed. "He's probably just repeating the same shit he hears from his parents. What do we want to do about that lie? Wanna nail him to it, try to get him to lie some more? Or go back to Landon?"

Mal looked into the observation room. Hunter's feet were on the table, in blatant defiance. He smirked, back on his phone, occasionally glancing up at the mirror, as if he knew she was there, watching, and pissed.

"As much as I'd like to wipe that arrogant grin from his face, I think Landon's the way to go. We should try the phone trick."

Mike laughed. "You think he'll fall for it?"

Mal turned and looked at Landon, fidgeting nervously in his seat, beads of sweat on his forehead even though the interview rooms were freezing.

"Definitely."

Chapter 41 - Mallory Black

MAL HANDED Landon the can of Coke, then took a seat opposite him. She pulled out her cell phone, then Mike's. She tinkered with her phone's screen, keeping it so that Landon couldn't see what she was doing.

She tapped the phones to each other, pretending to pair them, lowered the volume on Mike's phone and tapped the app she was looking for.

It was an app that you ran your fingers over, leaving trails of colorful patterns behind as the music changed depending on your movements. One of those time-waster apps that wasn't even a game, that Mike had been wasting time with for several weeks now.

Mal handed the phone to Landon. "Put your thumb on the center of the screen."

Landon did so, tentatively, a colorful red spilling from beneath his thumb as he pressed it onto the screen. "What is this?"

"Oh, you've never seen this?" Mal asked.

"No."

"Ah, don't worry. You just keep your thumb on it. And

whatever you do, don't move your thumb too much. It could throw off the results."

"*Results?*"

"Don't worry," Mal said. "Just tell us the truth like you've been doing and everything will be fine."

Landon swallowed.

She had him.

Mike stood next to Mal and looked down at his papers, preparing to ask the first question while Mal focused intently on her phone's blank screen. But Landon couldn't see her phone, as she held it under the table, using her body to block any reflection in the one-way-mirror.

"Okay," Mike said. "Can you run through exactly what happened again?"

"With what?"

"The whole thing."

"I mean, I already wrote it down," he said.

"Yeah, but this will help us. Don't worry, just say what you said before."

Landon delivered his story same as before, down to his choice of words, further reinforcing Mal's theory that this was a rehearsed lie.

When he got to the part about the girl in the treehouse, Mike asked, "What about the boy?"

"What boy?"

"We were talking to Hunter, and he said there was a boy with the girl in the treehouse." Mike pretended to look at his notes, just as he had done with Hunter. "Yeah, a dark-haired kid, around nine, with a green tee-shirt. He didn't remember if the shirt had a design on it or not, though. Do you remember the kid?"

After a long, confused moment, Landon said, "Oh, yeah, dark-haired kid. I think it was a Jets shirt."

"A Jets shirt?" Mike repeated. "You sure?"

"I think so. But I'm not sure."

"But he had dark hair, and he looked around nine, right?"

"Yeah," Landon said.

"Were you friends with Chloe?" Mike asked.

"No."

"Did you and Hunter pick on her?"

He looked down again. "I mean, sometimes, maybe, but we didn't mean anything. It was mostly because she was friends with John and Lucas."

"And who are John and Lucas?"

"John is friends with Hector. Lucas is his little brother. He's friends with Chloe."

"So, what was the issue between you two and John and Lucas?"

"Oh, I dunno. Landon just hates John, Lucas, and Hector. I don't know why."

"So, what? You just pick on people he doesn't like?"

"Well, I don't pick on them. I'm just, sorta there."

Mal kept her smart-ass comment to herself. She wasn't sure what she hated more, bullies, or their unwitting accomplices who never did anything to stop their reigns of terror.

Mike leaned down and gave the kid his Serious Tone. "Now, Landon, I need you to listen to me *very* carefully, okay?"

Landon's eyes widened. He shifted in his chair. "Okay?"

"That app is a lie detector. And I want to make sure that you're telling us the absolute one-hundred percent God's honest truth here, okay?"

He stared at Mal, then back at Mike. "I am."

"Okay," Mike said. "So, now I want to ask you another question."

"Okay."

"Why are you lying?"

"What do you mean?"

"You've been lying to us this entire time."

"No, I haven't," he said, putting the phone down.

Mal looked down at her phone, pretending to read results, "Lie, lie, another lie. Oh, here you were telling the truth, oh, wait, nope, that was a lie too. Hell, I have never seen so many lies on one test! And we were looking to cut you and your buddy a break, but I can't go to my bosses and ask for a deal when you give us bullshit like this!"

She held up her phone for emphasis.

Landon's eyes darted between them.

The last thing Mal wanted him to do was to make a run for the door, or ask for his parents — or worse, a lawyer. They needed to reel him in carefully or risk losing their prized catch.

Mal said, "Okay, Landon, here's the deal, Hunter lied, too. We've got him, on record, lying through his teeth. And now we have you. But, I don't think you're like Hunter. I don't think *you're* a bully. I don't think you wanted to go to Terrance's house last night and throw deadly objects."

"Deadly objects? They were just fireworks, bottles, and a few rocks!"

"Fireworks are classified as explosives. And given that two people died yesterday, and one is still in the hospital, that makes you and Hunter accessories to the crime."

"What? I didn't hurt anyone! We just wanted to scare the freak!"

"Yeah, well intent doesn't matter when the end result is murder."

"I didn't shoot anyone!"

"It doesn't matter," Mike cut in. "Man, don't they teach you kids anything about law these days? Surely you've heard of stories where a group of friends decides to rob a convenience store and one of the idiots brings a gun and accidentally shoots the clerk, and then they all wind up charged with murder."

Landon stared, eyes wide, brimming with tears. "No! I never heard of that."

Mal raised her voice, "Well, feel free to Google it when you get out of jail. Go ahead, Mike, put the cuffs on him."

"Wait!" Landon said, "You can give us a deal? What kind of deal?"

Mal sighed and leaned back in her chair. She looked at Mike. "You think we could get *all* the charges dropped?"

Mike put a finger to his lip, "Hmm, I don't know. I mean, he'd have to have something pretty good to give us. Something other than these lies."

"I've got something!"

"What?" Mal asked.

"I need to know I've got a deal."

"Well, see, that's not how it works. I can't make promises unless I know the value of what I'm getting."

"Okay," he said, sitting up, leaning forward like he was bargaining for his life. "Yeah, you were right. We lied about Terrance."

"How much of it?"

"All of it. Well, he *did* play with some of the kids in the woods, and I know he wasn't supposed to, but they weren't in the treehouse. And we never saw him touch anyone, or the girl buttoning up her shirt and pants."

Mal was relieved to know that her instincts weren't off and that there were no additional victims, though it also made Terrance's death all the more tragic and not some sort of karmic justice.

"Okay, that's a good start. Why did you lie?"

"Well, that's the thing I have for you. But I need to know I won't get in trouble."

"You won't get in trouble," Mike said. "As long as what you tell us has value."

"Oh, it does."

"What?" Mike asked.

"Someone paid us to lie about Terrance."

"Who?" Mal asked.

"Scott Isaacson."

Mal and Mike looked at one another, surprised. Mike asked, "Why did he pay you to lie about Terrance?"

"I'm not sure, but I think it might have something to do with the photos."

"What photos?"

Landon looked down, and his face flushed red. "Promise I won't get in trouble?"

"Promise," Mike said.

"Scott took some pictures of us."

"Who?"

"Me and Hunter."

"What kind of pictures?" Mike asked.

"Doing ... *stuff.*"

"What kinds of stuff?" Mike asked.

"I'm not a fag."

"We're not saying you are. Nor would we care if you were," Mal said. "What did he make you do in the photos?"

He made a hand motion of jerking off.

Mal knew it, the moment she laid eyes on Scott.

Artistic nudes, my ass!

"He made you do that to him?" she asked.

"No, ourselves. And each other. We weren't the only ones, though."

"Who else?" Mal asked.

"I'm not sure, but last week, I saw him giving money to John."

Mal said, "The John whose brother is friends with Chloe? The same John that one or both of you got into a fight with because you all were picking on his little brother?"

"Yeah."

Chapter 42 - Jasper Parish

JASPER, Alicia, and Ophelia were eating dinner, with the adults quiet, the child tense and uncertain, but knowing that something was wrong.

She'd asked where Aunt Karen was, but Alicia wasn't going to spill her fears that her sister had gone back to Clay.

It was a long quiet dinner, following a long quiet day, fear for Karen's welfare smothering them all.

As Ophelia gathered everyone's dishes, trying to do whatever she could to cheer her mother and Jasper, headlights splashed the front window.

Jasper and Alicia both got up and went to the door.

Karen staggered out of her car, laughing. Wasted.

"Where the hell were you?" Alicia yelled across the lawn.

"Sorry," Karen said, her voice slurred, stumbling like a baby giraffe into a hug with Alicia.

"Where were you?"

"Clay came by to ask me to come back."

"And?"

"I just went with him to his hotel to hear him out."

"And?"

"We talked."

"*And?*" Alicia asked, her voice rising higher with each repetition.

"I'm not going back."

"What are you on?" Alicia asked.

"Nothing."

"Don't lie to me."

Ophelia appeared next to Jasper. "What's wrong with Aunt Karen?"

"She's sick."

"Is she going to be okay?"

"I don't know."

Alicia asked, "What did you do with the money that Dennis gave you?"

Karen said, "I didn't do anything. It's in the envelope."

"Not all of it! What did you do?"

"I just needed a little something to carry me over."

"Little what?"

Jasper didn't hear what she whispered to Alicia, but judging from Alicia's screaming, "What the fuck? You're bringing that into my house?" he knew.

"Give it to me," Alicia demanded.

"What?"

"Give it to me."

"No."

"If you don't give it to me, you can't come in here."

"Please," Karen begged, crying. "Don't kick me out. I've got nowhere to go."

"You can go back with him."

"No," Karen shook her head. "I don't want to. I don't want that life."

"Then why the hell did you go with him today?"

She broke down crying, trying to hug her sister.

Ophelia cried beside Jasper. "Maybe we should go inside," he said, hugging her, then leading her back into the house.

They were in the kitchen, putting dishes back as Ophelia cried when the women came clomping into the house.

Alicia had Karen's drugs and was heading to the downstairs bathroom.

"No!" Karen screamed, following her. "Please, I need it!"

Alicia ignored her, dumping the heroin into the toilet.

Karen launched herself at Alicia, trying to wrestle her hand away from the toilet handle.

Alicia shoved her away and flushed.

Karen tried to dive after the drugs, but Alicia got in her way, holding her back.

The drugs disappeared down the drain. Karen yelled, "You bitch!" and smacked Alicia across the face.

Ophelia screamed, running from the kitchen to the bathroom. She pushed at Karen and cried out, "Stop!" at the top of her lungs.

Karen spun, smacking Ophelia across the face, even harder.

Ophelia fell backward, her eyes wide. Stunned. *Afraid.*

Karen sobered immediately, dropping to the ground beside her. "I'm so sorry, baby. I'm so sorry!"

She tried to help Ophelia up, but Ophelia pushed her away.

Karen turned to Alicia. "I'm so sorry. I'm—"

Alicia glared at her sister. "Get out of my face."

Karen turned toward the front door.

Jasper blocked her exit. "You're not driving now. You go upstairs."

Karen nodded, crying as she went up the stairs to the guest room, closing the door behind her.

Jasper looked at Alicia who was hugging a crying Ophelia.

Fucking moths and their flames.

Chapter 43 - Mallory Black

MALLORY AND MIKE approached Victoria Sutherland's apartment — the woman who ran the wedding service business that Isaacson had worked for. Mother to Lucas and John, a pair of Chloe's few friends, and potential victims of Scott's perverted photography.

The apartment was on the second floor, directly above Art Adleman's. The doorway was decorated with stringed lights and two potted plants along the left wall beneath an open window.

Lights were on inside, but Mal couldn't see much past the kitchen wall.

She rang the doorbell.

A shape moved in the window. She turned to see it dart quickly away. A kid, she figured, though she'd not gotten a good look.

No answer.

She rang again. "Creek County Sheriff's Office, please open the door."

Whispers from the other side, two boys arguing over whether or not to open the door.

"I can hear you," she said, pressing the doorbell twice more for emphasis.

The door opened.

A lanky brown-haired boy with azure eyes and olive skin answered. He was wearing what may have been a soccer outfit, black shorts, yellow and black knee-high socks, and a neon lemon tee. Judging from what Mal had looked up about the family already, this was probably John.

"John?" she asked.

He looked her up and down, then back at Mike, "Yeah?"

Behind John was a pudgy boy wearing jeans and a Minions tee, the eight-year-old Lucas. He was standing farther back like he was afraid Mal and Mike were going to come in and snatch them up.

MAL INTRODUCED HERSELF. Mike showed off their badges — kids always liked to see them — and asked if they could come in to talk about Chloe.

"Okay." John opened the door to let them in.

As she passed him, Mal noticed his fading black eye, almost vanished, but not quite. "Is your mother home?"

"No, she's with a client," John said, leading them into the small apartment, standing in front of his little brother, who was peering at Mal and Mike with curiosity.

Their home was the same layout as Art's place downstairs, but feminine, with crafts, flowers, and other decorations on display. Instead of white walls and old perfectly preserved furniture, the walls were a deep beige with cozy, well-lived in furniture in autumnal oranges, browns, and reds.

The place looked like it was ready to be featured in one

of those magazines that Mal leafed through while at the doctor's office.

"Is there somewhere we could talk?" Mal asked.

John pulled out a chair for Mal, and another for Mike at the closest end of the rectangular table. He then took a seat at the far end, as far away from Mal and Mike as possible at a table that seated only six.

Mal turned to see Lucas standing in the rear of the house, near the L-shaped red sectional, as if trying to disappear.

"You too, please," Mal said.

Lucas shuffled over, walking around his brother, and took a seat beside him, the second furthest from Mal.

"You were both friends with Chloe, right?"

Lucas nodded.

John said, "She was his friend. I didn't know her as well."

"Do you know anyone who might have wanted to hurt her?"

Lucas shrugged, still silent. His brown eyes were big, and he was blinking more than he probably should be.

"How about you?" Mal asked, John. "Did you know anyone who might have wanted to hurt her?"

"I dunno."

"Did you get in a fight recently?" Mal asked.

He nodded, looking down at his hands, folded on the table.

"Who with?"

"Just a couple of kids."

Lucas looked at John like he wanted to say something, but didn't. He sat on his hands as if that might keep him from bursting with what he seemed desperate to say.

"What were their names?" Mal asked.

Still looking down, "Hunter and Landon."

Lucas blurted, "They were picking on me! They took my lunch at the bus stop."

"So, your brother defended you?" Mal asked.

Lucas nodded. "He punched one of them—"

"It's not a big deal," John interrupted. "They're jerks. They pick on lots of kids."

"Did they pick on Chloe?"

Lucas nodded. "Yeah, they called her names."

John pursed his lips and sighed, probably wishing his brother would shut up.

"It's okay, John. We're not here about your fight."

"Okay. How can I help you then?"

John's words landed somewhere between polite and wanting to get this whole thing over with. Mal had a feeling why he was being short, and it had to do with the money Scott had given to him.

"We're just talking to neighbors, trying to figure out what happened to Chloe on Friday. Did you see anyone with her that day?"

"I didn't see her," John said. "Neither of us did."

"You didn't see her at all in the morning, Lucas?"

Mal recalled Art saying that the boy had been with her before his mother had driven he and his brother to school.

He shook his head no.

"How about at school?"

"We didn't have the same class. I might have seen her at recess, but I don't remember. We didn't play together. I like kickball, but she just kinda sits by herself, reading a book or something."

"How about after school? Did you see her then? Did you take the bus home?"

"No," John cut in. "Our mom picks us up from school. We came right home and did our homework."

"Your mom makes you do your homework right

away?" Mike said, trying to establish rapport with either of the kids.

Neither bit.

They both just nodded.

"So, you didn't go out or see Chloe? Maybe looked out your window and saw her with someone else?"

They both shook their heads.

The tension in the room was thick, though the kids were doing their best to pretend there was none. Mal had been a mother long enough to know they were hiding something. She decided to do something to test their response.

Mal pretended to sneeze, a big, violent, obnoxious outburst, while keeping her eyes on the kids.

They both jumped.

And then they both stared at her before John thought to say, "bless you."

"Thank you," she said, meeting his eyes. "So, I'd like to ask you about some of your neighbors, if you don't mind. Just to get your feel for them."

"Okay," John said.

"What do you think of Art Adleman?"

"He's nice," Lucas said immediately. "His cat is chubby like me."

Mal smiled. "He is a cute cat, isn't he?"

Lucas smiled.

"Okay," Mal said, "how about Megan Hudson and her mom?"

John shrugged. "She's alright. She's smart. In middle school early. I don't know her mom too well, though."

Lucas nodded. "Sometimes she plays with me at the park. But I don't see her there a lot."

"How about Terrance Burridge?"

"What about him?" John asked, his eyes as serious as Lucas's frown.

"What did you think of him?"

"He was nice, I guess."

She turned to Lucas. "What did you think?"

"He was nice. Chloe liked him a lot. She didn't think he did what everyone said."

"What about you? Did you think he did it?"

"I dunno," Lucas said. "My mom didn't want us talking to him, though."

His use of past-tense suggested that they'd heard what had happened with Terrance yesterday. She didn't press it.

"Did you talk to him?"

John shook his head no, but Lucas nodded.

John gave him a look.

Lucas said, "What? I wasn't going to be rude."

"When *did* you talk to him?"

"Sometimes he'd come to the park, or into the woods with Chloe. And I'd play with him if he was with Chloe."

"And did he ever do anything inappropriate around you, or to Chloe, that you know of?"

"No," Lucas said. "He was always nice. Like a big kid, but a grown-up. He wasn't very smart, but that's okay."

Lucas's eyes started to water, and he sniffled.

"Are you okay?" Mal asked.

"Just … sad what happened to him. And to Chloe."

"You can go to the bathroom and blow your nose if you need to."

"Thank you," he said, starting to cry louder as he walked away, his face turning red.

Mal turned to John. He was staring at her as if expecting her to question him harder without his little brother around.

"What about Scott Isaacson? What do you think of him?"

John shook his head. "Nothing."

"Nothing? That's an odd way to feel about someone who gives you money."

He blinked, caught.

He said nothing.

Mal asked, "It's okay. You can tell me about the money. You're not in trouble."

"I don't want to talk about it."

"Did he take pictures of you or your brother?"

John closed his eyes, looking down, crossing his arms over his chest. "Please, I don't want to talk about him."

Mal felt so bad for him and whatever pain he was holding inside. She wanted to give him a big hug and tell him that everything would be fine.

"It's okay. We know about the pictures." Pretending that she knew if John or Lucas had been in any of the pictures might ease the admission from his lips.

But he said nothing, still looking down, now blinking. He might've been crying, his hair falling over his face just so.

Mike cut to the chase. "Did he pay to take photos of you?"

John nodded.

"Were you naked?"

Another nod.

"What about Lucas? Did he take pictures of him?"

John shook his head.

"And what about Chloe?"

John nodded again. "He made us pose with her."

"Who?"

"Me, Landon, and Hunter."

Mal had to lean back in her chair, her head spinning, anger like fire inside her.

Lucas came back from the bathroom, no longer in tears.

John looked up, wiping the tears from his eyes, then got up, and went to the fridge, trying to keep Lucas from seeing that he'd been crying.

"Hey, Buddy," he said from the kitchen, out of sight, "you want some Kool-Aid?"

"Yes, please," Lucas said, sitting back down at the table.

John came back, handed Lucas the cup of grape Kool-Aid, and put an arm around his brother.

Mal's heart was already in pieces.

She had to get out of the house before she cried. "Okay. We'll be in touch later. Thank you both for your help. We appreciate it."

Mal headed toward the door, quickly, vaguely aware of Mike following behind her.

As she hit the balcony, her stomach was a ship in a violent storm. She stood still for a moment, clutching the balcony to keep from hurling.

She looked down and saw Isaacson getting out of his car.

He looked up.

She called out his name.

And once again, the asshole ran.

Chapter 44 - Mallory Black

THE MOMENT SCOTT broke into a sprint, heading along the
path that ran along the first-floor apartments, Mal jumped
off the balcony, landing with a roll in the garden instead of
the sidewalk.

She popped up and saw Scott run past his apartment,
then keep going toward the end of the building.

She followed him at a sprint, heart racing, legs burning.

He reached the end of the building twenty yards ahead
then disappeared around the corner.

From there, Mal figured he would either make a
beeline toward the left parking lot and try to hide or keep
running to the next building and hope to lose her.

She didn't have time to reach for the radio in her jacket
pocket and assumed Mike was calling in the pursuit.

No fucking way she was going to let this asshole
escape.

She approached the end of the sidewalk where the
building gave way to grass, where she'd seen Scott slip left.

She reached the corner, went to turn, and crashed into
Scott.

He was already swinging, his hand clutching what she barely registered as a rock.

No time for her to react before it hit her hard in the head, hard.

She fell back, the pain dizzying.

She sat up, wiped the blood from her eyes, and screamed, "Stop!"

He didn't.

Mal grabbed her taser and took aim.

The wires shot forward, hitting him in the back and sending him to the ground in twitching convulsions.

Mal raced to him, cuffs in hand.

As she reached him, somehow, he was still able to control himself enough to sweep his legs, knocking her down, flat on her back, knocking the breath from her body.

She didn't see where the cuffs went as she lost her grip.

Isaacson was already on her, arms at her throat, choking, his eyes enraged, veins bulging in his neck as spittle rained from his mouth.

"You ruined everything!"

Her instincts and years of training kicked in.

Mal brought her arms up in a swift compact motion, then spread them out, breaking his hold on her.

As he let go of her neck, she reached up, grabbed him under the neck with one hand, and by the side of the head with the other. She twisted his skull sideways, using the leverage of potentially snapping his neck, along with her legs wrapped around him, to flip Isaacson over and straddle him.

Before he could launch a counter attack, Mal punched him, connecting with his cheekbone. Her hand was already throbbing, but she followed up with a second hit to his face, then leaped backward to her feet, drawing her gun.

"Don't fucking move!" she shouted, training her weapon on him.

Mike raced up behind her.

"Cuff him," she said, keeping the gun on the Isaacson, closing her eyes to the sting of sticky blood dripping from the gash in her forehead.

Mike flipped Scott over and got the cuffs on his wrists.

Scott tried to resist, bucking and squirming.

Mike ended his struggles with a hard knee into Scott's wriggling back.

"Stay down!" Mike barked.

Sirens approached as Mal holstered her gun.

She pulled out her phone and snapped a photo of Mike on top of the bastard.

"You like taking pictures so much?" Mal said, smiling. "Say cheese, motherfucker."

Chapter 45 - Jasper Parish

JASPER WAS WORKING out at the park as evening rolled in. He'd missed his morning routine two days in a row, not wanting to leave Alicia alone to deal with her sister until he thought things were stable.

Something about pushing his body to its limits always calmed him. Even as the world went to hell around Jasper, to focus on one thing he had control over helped reduce his anxiety before it spiraled out of control.

He ran along the trail, pushing himself to go another lap, considering all that had happened in the past two days.

Karen had apologized, and the girls forgave her, but it was the tenuous sort of absolution, the kind which could make you regret letting that person back into your life. Typical with addicts.

Karen, for her part, had gotten a hold of that friend in New York and was planning to leave in the morning. She didn't have a job lined up yet, but Jasper's money would help her get by for a while — assuming she didn't shoot it into her veins.

Alicia made Karen promise to get help. Jasper had even offered to send more money, regularly for a while, if she could prove that she was in a program and getting clean. He hated having to monitor an adult to do what they were supposed to do. But at the same time, he didn't want to enable her habit.

Jasper was soaking with sweat, and thirsty. He stopped at the water fountain and gulped for a minute.

Motorcycle engines roared down the road. A rare sound around here, especially in multiples.

Clay!

Clay had tried to call Karen several times yesterday. She ignored the calls, sending them all to voicemail. And to her credit, Karen said that she hadn't listened to a single one.

They hadn't heard from Clay at all today. Jasper had hoped that he'd given up and that Karen would be able to sneak out of town in the morning.

But now, that appeared to be wishful thinking. He was visiting the house again, maybe find out why Karen wasn't answering her phone.

The park was several blocks from Alicia's, and Jasper hadn't taken the car. He would need at least five minutes to get there, if not more.

Jasper ran.

Eight motorcycles littered the driveway and street. Several thugs were outside Alicia's home as if standing guard.

The front door was wide open.

From the house, he heard women screaming.

Fuck!

Jasper was two houses away when one of the thugs, standing in the driveway, spotted him.

The man's eyes widened as Jasper barreled toward him.

He threw out his hands, to try and stop Jasper.

Jasper grabbed the man's arm, twisted it behind his back, fast enough to rip the man's shoulder from its socket.

The man screamed and crumpled to the ground.

A second thug came at Jasper, knife in hand, swinging.

Jasper dodged, grabbed his hand, twisted his fingers back, and forced him to drop the blade.

Jasper fell to the ground, grabbed the knife and jumped back up, driving the knife right through the man's eye socket.

The man screamed as Jasper yanked the blade from the man's skull and kicked him forward.

A gunshot rang out.

At first, Jasper thought someone had shot at him, but no, it had come from the house.

He had to get inside.

Three bikers stood in his way.

One was armed, and aiming at Jasper.

Jasper threw the knife at the man, hoping to lodge it in his throat or gut. But the blade went wide.

The man fired.

Jasper dodged, ducking behind his car.

The man fired again, shattering the front window.

Jasper reached up, used his fingerprint to unlock the door, opened it, and reached for the glove compartment.

Another two shots. Windows exploded overhead.

Jasper grabbed the Glock, brought it up and fired through the shattered window, hitting his target in the head and chest, bringing him down.

Jasper's right arm and hand exploded in pain, the gun

falling from his fingers as a chain coiled and wrapped around his forearm.

The biker on the other end of the chain, a big fat man with just two teeth, smiled, "Gotchya, ni—"

Jasper yanked the chain. That surprised the man, stopping him mid-slur, as he stumbled forward.

Jasper moved out of the way, just before the man fell on him, then wrapped the length of chain around the man's neck and squeezed tight.

The man gasped, kicking, squirming, and trying to pull it from his neck.

Jasper yanked tighter.

Footsteps approached from behind.

Jasper released the chain before he could choke the man's life from him, then ducked, grabbed his gun, and raised it in time to shoot the oncoming biker in the face.

Jasper turned the gun on the fat man, who was rising to his feet, and shot him right through the top of his skull.

Jasper looked around.

Nobody else standing outside.

But lights were on all around the neighborhood.

Cops would be on their way any second.

Jasper reloaded his pistol and went inside to finish taking out the trash.

Just inside the doorway, a biker was waiting with a shotgun.

But the biker was too late.

Jasper fired, hitting him in the head.

The shotgun blasted into the floor as he fell.

Jasper stepped past him, looked into the living room.

One biker with a knife to Ophelia's throat, and Clay holding a gun to Karen's head.

Alicia was on the ground, bleeding, whether from a knife or gun wound, Jasper didn't know.

She looked at Jasper, eyes pleading for him to save her, to save her sister and daughter.

She tried to talk but coughed up blood instead.

She would bleed out in minutes without help.

The sirens were insistent, and getting nearer.

Good.

"Let them go," Jasper growled, aiming his pistol at Clay.

Clay grinned like a fucking maniac.

Karen cried, "Please, I'll go with you. Just let them go."

"You hear that?" Clay said. "We're going now. So I suggest you stand the fuck down or I'll—"

Jasper fired into the man's open, ugly-toothed mouth, then spun around and fired again, this time at the man holding the knife to Ophelia's throat. The man took three bullets to his face and dropped the blade.

Ophelia ran to her mother.

Jasper turned just as Clay's gun went off in a death-grip-twitch.

Jasper's heart dropped. He didn't know where the bullet had gone. He looked at Karen, now running toward them, certain she'd fall down dead.

But she kept on coming, seemingly okay.

He turned back toward Ophelia, afraid he'd see her standing there, a bullet hole in her forehead.

But she was okay, too.

The bullet must've gone into the ceiling.

Or into him, and he just hadn't felt it yet.

Jasper went over to Clay, pumped another two rounds into the bastard's body to make sure he was dead.

The sirens sounded inches away.

He knelt next to Alicia. Ophelia was hugging her, crying, "Please don't die, mommy. Please don't die."

"You need to put pressure here," Jasper said, telling

both Karen and Ophelia how to keep the right compression on Alicia's wound.

Closer, Jasper could tell it was a knife wound to the gut. Not good.

She stared at him, then with her voice weak and blood still coming from her mouth she said, "Who are you?"

"Shh. I've gotta go. You all keep pressure on her wound."

"You can't go!" Ophelia cried. "Mommy needs you."

"She'll be okay," he said, hoping the words might make it true. "When the paramedics have her, I need you to make sure that there aren't any photos of me around. Delete anything you have on any of your phones."

"Who are you?" Karen repeated her sister's question.

"It doesn't matter."

"What do we tell the police?" Karen asked.

"The truth. You can tell them the name I gave you. As long as they don't have my photo, it's all good."

Jasper kissed Ophelia on the head, then Alicia. "I love you, both. I'll be in touch when it's safe."

He left, driving into the night, just another ghost who thought he could have a life.

Chapter 46 - Mallory Black

MAL SAT in the observation room between Interview Rooms One and Two, as exhausted as she was exhilarated. She held a cold pack against the stitches on her forehead, the pain mostly a dull throbbing, but not enough to put her on the sidelines.

Hell, even if she'd been more seriously injured, the adrenaline from chasing Scott could coast her through the rest of this day and into the night.

Isaacson was in Room One.

John and Lucas were in Room Two, with their mother, Vicky.

It was time to get to the bottom of this shit once and for all.

The sheriff and Captain Wilson were both present, listening as Mike updated them on everything that had gone down, and what they'd learned.

Aanya entered the observation room. She'd gotten a program from a friend in the FBI which broke the encryption on Scott's hard drives.

She brought her laptop with some of the photos copied onto it.

Mal's gut churned as she thumbed through the photos on-screen.

She didn't want to look. Didn't want to bear witness to the abuse these kids had suffered. But it was Mal's job to see the worst in humanity. That was how she delivered justice and prevented monsters like Isaacson from ever harming another child.

There were photos, mostly black and white, of at least six different kids in various sexual acts, by themselves and with one another. Among the photos were John, Hunter, Landon, and Chloe. There were also two other kids that Mal hadn't recognized.

John and Chloe were naked in the photos. Chloe was laying in a bed with her eyes closed. Mal wasn't sure, but she seemed unconscious. John was lying next to her, touching himself, not her.

Seeing these children, the youngest not even at puberty, posed in sexual situations, repulsed her. Mal couldn't imagine the sick fucks that got off on these debasing images. It filled her with rage and made her want to march into the other interview room, and put a bullet in Isaacson's head so this thing would never go to trial and become an ordeal for the victims that they could never forget.

She wondered if he took these photos for himself or if Isaacson was selling them online to other perverts and monsters in hiding.

"This is just some of them," Aanya said. "I'm still decrypting the other drives."

"Print them and put them in a folder, please," Mal said.

After Aanya left the room, a silence descended, the

gravity of what they saw settling into their bones, images branding themselves into their minds.

And yet, as awful as it was for them to see, it was worse for the children whose innocence had been stolen from them. Children might never know normal loving, trusting relationships because of what some monster did.

Mal stared at Isaacson in the interview room, wishing she'd taken a shot with her gun instead of the taser.

Wilson stepped next to Mal at the one-way mirror. "You okay?"

"This?" she said, holding the ice pack away from her head an inch.

"Yeah. Do you need to rest or anything?"

"No resting until we get answers."

MAL STEPPED into the interview room, her chest tight as she carried her iPad with her, not wanting to do what she about to do.

Deputies had brought a card table into the room, setting it next to the metal table bolted to the ground. Now John, Lucas, and their mother could all sit on one end with Mal and Mike on the other.

Vicky sat between the boys, her forehead creased with concern. Mal wasn't sure what Mike had told the woman to get her down to the station, or what her kids had said after that earlier conversation.

"What's going on?" she asked.

Mal looked to John and Lucas. Sure enough, the job of telling her fell to Mal.

Mal gave Mike a look. He said, "Hey, Lucas, do you want to pick out a snack and drink from the vending machines?"

Lucas looked at his mother. "Can I?"

"Go ahead," Vicky said.

As Mike left with the younger boy, Mal inhaled, bracing herself as she brought Vicky up to speed.

Vicky went through all the usual emotions — shock, disbelief, crying, then hugging John close, which, of course, prompted him to start sobbing as well.

Mal set her tablet on the table, glad that Vicky had believed her. This meant that Mal didn't have to show her the photos, something that could have traumatized John yet again.

"How could I not have seen this? To think, I had that man over to my house. I worked with him. I entrusted my clients to him. And he's been preying on these children all this time?" Vicky turned to her son. "Why didn't you say anything to me?"

He shook his head, crying. "I don't know. It just happened, and ... and I thought I'd get in trouble. That we'd *all* get in trouble."

"How and when did he first approach you?"

John shook his head. "Do I have to say?"

Vicky squeezed his hand. "It's okay, baby. I'm right here. Just tell her what happened."

He blinked, biting his trembling lip. "I ... I don't think I can."

"It's okay. No matter what happened, I still love you. It's not your fault."

"Scott, he found out about me and Hunter."

"What do you mean?"

"Me and Hunter ... we were seeing each other."

"What?"

"I'm gay, Mom."

She stared at her son for a long moment, maybe even more shocked than she'd been by Scott preying on her son. And then she hugged him. "Why didn't you tell me?"

"You're not mad?"

"Why would I be mad?"

"I just thought you would be. You were going off when that gay couple asked you to to help with their wedding last year, saying how it was unnatural and against God."

Vicky swallowed. "That doesn't mean I don't love you. You're my son. I love you no matter what."

She hugged him again, tears now streaming down both their faces.

Mal handed them tissues to blow their noses and wipe their eyes. Then she said, "So, Scott found out you were seeing each other and then what?"

"He had us over to his place one day. Hunter modeled for him and asked if I wanted to watch. Then he asked me if I wanted to model too. I said no, I'm not a model. Hunter said not to be a pussy, so I stood with him, not thinking about it too much. Then Scott told us to take off our shirts."

Vicky looked down, closing her eyes, doing her best to listen as John continued.

"And then he asked us to take off our pants, to take some 'fashion shots.' That's what he called them when we were in our underwear. One thing led to another, and he started offering us money to kiss.

"I said 'no way, dude' and Hunter said it was okay, that Scott knew that we were seeing each other."

"And what then?" Mal asked.

"I was pissed at Hunter for saying anything. Then Scott said if I didn't kiss Hunter that he'd tell my mom I was gay."

"That bastard," Vicky said.

"So I did it. He gave us each two hundred bucks. And I was like, 'woah, this is a lot of money.'"

"You could have come to me if you needed money," Vicky said.

"No, you're always complaining about how slow work is, and how dad left us high and dry. I thought I could help out, buy some groceries and stuff."

Vicky shook her head, her anger obviously boiling, though Mal wasn't sure if she was mad at her son, Scott, both, the situation she'd found herself in, or that she hadn't seen the predator preying on her son.

"So, what happened after that?"

"We started taking pictures, and he kept on giving us more and more money. He put the photos up on some website, though he blurred our faces. Dudes would send him clothes for us to wear. We'd model in them, and kiss some more."

Vicky continued crying as John continued.

"Then he offered us a lot of money if we got naked. I said no. *No way.* But then Scott said if we didn't, he'd send the photos, without our faces blurred, to my mom and to everyone we know on LiveLyfe. He—"

"I want to kill him," Vicky interrupted. "I want to fucking kill him."

"So," Mal said, "how did Chloe get involved?"

"It was just the once. Some rich dude said he'd pay a lot of money if we posed with a girl. Hunter convinced Chloe to come over to Scott's place to hang out. And Scott gave her some drink that made her sleep."

Vicky shook her head again.

"And then what?"

John started crying again. "He made me touch myself."

Vicky couldn't take any more.

She screamed. Loud and long, venting every bit of

anger that had been brewing inside her. Then, to Mal's surprise, she turned the anger onto John. "You let him do that to that poor girl?"

"I didn't know what he was going to do!"

"You abused her, too!"

"No, I didn't even touch her."

She stood, turned away from her son.

"Mom," he said, reaching out to her.

She shrugged off his touch. "Don't. That girl wasn't right in the head. She was your brother's friend. She was your brother's age, and you let him take pictures of her naked?"

"I'm sorry, Mom. I didn't know what else to do. He threatened Hunter and me."

Mal interrupted their fight to ask a question that had been simmering for a while in the back of her mind. "If you and Hunter were going out, why did he pick on your brother? Why did you two get in a fight last week?"

"He got mad at me when I said I wouldn't do any more photos with him. After that whole thing with Chloe being drugged, I said no more. I'm out. He got mad and threatened to out me. Then I got mad and told him I didn't want to see him anymore. He started coming around and messing with Lucas, just to get to me. So I went after him."

Vicky turned to Mal. "Can we have a moment?"

"Sure," Mal said.

Vicky looked around the room, probably assuming there were cameras recording their every word. "Can we go somewhere more private?"

"Yeah," Mal said, leading them out of the room, down the hall, and into a victim's services room. "You all can hang out here. I need to take care of something. I'll come find you as soon as I'm finished, okay?"

"Thank you," Vicky said.

Mal went back to the observation room, where Wilson and Gloria were sitting there solemnly.

Mal looked in on Isaacson, still sitting in the interview room, his head now in his arms as though taking a nap.

She wondered if he knew how much shit he was in and if he'd immediately ask for a lawyer. He'd asked for one the last time they brought him in, but they cut him loose, so he never did call, and didn't have representation, so far as she knew. Asking for a lawyer would be his best move, but Mal hoped to avoid that, though she wasn't sure how. She wanted a full confession so Isaacson's victims wouldn't be dragged in for a lengthy sensational trial.

She might be able to get him to confess to what he did with the kids, but nailing him for Chloe's murder was another story. She didn't have anything to link him to her death. But he had to have *something* to do with it. Maybe the girl remembered being drugged and went to one of the kids, or even Isaacson, and said something. Maybe he decided that only death guaranteed her silence.

She radioed Mike. "Hey, Vicky and John needed some time to talk, so I put them in victim's services. I want to interview this asshole now. Is there anyone you can leave Lucas with so you can join me?"

"Yeah, I'll see who's around."

A few minutes later, Mike came into the observation room saying, "I left him with Aanya. They're talking about video games, so that should keep them busy for an hour or so."

"Good. You ready?" Mal looked in at the monster who had abused who knew how many kids in his own back yard.

"Let's get this fucker."

Chapter 47 - Jasper Parish

JASPER DROVE HOME IN SILENCE, praying for Alicia's survival, and hoping that his anonymity would survive.

But that no longer seemed likely.

If either Alicia or Ophelia had gotten a photo of him, he was done for. Even if they deleted them, the authorities might be able to find them in the cloud.

Jasper Parish, a man who had faked his death to live a new life in the shadows, would be breathing again.

And if his identity were exposed, it wouldn't be long before the authorities began searching for him. Maybe they'd link him to his crimes, in which case, he'd likely become an FBI's Most Wanted criminal. His photo would be everywhere. His name, and his crimes, out there for all the world to see.

Exposed like the criminals he hunted.

He would have nowhere in the country to hide.

And, as his mind raced over the evening's events, he kept seeing one thing over and over — Ophelia cradling her mother as Alicia's eyes widened to the realization that he wasn't who he said that he was.

No, he was a monster.
And monsters weren't meant to have love or families.

Chapter 48 - Mallory Black

MAL AND MIKE entered the interview room just as Isaacson lifted his head, the chains connecting his cuffs to the table jangling as he sat up.

Mal took a seat at the table and placed a folder in front of her with the photos she'd printed.

Mike stood next to her, arms folded across his chest.

"So," Mal said as she opened the folder and tossed the first of the photos at him, "are…"

She tossed another, "these…"

And another, "art?"

His jaw clenched.

"You are fucked, friend," Mal said. "You can bitch out and ask for a lawyer again, but I guarantee you that with these photos, you're going to have a hard time finding anyone decent to represent you. Your best move is to come clean and tell us what happened with Chloe. Prosecution can ask the judge to show some leniency. And if you *don't* work with us, we're going to bury your ass."

Isaacson showed no emotion as he stared at the three photos, two of Hunter and Landon and the other of Chloe and John. He looked tired. Probably from hiding, living a lie, and pretending to be something resembling a human.

His eyes were almost glazed. He shook his head, ever so slightly. "I didn't kill her."

Mal sighed. "Tell us about these little photo sessions."

"What's to ask? You already saw the photos."

"Why?"

"A teen modeling site I run. It's perfectly legal."

"These photos are *not* legal," Mal said, pointing to the two where the kids were nude.

"It's art. And those photos aren't on the site. Those are custom sets for discerning patrons."

"Why?" Mal asked. "You're a talented photographer, why peddle this shit? Does it get you off?"

"No. It happened by accident. I was posting some portrait photos on a forum, looking for work after that unfortunate bathroom incident cost me my livelihood. That little bitch's lie ruined everything." He took a moment to compose himself, then continued, "Anyway, I started getting a bunch of people asking for custom sets. And offering to pay me. One thing led to another until I was finally able to make a living again through my art."

"Peddling child porn, you mean."

"One man's art is another's porn. Not for me to decide."

Mal wanted to lay into him, but arguing wouldn't earn the man's cooperation. And it wasn't as if she could change his mind on obscenity.

"So, what then? You blackmailed kids into modeling for you?"

"No, I paid for their time, and quite well."

"Not from the way John Sutherland tells it."

Isaacson smiled. "Oh, yeah, what does *he* say?"

"That you threatened to out him, got him to kiss

Hunter, then used those photos to blackmail him into doing nudes."

"Why don't you ask Hunter how it went down. You're more likely to get the truth from him."

"Why don't *you* tell me how it went down?"

"John was totally into it. Hunter had told him about the modeling he was doing, and John asked if he wanted to make some money. We shot a few photos then he asked if he could make *more* money, doing the shots Hunter had told him about."

"So, you're saying he asked if he could pose nude?"

"More or less. The kid wanted cash, and my clients want art. Win-win, way I see it."

"What about Chloe? How does she play into all this?" Mal asked.

"A client wanted something with a girl, so I asked her if she'd be interested in making some money. She said yes, and we shot."

"She was passed out on the bed! You drugged her."

"No, I didn't. It's acting. Kids love to play pretend. We were re-enacting *Sleeping Beauty.*"

"Naked?"

He shrugged, staring smugly at Mal.

For all the fear and anger she'd seen in him before, Isaacson seemed remarkably cool at the moment, as though he wasn't about to do time for child porn, and maybe murder.

Mal shook her head.

Isaacson smiled. "You sit there judging me, acting like you know me, like you've got this all figured out, but you're so damned blinded by your prejudice against supposed pedophilia that you don't see what's right in front of you."

"What?"

"The killer, you're so blinded by your hate for what you *think* I am, that you're missing the obvious."

"What are you talking about?" Mike asked.

"Here's what's going to happen. You're going to come to your senses and give me a deal on these photos, and I'll tell you who the murderer is."

Mal glared at him. "No. We don't make deals with sick bastards. You abused children, selling that abuse to other sick fucks. There's no way in hell you're walking away from that."

"Well, then, good luck finding that murderer, detectives. And, oh yeah, … I'll take that lawyer now."

Isaacson smiled and winked.

It took everything Mal had in her not to slug him in the face.

Chapter 49 - Mallory Black

MAL WALKED to the break room for drinks. Mike followed, asking, "What does he mean we're missing the obvious? You think he's trying to misdirect us, or does he know who the killer is?"

Mal repeatedly shoved a dollar bill into the soda machine until the piece of shit finally took her money and dropped a Coke down the chute.

She cracked it open and gulped, eager for a dose of sugar and caffeine.

Scott's words echoed in her head: *you're missing the obvious.*

She considered their clues, the suspects they'd interviewed, and the leads still to pursue. She wondered how much Scott fit with the other pieces. How well did he know Kelly? Did he know Dixon or the drug dealer that guy was into for twenty large?

It didn't seem likely.

Missing the obvious.

Her mind flashed to when she first met John and Lucas, talking to them in their kitchen.

John putting an arm around his brother, hugging him.

The way he stood between Lucas and Mal and Mike when they'd first arrived.

And while she'd not registered it at the time, John's actions seemed even more significant in retrospect — a protective older brother.

But protecting Lucas from what?

Mal grabbed her phone and called Aanya.

"Is Lucas still with you?"

"Yes, we're about to head over to victim services."

"Don't. You at your station?"

"Yes."

"Okay, keep him busy until I get there." Mal turned to Mike. "I think I know who the killer is."

MAL TOLD Mike to head over to victim services, and make sure Vicky and John didn't go looking for Lucas. She didn't want any interruptions. Mal also thought she might get answers more easily on her own, that one cop versus two would be less intimidating to the skittish child.

Mal headed to Aanya's office, a long room where she worked computer crimes and computer forensics with a couple of other detectives. But Aanya was the only one currently on duty, so they had plenty of privacy.

"How's it going?" Mal asked them both.

Lucas was sitting next to Mal at a computer where he was watching YouTube videos of someone playing *Minecraft*.

"You like *Minecraft?*" Mal asked.

"Yeah. Do you play?"

"No, but my daughter, Ashley did."

"*Did?* She doesn't anymore?"

Mal took a seat next to the kid.

Aanya, taking a hint, went to another workstation, giving them space.

"No, she passed away."

"Oh," he said, staring for a moment before asking, "How?"

"Someone killed her."

His eyes widened. "Really?"

"Yes," Mal said.

Lucas was quiet for a moment. She wasn't sure if he was paying attention to the goofy sounding British guy with a cat avatar playing *Minecraft*, or if he was lost in thought.

"Do you miss her?"

"Every day I wake up," Mal said.

"What was she like?"

"She was a year older than you when she died. She was bright, kinda shy around people she didn't know, but once you got to know her, she could be goofy." Mal smiled, remembering how Ashley would put on impromptu "concerts" for her and Ray in the living room, making them watch her lip sync or dance to whatever song she was obsessed with at the moment.

"She was also really sweet. Never had a mean word to say about anyone."

Lucas stared at the computer, his eyes watering.

"Does that sound like Chloe?"

He nodded.

"What was she like?"

"She was always nice to me. Other kids would make fun of me for being fat. And even the ones that didn't call me names would make me feel bad. They'd never pick me for teams at recess, or they just wouldn't play with me.

Girls would call me gross. But not Chloe. She was always nice to me. *Always.*"

Tears spilled down his cheeks.

Mal could feel the boy's pain, born and blooming inside her.

"Was she your best friend?"

He nodded, sniffling.

Mal reached into her jacket and pulled out a pocket tissue pack. She handed it to him.

He pulled some tissues free and blew his nose, then wiped at his cheeks.

Mal grabbed a plastic trash can from next to her and put it between herself and Lucas.

He dropped the tissue and went back to staring at the monitor.

Mal put a hand on his shoulder. "You know the hardest part when my daughter died?"

"No." He looked at her. "What?"

"For a while, I didn't know what happened. I didn't know who killed her, or why. And even more than her death, that hurt. The not knowing who did it. Was it a bad guy who hurt her, or was it an accident? And I was up nights imagining the horrible things that might have happened to her, and all I wanted was to know that she didn't die in some awful way. That it was over quickly."

Lucas swallowed, his lips trembling.

"Was it?"

She lied. "I don't know. I still don't know. I would like to think so. Did you know Chloe's mom?"

"Not really. I went to her house a few times, and her mom was nice to me and gave us cookies and stuff. But she seemed to be busy a lot. Didn't have a lot of time for Chloe."

"Did that make Chloe sad?"

"Yes."

"Did Chloe love her mom anyway?"

"Yes."

After a long silence, Lucas finally arrived at the door Mal had been leading him to. "Do you think her mom is sad because she doesn't know what happened?"

"Yes, I think she's very sad. Do you think Chloe would want her to be sad, to not know what happened?"

"No." His lip trembled. Tears spilled faster.

"Do you know what happened, Lucas?"

He nodded.

Mal swallowed.

"Don't you think Chloe would want her mom to know so that she won't suffer anymore?"

He nodded again.

"You think Chloe would want you to tell what happened?"

He nodded. "John said not to, though. That we'd be in trouble."

"Sometimes not telling the truth leads to even more trouble. At least if you tell the truth, then people can understand, right? It's got to feel better than lying, right? It's the first step to going back to the way things were."

He nodded.

"It's okay," Mal said, rubbing his back. "Just start at the beginning."

"It was an accident."

"Okay, accidents happen, all the time."

"Chloe was at our place. We were in my bedroom, the room I share with John."

"Where was John?"

"In the living room, playing Nintendo."

"So, okay. You and Chloe were in your room. What were you doing?"

"Playing with my stuffed animals. She was the only person who didn't make fun of me for having them. Anyway, one minute she was normal, and then all of a sudden she started getting all scared."

"Scared of what?"

"I don't know. She said something about John, and that she remembered."

"Remembered what?"

"She started talking crazy, saying that she was naked, and he was naked, and she just kept saying over and over that she remembered. And at first, I thought she was joking, but she wasn't. She started screaming. And then John came running into the room asking what was wrong."

Lucas paused, wiping at his eyes.

"And then what?"

"She screamed at him and went running at him, knocking him into his dresser, knocking over all of his trophies and stuff. And then she was on top of him, hitting and scratching at him. I was really scared. I tried to pull her off of him, but she wouldn't stop. And I know he didn't want to hurt her. He was just trying to get away from her, but she was like a wild animal. Her eyes were crazy. She grabbed one of his trophies off the ground and hit him in the back of the head. And he just fell down."

Lucas wiped at his eyes and blew his nose again.

"And I thought he was dead. But she jumped on top of him and was hitting him more. I yelled at her to stop, but it was like she didn't even hear me, so ... I grabbed John's bat from the closet."

Mal swallowed a knot. As much as she wanted closure on the case, to know what happened, she didn't want *this*.

"And I hit her. Just once. Just to get her off, and she stood there for a minute like nothing happened. Then ... she just dropped."

Lucas shook his head. "I didn't mean to hurt her. I just wanted her to stop. And then I was standing there, and I thought they were both dead. And I was scared. But then John got up, and he saw what happened. He tried to get her to wake up, but she ... she was .... dead."

Mal rubbed his back again, trying to comfort him while his confession kept rolling. "What then?"

"John was dizzy for a bit, seemed confused. His head was still hurting. He said we had to get Chloe out of here, that nobody would understand that it was an accident, that we'd both go to jail forever."

He turned to her, crying harder. "Are we going to go to jail forever?"

Mal shook her head. "No, Lucas. I'm not sure what will happen, but it was an accident. I'm sure we can figure something out."

"I didn't mean to do it. I loved her. She was my only real friend," he crashed into Mal and cried hard into her shoulder.

She struggled to throttle her tears. She needed the details.

"So, what did John do with Chloe?"

"He wrapped her up in his old baseball bag and snuck her out to the woods. I don't know what he did after that, but he said that he made it so the police would think someone else killed her."

Lucas looked up at Mal. "John isn't going to be in trouble, is he? He didn't kill her. I did. He was just trying to protect me."

Mal didn't have an answer, at least not an honest one. She hugged him, her heart breaking as she held this accidental murderer tight against her, a child she was about to arrest. "I'll do what I can."

And as she held him, Mal thought of all the guilt and

neglect that led to Chloe's death and Terrance's tragic suicide via lynch mob.

An irresponsible, selfish mother in Kelly Conlan, a drug-dealing scumbag boyfriend, a career politician grandfather more concerned with appearances than justice, a blogger pushing a narrative to try to oust the sheriff. Beneath it all, a sexual predator hiding behind a camera, using money and blackmail to keep kids quiet while peddling these kids' betrayed innocence to online perverts.

The whole thing made Mal sick, especially knowing that all the guilty parties would never be held to justice for what had happened.

No, instead two children would likely go on trial.

Their lives, as well as their mother's, would be pored over in the national and local media by parasites feeding vultures. People asking *How Can This Happen?* — many hypocritically so, never acknowledging their role in the tragedy.

John and Lucas might be able to get a deal and stay out of jail, but the tax would last the rest of their lives.

Mal could only beg Gloria to pressure the DA's office to make sure that Isaacson's sexual predation, the lynchpin without none of this would have happened, was prosecuted to the full extent of the law. And that if anyone was ultimately held culpable for Chloe's death, it would be him more than any other.

For now, Mal held Lucas as his childhood ended.

Chapter 50 - Mallory Black

MAL SAT in her cubicle watching the live Wednesday morning press conference. Felicia Day, Sheriff Bell, and Captain Wilson updated the packed room full of journalists — and wannabe journos like Cameron Ford — on the details of the Chloe Conlan case. They announced the arrests of two youths whose names were momentarily protected.

Mike strolled in twenty minutes late, holding two boxes of donuts and a tray with four coffees, because an officer holding donuts could do no wrong.

He set the box down and said, "Donuts!"

Heads popped up from behind cubicle walls like prairie dogs. Soon, detectives, deputies, and other staffers descended on the donuts like savages.

"One of those coffees better be mine," Mal said approaching Mike and his mayhem. "And you fuckers better leave a donut in the box, and not a plain one!" Skippy sprinted away with two donuts like the greedy bastard he was. "One per person, Skippy!"

"It's for Baylor," he said, "he's in the shitter."

"TMI, Skippy, TMI," Mike yelled as Skippy headed back to his cubicle in property crimes.

Mike handed Mal one of the two coffees left in the holder. "Here ya' go, Mal."

"Thank you."

There were two donuts left in the box when she got there. A plain and a cinnamon. No chocolate, no glazed, no jelly, not even one of those awful pink frosted.

"Okay, fuck all of you," Mal said, reluctantly reaching for the plain.

"Trade you." Mike handed her the chocolate frosted in his napkin.

"You sure?"

"Hey, you closed the case, you get the chocolate frosted donut."

"Thanks." She grabbed it and took a bite. The donut was still warm, the chocolate rich. She closed her eyes. "Damn, that is good."

"You actually ate it?" Mike shook his head. "I can't believe you. I was offering it to be nice."

"And I appreciate you being nice." Mal grinned, walking to her desk.

They watched the rest of the press conference together. When it ended she said, "Funny. Not a peep from Cameron Ford."

"He's probably waiting for Conlan to give him new talking points.

"Did you ever get a hold of Kelly last night to tell her we found Chloe's killer?"

"No, she wasn't at her mom's and wasn't answering her phone."

"You didn't call Shapiro?"

"No, but you're welcome to, partner."

"Well, I'm sure she's hearing about it today. You know, there are still a few things that aren't adding up."

"What's that?" Mike asked.

"Well, who did those Google searches on her phone? And there were signs of prior sexual abuse with Chloe."

"Do you think John or some other kid did it? Maybe it wasn't the first time Scott had Chloe knocked out?"

"I dunno," Mal said, taking a long sip of her coffee. "But I am going to find out."

"I'd expect nothing less."

Chapter 51 - Mallory Black

MAL WATCHED the blonde in jeans and a red Georgia Bulldogs sweatshirt pull into the driveway of her cozy two-story home, then out of her car and go to the trunk.

Mal had been sitting on the house for twenty minutes. She'd knocked on arrival but got no answer. She'd driven too far to turn around.

Before the woman could open her trunk, Mal was out of her car, approaching.

"Bree?"

The young woman looked at Mal, confused. "Do I know you?"

"I need to talk to Kelly."

"Piss off." She opened her trunk and grabbed two bags of groceries, then slammed it and started walking.

"It's about Chloe," Mal said.

"She's not doing any interviews, now leave before I call the police."

"I *am* the police," Mal said, pulling the badge from her pocket.

Bree looked at it. "Creek County? You're a long way from home."

"It's important that I talk to her. Please. It's about Chloe."

"She didn't do it."

"I know. I want to apologize."

"Hold on," Bree said, carrying the bags up the sidewalk to her house.

Mal waited.

She'd driven all day and into the night to find one of Kelly's oldest friends, one of the only people who'd spoken with Kelly regularly on LiveLyfe before she killed her account. Mal wouldn't leave empty-handed.

After a few minutes, Kelly appeared at the door. She was wearing a long sleeve tee and jeans with her hair pulled back in a ponytail. Her eyes were tired, but she didn't look as distressed as the last time Mal had seen her.

"Yeah?" Kelly stood in the doorway, neither inviting Mal in or coming out to join her on the porch.

"First, I want to say sorry for all the media bullshit. If it means anything at all, we didn't put that camgirl story out there. I hate Molly Grant more than you do. Her sensationalism creates more problems than it solves."

Kelly nodded. "My dad has lots of enemies. It could've been anyone."

"Politics should have no part in any of this."

"Why are you here, detective? You didn't drive all this way to say sorry."

"Not just to say sorry, no."

"Then what is it?"

"I lost my daughter, too. I know how rough it is. And I'd be lying if I said it gets easier. But I think you should take some small comfort in knowing that your daughter's death was an accident."

"Yeah, accident. Whatever. Is that all?"

The press conference had given few details, but it did include the suspect saying that the death was an accident and that the sheriff's office was investigating his claim.

"Can I come inside? I think you should know what we found."

Kelly looked her up and down, untrusting. But then she nodded. "Okay. You get five minutes."

Mal followed her inside, joining Kelly in the living room where Bree sat on the couch beside her, their hands clasped as Mal explained everything from Isaacson's involvement to Lucas's confession.

Kelly cried, the exhausted sobs of someone nearly out of tears.

After Mal finished, she broached the reason for her being there.

"Two things still bother me about the case."

Kelly flinched as if Mal had tricked her, was going to cuff her, and drag her back to Florida.

"Those searches on your phone."

"I didn't do them."

"Eddie says he didn't do them, either. Did anyone else have access to your phone?"

She stared at the ground. "I dunno."

"One other thing that's left unresolved. Your daughter had signs of past sexual abuse. We're looking into whether Isaacson may be involved, but —"

"It wasn't him," she said, blankly.

"Do you know who it was? Was it Eddie?"

"No," she said, still staring at the ground.

Mal realized why this woman was so tired. She *knew* that her daughter was being abused. And she'd been fighting that knowledge for a while. But now she seemed conquered.

"Who was it? Who was abusing Chloe?"

"Her father."

Mal leaned forward. "You said you didn't know who her father was."

"I lied. It was her father. I stopped it, but I couldn't bring myself to go to the police."

"Why not?" Mal asked.

"Because her father is my father."

Mal stared.

"He abused me too, from the time I was thirteen until I was pregnant with Chloe. It's what made my mom leave him. She found out."

"And nobody went to the police?"

"He said he'd destroy us if we did. And if you knew my father's dark side, you'd know what he was capable of."

"God," Mal said.

"I think he also searched for those things on my phone. He's been paying me and my mom to keep our mouths shut for years. A few months ago, he asked me to bring Chloe to his house to spend the weekend with grandpa, like she sometimes did with my mother. I said no way in hell. He was lucky to see Chloe when I was *there*. No way I was going to leave her with him, even for an hour. You'd have to kill me for a weekend. But then he did something I didn't expect. He picked her up from school and brought her to his house.

"I freaked out. I went over there, but I was too late. He'd already hurt her. She was passed out. He'd drugged her, but I knew what he'd done. I went into the bathroom with her, tried to wake her up. When I came back out, he had my phone. I thought maybe he'd taken it so I couldn't call anyone, but when you said those searches came up on my history, I figured he must've done it. Not sure if he was trying to set me up, but I wouldn't put anything past him."

Drugged her, just like Scott.

Fucking cowards trying to hide their evil deeds.

"Why didn't you tell someone?"

"I … I don't know. I didn't think anyone would believe me. I was scared that it would ruin Chloe's life. My father knows a lot of powerful people. You'd be surprised what he can do. But, also, she didn't even know what happened to her. If I had him arrested, the whole thing would go to trial, and because he's a big deal, it would be public knowledge. This would become the thing that defined her, and I didn't want that for my daughter."

"So, she had no memory of the incident at all? Wasn't she in pain?"

"Yes. It was terrible when she woke up. She was confused, bleeding. At first, I tried to see if she remembered anything, but thank God she didn't. I told her that she must've fallen on something, but that she'd be okay. She just had to let herself heal."

"Then what?"

"I told my father I would kill him if he ever came near Chloe again. And that's the last time I saw him until all this happened." She shook her head. "I can't believe that two men abused her, one of them selling photos of that abuse and I didn't even know it! What kind of fucking mother am I?"

Kelly cried into Bree's arms. Mal felt her pain, and also some guilt for being so judgmental. Yes, Kelly was a neglectful mother, but she seemed to have been trying, at least. She was a kid herself when her father got her pregnant, after years of raping her. What chance did she have? What chance did either of them have?

Mal stared at her. "You can't let him get away with this."

"He already has. What would the point even be now?"

"Justice. For you and Chloe."

Mal didn't need Kelly's permission to go after her father, but she'd probably need her testimony to ensure a guilty verdict. She needed Kelly on board, needed her to believe that she had some power.

"There is no justice for men like him. They do what they want, hurt who they want, and never pay the price."

"He has no power over you anymore, Kelly. You hold the cards if you're willing to play them."

"I don't know."

Bree, still holding Kelly's hand, said, "You need to do this, Kelly. Fucking burn him."

"You think?"

Bree nodded, her eyes welling up as she turned to Mal. "Will you help her?"

"I would love nothing more than to get justice for you, and for Chloe."

Chapter 52 - Mallory Black

MAL AND MIKE didn't typically make arrests, but they both wanted to be there when deputies kicked in the door to Harry Conlan's beachfront cottage.

The breacher burst it like a melon. Three deputies stormed the home's first story while Mal and Mike waited with Wilson across the street in an unmarked van, listening to the radio and watching via monitors in the back.

As they went room to room, Mal's heart pounded, waiting for the moment they'd find and cuff him.

But that moment never came.

After a complete sweep of the home, Deputy Gossard announced, "He's gone."

"What the fuck you mean he's gone?" Wilson shouted.

"Clothes all over his room, dresser drawers left open, open safe in the closet. Looks like he left in a hurry. Hold on, there's a note here. It says, 'I refuse to be a political pawn in your game, Sheriff Bell.'"

"Who the fuck tipped him off?" Mal screamed. She opened the rear door of the van and walked away, venom boiling in her gut.

NOLON KING & DAVID WRIGHT

Mike followed.

Mal turned to him. "Someone in the DA's office tipped him off. He's probably already out of the country."

"We'll put in calls. We'll find him before he gets out."

"No," Mal said. "Kelly was right. There is no justice for men like him."

Epilogue 1

Councilman Harry Conlan sat in the back of the small bar in Havana, Cuba, drinking a bottle of Bucanero Fuerte with a beautiful sixteen-year-old *Jinetera*.

He'd been in Cuba for less than a week and had already slept with three different girls under eighteen. He hoped that after he became better known in the city, and those who controlled the prostitution knew he was willing to pay, that he could get younger girls.

For now, sixteen would do nicely.

Her name, or at least the one she gave him, was Charo. She didn't speak a word of English, but he knew enough Spanish to get by.

Harry asked her if she wanted another drink. She was just about done with her first.

"No." She smiled.

He asked if she was ready to go back to his hotel.

"Si." She batted her lashes.

He took her hand and led her out of the bar. The live music followed them to his hotel, one block from the bar.

He was already aroused. A part of him wanted to take

her into a back alley or a bathroom and fuck her right there. Something about fucking trashy girls in trashy places aroused him more than a hotel room ever could. But he wasn't sure how well that would go down with local officials. Sure, they could be bribed, but he wasn't sure how they'd take to some American doing whatever he wanted, wherever he fancied. He didn't have *that* much money.

He'd been to Cuba twice before and had partaken of the local prostitutes both times. But he'd only slept with women, not girls. Now on the run, and living under an assumed name, with enough money to last him a few years, he may as well enjoy himself.

His old life was over.

And he would miss it.

He liked the power.

If someone had asked Harry what he enjoyed most about being a councilman, he would have said, "serving his citizens." He lived to make a difference in the community. While that was partly true, he also loved the power. He liked wealthy landowners coming to get their projects approved. He liked businessmen coming to him for input. He liked the insider tips and benefits of his position.

He also enjoyed the game of politics. He'd looked forward to bringing down Sheriff Bell, who had been a pain in his ass forever. He'd looked forward to getting Claude Barry back into office, and the associated perks that would come with his old friend returning to power.

But now he had nothing, except his money.

He'd have to find a way to recover what he had lost.

For now, he'd enjoy his dominion over these poor girls. He'd fuck them rough, but not too rough. Not yet.

Perhaps in time, he could fuck them like he really wanted. And hurt them. Hurt them like he wished he could hurt his daughter for ratting him out.

Epilogue 1

In front of the hotel his erection was rock hard.

Harry opened his second story hotel room door and went inside.

Charo asked if she could use the restroom.

He said yes.

As she freshened up, he took his clothes off, laid them neatly on a chair, and went to the bed in his boxers, stroking himself through the silk.

The bathroom door opened, but Charo didn't step out.

She sat on the toilet, counting cash. A black man wearing clothes the color of midnight stepped out, gun aimed right between Harry's eyes. And the gun had a silencer.

Harry couldn't believe that the bitch had sold him out, walked him into a trap.

Fucking Cubans!

He had prepared for robbery, leaving the bulk of his money in a safe with the hotel's management.

He held up his hands, pleading with the man, in Spanish, not to shoot. *He had money.* His heart raced. He pointed to the dresser, telling the man that all of his money was in the bottom drawer, stuffed in a sock.

"I don't want your money," the man said, in perfect English.

"You're American?"

"Yep," the man said slowly approaching the bed, gun still trained on Harry.

"You a bounty hunter?"

"Nope," the man said.

"A cop? A fed? I don't know what you've been paid, but I can pay you more. Just name the price to walk away and tell them you didn't find me."

"I already told you I don't want your money."

Harry's heart raced faster, working to untangle this man's intentions. Cops and law enforcement didn't carry silencers, as far as Harry knew. Silencers were the domain of special ops and hitmen.

"What *do* you want then?" he asked, afraid that he might not be able to bargain with this man.

"Justice for your daughter and your granddaughter."

Harry looked from the open second-floor window straight ahead, and the door to his right.

No way he could make either of them.

But he had to try.

He never got the chance.

The last thing Harry registered was the impact of a bullet finding his skull.

Epilogue 2

Jasper Parish sat at a wobbly table in a rickety chair watching the news on a staticky TV, eating cold pizza he'd ordered hours ago.

He was alone, with not even Carissa coming to visit these days. She didn't want to see Jasper, and she definitely didn't want to see Tom Wilson, his newest identity. Maybe she was done with South Florida.

He laughed. A dry, ugly croak. He'd stopped taking the pills in hopes that she'd come back, but alas, she had not. Nor had Jordyn.

He'd alienated them both and was more alone than ever.

He tossed the last piece of crust into the box then picked up his burner and hit redial. "Come on, Karen, pick up."

He'd just gotten her number last night from a PI he sometimes employed but had yet to get an answer despite his many attempts.

He needed to know if Alicia was okay.

The news reports from days ago said she was in a coma.

Come on.

"Hello?" Karen said, sounding a million miles away.

"It's Dennis."

"Oh my God," she said, sounding relieved. "Where are you?"

"I'm on the road. Is she okay?"

"She came out of the coma earlier. The doctor thinks she'll be fine. I'm at the hospital, in the lounge. Do you want me to see if I can get her on the phone?"

"No. Let her get better. She doesn't need to hear from me now. I just wanted to make sure she's okay. How is everything going?"

"Okay. The police have been up my ass, but I think they're just looking to wrap the case as quickly as possible. I told them pretty much everything that happened except we said we didn't know you. You were some stranger that came in and saved us. Also, you don't need to worry about your photo. Ophelia said they never had a picture of you."

"Good," he said, though it also reminded him that he didn't have a photo of them, either.

"We described you as if you were short, in your early twenties, maybe, with a big giant afro, and, oh yeah, pudgy, with a lazy eye."

Jasper laughed. "Thank you."

"No. Thank you. For everything. You saved us all."

She was crying on the other end. "Hey, someone wants to talk to you."

Before he could stop her, Karen put Ophelia on the phone.

"Dennis?"

"Hi, Ophelia," Jasper said, tears stinging his eyes. "How are you?"

"Okay. When are you coming back?"

"I don't know, honey."

"Mommy's awake."

"I heard. That's really good."

"Are you going to come see her?"

"I can't."

"Why not?"

"It's complicated."

Her soft crying on the other end burned his eyes even more. "Are you a bad guy?"

"No, honey. I don't think so."

After a long pause, she said, "You're not coming back, are you?"

He wanted to say he didn't know.

He wanted to say maybe.

He wanted to say yes.

But any of those would give her hope, and hope was an endangered species on Planet Jasper. Everything he touched turned to shit, and killing was his gift. He wanted to say yes. To hang up the phone, drive up there, and take her and her mother in his arms. To hold them all night.

"No."

Her voice hitched as she cried louder, "Okay."

He heard her pass the phone to Karen.

"What did you say to her?" Karen asked.

"That I won't be back. I can't explain it, but trust me, it's better for all of you. I'll call in a few months. And if the three of you need anything, it's yours. But I can't come back. Tell the girls that I love them."

Jasper hung up.

And closed his eyes.

He drifted off.

He woke to hands on his shoulders.

He jumped, turning to see Jordyn standing behind him.

"Hi, Daddy."

"Jordyn?"

"I'm sorry," she said.

"No, *I'm* sorry. I shouldn't have killed Calum. You were right. And it's been eating me ever since."

"It's okay," she said, hugging him.

He inhaled her familiar scent, her fruity shampoo. He thought he'd never smell her again, and here she was, holding him.

Back.

"I'm sorry about Alicia and Ophelia, too," she said.

"You saw them?"

"I know you didn't see me, but I never left you. You're my father. I'll always be near."

He cried again and held her tighter than ever.

Jasper and Jordyn spent hours catching up.

They watched horrible sitcoms on the crappy TV until Jasper drifted off.

Then he woke with a scream.

Jordyn, sitting at the wobbly table, reading a book on her phone, set it down and ran to his side. "What is it?"

"I saw something."

Epilogue 3

Mal was asleep when her phone rang with an unlisted number.

She was exhausted and wanted to let it go to voicemail, but something, whether intuition or martyrdom, told her to answer.

"Hello?"

"You're looking for me?"

"Jasper Parish?"

A pause, then, "Yes."

"Why are you calling me? Is this some game?"

"No. I'm calling because you need me."

"Why do I need you?"

"So you can stop Paul Dodd before it's too late."

THE END

The story continues...

Jessi Price is missing. Mallory Black's past catches up with her and gets her suspended. Helping Mallory could cost Jasper Parish his freedom. But he will stop at nothing to save Jessi ... even if it costs him everything.

No Return is the fourth book in the *No Justice* series.

GET NO RETURN TODAY

A quick favor...

If you liked *No Hope*, then *would you kindly* * consider taking a few minutes to leave a review on your favorite bookselling site. If you're a book blogger, we'd love any mentions on your blog or YouTube channel, also. Every bit of word-of-mouth helps to introduce us to new readers.

As always, thank you for reading,
    David Wright (and Nolon King)

(* *Bonus points if you got the* Bioshock *reference.*)

About the Authors

Nolon King writes fast-paced psychological thrillers set in the glitzy world of entertainment's power players with a bold, insightful voice. He's not afraid to explore the darker side of human nature through stories featuring families torn apart by secrets and lies.

Nolon loves to write about big questions and moral quandaries. How far would you go to cover up an honest mistake? Would you destroy your career to protect your family? How much of your soul would you sell to get the life of your dreams? Would you cheat on your husband to keep your children safe? Would you give in to a stalker's demands to save your marriage?

David W. Wright is the co-author of edge-of-your seat thrillers including the best-selling post-apocalyptic series *Yesterday's Gone*, the paranoid sci-fi *WhiteSpace* series, and the vigilante series, *No Justice*, as well as standalone thrillers *12*, and *Crash* which was recently optioned for a movie.

David is an accomplished, though intermittent, cartoonist who lives in [LOCATION REDACTED] with his wife and son [NAMES REDACTED.]

He is not at all paranoid.

He is "the grumpy one" on the *The Story Studio Podcast* with fellow Sterling and Stone founders, Sean Platt and Johnny B. Truant.

You can email him at david@sterlingandstone.net

We swear, he almost never bites. Unless you feed him after midnight.

Also By Nolon King

Hidden Justice

Hidden Justice

Hidden Honor

Hidden Shame

Hidden Virtue

No Justice

No Justice

No Escape

No Hope

No Return

No Stopping

No Fear

Once Upon A Crime

Once Upon A Crime

Twice Upon A Lie

Three Times a Murder

Dead For Good

Dead For Good

Left For Dead

Dead Of Night

Wake The Dead

Dead For Life

Stand Alone Novels

Pretty Killer

12

Blown

Miserable Lies

The Target

Secrets We Keep

Close To Home

Heat To Obsession

A Simple Kill

Tell Me No Lies

Red Carpet Black

Fade To Black

Victim

Also By David W. Wright

Hidden Justice

Hidden Justice

Hidden Honor

Hidden Shame

Hidden Virtue

No Justice

No Justice

No Escape

No Hope

No Return

No Stopping

No Fear

Karma Police

Jumper

Karma Police

The Collectors

Deviant

The Fall

Homecoming

Yesterday's Gone

October's Gone

Yesterday's Gone Season One

Yesterday's Gone Season Two

Yesterday's Gone Season Three

Yesterday's Gone Season Four

Yesterday's Gone Season Five

Yesterday's Gone Season Six

Tomorrow's Gone

Tomorrow's Gone Season One

Tomorrow's Gone Season Two

Tomorrow's Gone Season Three

Available Darkness

Darkness Itself

Available Darkness Book One

Available Darkness Book Two

Available Darkness Book Three

WhiteSpace

WhiteSpace Season One

WhiteSpace Season Two

WhiteSpace Season Three

Stand Alone Novels

12

Crash

Emily's List

Threshold

www.ingramcontent.com/pod-product-compliance
Lightning Source LLC
Chambersburg PA
CBHW010530100726
47903CB00011B/2958